Tall Grass

By

S. R. Larson

ISBN: 1-4033-8781-8 (electronic)
ISBN: 1-4033-8782-6 (softcover)

Library of Congress Control Number: 2002095301

This book is printed on acid free paper.

Printed in the United States of America
Bloomington, IN

1stBooks – rev. 02/28/03

Dedication

This book is dedicated to my parents, Dr. C. Robert Larson and Carla Jacobson Larson, to my wife, Sharon Witwer Larson, and to my brothers, Mark and Leif, and their wives, Lynn and Marie and to my friend Dale Schatzberg all of whom showed me how to adapt and adjust and cope.

About This Book

What would you do if...
Things that could kill you were hiding
in the tall grass?

Would you run and hide? Would you evade and avoid? Would you become enraged and move to destroy? Would you ask for and expect help? Would you take on the responsibility of having to decide? What would you do?

This is very human book about very human people involved in situations not of their own making.

Chapter 1

The sunrise was not spectacular. It was gray and dull. The monsoon was to blame for the lack of significant spendor as the monsoon was just being the monsoon and the monsoon was not spectacular. It was just bringing the rain.

The Fire Base onto which the rain fell was on top of a low hill in I Corps, Republic of Vietnam. Near the south gate there was a canvas tarpaulin stretched above and between four wooden poles and, under the tarpaulin, an American soldier laid his pack on the damp ground and sipped coffee from a tin cup. The soldier's uniform was new and clean and the canvas on his jungle boots was bright green. The nametag sewn above the soldier's shirt pocket read "MAJEWSKI" and, in rank, he was a Private First Class.

The soldier watched the eastern sky for a few minutes and listened to the rain. He seemed to be quietly bringing the morning into himself with his senses. He concentrated on each sound and on each sight and on each smell until that solitude was broken by the arrival of another soldier.

"Where're the others?" Majewski asked.

"I talked to Burke a couple of minutes ago," the soldier said, "and he said the rest are finishin' chow."

"Where did ya see Burke?"

"Down by the mess hall. I think he went to take a leak or else he's gettin' some ammo."

Majewski turned and watched the sky lighten while he waited for the other soldiers in the platoon to gather under the tarpaulin. The arrival of each soldier was announced by the sounds boots make when men walk through mud and by equipment noises and by complaints about the weather. The last soldier to arrive was a Staff Sergeant and he was holding a piece of soggy white paper.

"Listen up men," the Staff Sergeant said. "We've got a couple of new guys with us today to take the place of whoever it was that got killed the last time we were out."

One of the soldiers said "Crandal."

The Sergeant remained quiet for a few seconds and then repeated what the soldier had said. "Crandal. Yes. Crandal. Randall Crandal. Randy Crandy. Randy Candy."

Someone under the tarpaulin said quietly, "he was all right."

"Anyway," the Sergeant continued, "for you new guys, I'm Sergeant Jackson and for you old guys…" Jackson looked at the piece of paper…" one of these guys is PFC Noland and the other one is PFC…Majen…Mahjew…"

"Majewski. Pronounced mah-jes-key. The 'w' is silent."

Sergeant Jackson slowly lowered the paper.

"Are you a Jew, boy?"

"No," answered Majewski.

"Catholic?"

"No. I'm an anesthetist."

Jackson stared at Majewski. He seemed to know that whatever Majewski had claimed to be may not have had anything to do with Religion but he was not certain so he glared at Majewski and said "Don't be givin' me no shit. I don't need no shit from you. You jus' do what I say and everything'ill be fine. If I need to know your name I'll learn it but, for now, you ain't nothin' and you don't know nothin'."

Majewski said nothing.

Jackson returned his attention to the assembled soldiers.

"Listen up, men. We'll be headin' west for about a mile and then south down to the creek. I don't know if we'll find anything 'cause it's been pretty quiet and we haven't been out for a while either. This weather must've been a bitch for them, too, because the recon patrols haven't noticed any activity. We won't be settin' up any ambushes so we should be back late this afternoon.

"Sergeant Bible, you take the point and Lewis you take slack. You two cherries, Noland and Whatever, fall in behind Ortega and the rest of you fall in behind the cherries and, Norris, you've got the back of the bus with me. There will be no talkin' or bullshittin' around and there will be five meters...them's yards for you new guys...between each swingin' dick. No clips in

the weapons until either I say so or we start catchin'
some shit.

"Ortega, you run a commo check and make sure
that damn radio works." Ortega made a commo check
and the platoon formed up and moved out through the
gate into the wet Asian countryside.

Majewski and Noland fell into their assigned
places and the platoon moved out. Majewski's hands
began to sweat with apprehension when he realized
that he was exchanging the relative safety of the Fire
Base for the muddy uncertainty of the Vietnamese
countryside. He found himself wanting to look back
over his shoulder to see if he could tell what Noland
was thinking but he didn't. He looked forward out
over the misty countryside. In front of him the
landscape presented itself like a fine Chinese
watercolor, beautiful and serene. Majewski allowed
himself to briefly study the distant hills but the hills
were not a threat. Harm would not come from the
foggy hills. It would come from nearby or underneath
so Majewski turned his eyes downward and

concentrated on the wet matted grass at his feet. He did not want to trigger a booby trap.

Each man in the patrol was paying strict attention to the area around him and, as they covered the first rainy mile without incident, the tension subsided somewhat. Majewski began to feel that maybe the infantry wouldn't be so bad if all he had to do was follow other soldiers through terrain that seemed pretty safe.

As the patrol swung south toward the creek that Jackson had mentioned in his briefing the rain changed to a gentle mist. Majewski had no idea where the creek was and he didn't care. Jackson knew and Jackson was leading.

The patrol proceeded cautiously for about an hour and then, as they approached the crest of a hill, Sgt. Bible ordered them down. Quietly the men spread out on the wet grass and wondered what was happening. Sgt. Lewis and SSG Jackson crawled up to Bible and the three of them peered over the crest of the hill. Majewski watched the three sergeants and wondered what was commanding their attention. He didn't have to wonder for long. SSG Jackson crawled away from the other two and down to the rest of the men who, when he arrived, gathered quietly around him.

"Somethin' we didn't friggin' expect came up. There're five of 'em down on the other side of the creek so we're going to shoot 'em up. They'll be to our right so what sun there is will be at our backs. I want you shits to spread out along the ridge and let 'em have it when I give the word."

Majewski could not believe what was happening. He was wet from rain and sweat and he was frightened and apprehensive. Glancing to his left he saw Noland's look of equalled bewilderment. Both Noland and Majewski seemed to realize simultaneously that room would have to be made in their minds for a brand new experience.

Quietly and deliberately each soldier positioned himself along the ridge and Majewski, from his vantage point high above, had an unobstructed view of the Vietnamese soldiers. Completely oblivious of the Americans on the ridge, some of the Vietnamese were cooking rice, others were cleaning their rifles and passing around a cigarette. Majewski was surprised because the Vietnamese did not seem to be ready for war. They looked instead as if they were waiting on a street corner for a bus to take them to work. For the Vietnamese the bus came in a torrent of M-16 fire. They danced like spastic puppets for a few seconds as bullets ripped them apart and then they crumbled to the ground and lay motionless as pools of blood expanded beneath them.

When the firing began Majewski had raised the sights on his rifle well above the soldiers' heads and threw eighteen rounds into the tree trunk behind the Vietnamese.

Majewski's bullets were not needed but his body was. SSG Jackson walked up and ordered Majewski, Noland, Norris and Burke to accompany him down to the bodies. The rest of the patrol stayed on the hill to provide cover in the event that cover was needed.

The firing ended almost as soon as it had begun and Majewski was stunned by the event. Cautiously the men descended the hill, crossed the stream and began to search the bodies. The dead Vietnamese looked very young and innocent. Majewski looked at the contorted face of one of the Vietnamese and thought he noticed a look of complete surprise.

Not far from Majewski Sergeant Burke kneeled over one of the soldiers and then called for Jackson.

"This one ain't dead," Burke said softly.

Jackson walked over and peered down at the bleeding soldier. The soldier was clutching his stomach and blood was oozing out between his fingers. When his eyes focused on Jackson the Vietnamese soldier squirmed and tried to move away.

"You're right. This one ain't dead yet," SSG Jackson said as he swung his rifle out in a gentle arc and fired four shots into the wounded soldier's head. "But he is now."

Burke's eyes burned into Jackson's.

"Jesus, Sarge! He might have known somethin'!"

"Shit," laughed Jackson. "He don't know nothin' except how to die. Some of 'em can't even do that right."

Burke slung his rifle over his shoulder and began searching the dead man's pockets. Jackson turned and began searching what was left of another dead soldier. Reaching into the shirt pocket Jackson extracted a pack of Salem cigarettes and a roll of American Military Payment Certificates which caused him to fly into a fit of uncontrollable rage. Jackson began jumping around and swearing at the dead man.

"You son of a bitch! American money and cigarettes! I'll teach you, you fuckin' son of a bitch! You'll pay for this…"

Jackson put another clip in his M-16 and began firing at all the lifeless Vietnamese. He expended the entire clip and then began to kick the nearest dead soldier. Burke had seen enough and ran over to Jackson but Jackson pushed Burke away and continued to kick the corpses and, as Jackson flailed his arms wildly, he pushed Majewski, who happened to be standing in near enough proximity, and Majewski fell on top of one of the dead men.

Feeling the warm blood and entrails, Majewski panicked immediately. He tried to jump up but couldn't get any footing and fell back. He realized, as he tried to roll over and push himself up, that all the warm blood he was feeling had been flowing peacefully through a living man just moments before. That realization was making him sick. He pushed himself up, got his feet under him and stumbled into the creek where he immediately began splashing himself with water.

Still enraged, Jackson took out his machete and hacked furiously at the neck of the soldier he had been kicking.

Majewski stood in the water and watched in disbelief. The head came off. When it did Jackson grabbed it by the hair and shoved a unit patch into the bloodied and gaping mouth. Then he took the head and wedged it into a fork in the tree. and left it as a trophy.

Jackson stepped back and surveyed the trophy with delight and satisfaction. He was so proud of his feat that Majewski, dirty and wet and distressed by blood, vomited.

Chapter 2

Majewski didn't remember much about the misty return to the Fire Base. His clothes were wet, sticky and psychologically uncomfortable. His mind dwelled on the dead Vietnamese soldiers while his eyes checked the ground at his feet. The Vietnamese had seemed so carefree and pleasantly alive until the M-16s opened up and pulverized them. He kept wondering what had gone through their minds when the first bullets crashed into and tumbled through their bodies. Did they cry out in terror or did they resign themselves quickly to the fact that they were being killed? Was there time for pain or prayer? Was there time at all for thought before their lives exploded? Did they try to see where death was coming from? Did they think of trying to hide? Would they have done the same thing Jackson had done if the situation had been reversed? Majewski didn't know. Speculation answered nothing. The only way Majewski could ever know what had gone through the minds of the dying

Vietnamese would be to get shot himself. He didn't really want to find out that badly. Speculation would do afterall.

Majewski allowed his thoughts to return to his time in the creek. He vaguely remembered that, while he was washing in the water, Jackson was yelling at and threatening Burke, Norris and Noland. Though Majewski was not paying conscious attention he did know that Jackson did not appreciate any interference into his activities and, when the patrol reformed to return to the Fire Base, Jackson stated emphatically that he would meet and deal with Burke, Norris, Noland and Majewski that night but Majewski didn't really care.

The Fire Base consisted of several buildings constructed of plywood, wire screen and sandbags. The roofs were corrugated tin and sandbags were used to strengthen the walls. Sandbags had also been used to construct bunkers and to give protection to various parts of the base. The buildings where the soldiers were billeted were called "hooches" and personal areas inside the hooches were called "Areas of Operation" or

"AOs." One of the buildings was topped by a large water tank that rarely contained much water, even during the monsoon rains. Pipes running down from the tank connected to showerheads but a master valve controlled the flow of water.

When the patrol entered the Fire Base Majewski entered his hooch, grabbed his bar of soap and a towel and ran to the shower. He stripped off his bloodied clothes, stepped under the showerhead, turned on the faucet but nothing happened. He moved to another showerhead and tried it but still nothing happened. He swore and moved around the shower room but each time he turned on a spigot, nothing happened. The master valve was turned off and the handle had been removed.

Dejectedly Majewski turned all the faucets back to "off" and put on his green underwear. Then he stood in front of the mirror and noticed that he had dried blackish blood on his neck. He tried to rub it off but touching it repulsed him and knowing that the blood was on his throat made him want to vomit again. Collecting his clothes he walked outside where he tried to throw up but could only gag. He felt totally degraded and humiliated as he stood on the wet sand. The realization that he had no control over anything crept coldly over him and, in exasperation, he screamed "Shit, I can't even puke anymore!" Then he sat down on the sand and began to tremble. There were no tears and gradually he regained some selfcontrol. He sat quietly for a few minutes and felt the mist fall on him. He allowed his towel to become damp enough to remove the dried blood on his neck and then he returned to his hooch.

Norris, in the AO at the far end of the hooch, was rummaging around in his footlocker. Majewski startled him by calling his name. Norris spun around, slammed the lid down on his footlocker and sat down on it all in one set of nervous and clumsy motions.

"Shit, man," Norris sighed, "You beaucoup scared the hell out of me. I thought Jackson or one of them lifers had come in. I was lookin' for my dope, man."

"Sorry," said Majewski, "I just wanted to ask you when they turn on the showers."

"Bout seven."

"Thanks, I just wanted to wash off any blood that's left."

"How did you get all bloody?"

"Jackson pushed me onto one of those dead Vietnamese."

"Oh, I was wonderin' what you were doin' in the water. I was checking the tree line and looked down and you're down there splashin' like a fuckin' bitch."

Majewski again wiped his neck with his towel.

"Ya know," Norris said, "that really gave me the ass out there. Jackson had no call choppin' that guy up. Shit, man, he was mutilated enough without Jackson jumpin' in and cuttin' off his fuckin' head. The weren't no reason for him to do that."

"I know. I never even imagined doing anything like that."

"Burke's over bitchin' to the CO now. That other new guy is with him, too."

"Who? Noland?"

"Yeah, if that's the guy in the AO next to yours. They went straight over as soon as they got back inside the wire."

Majewski shook his head and said, "Noland was a freak back in the world. He and I got drafted together and went through Basic and AIT together and we made a pact that we wouldn't kill anyone over here. We're serious about that."

Norris shook his head. He had found his dope and was sprinkling marijuana onto a cigarette paper. He looked at Majewski and said, in a very even voice, "it ain't no big deal."

"But how do you cope with this?"

"With what?"

"With killing people."

"I smoke shit, man."

"Yeah, but that doesn't always help, does it?"

"No. The first few times I was out I was really fuckin' scared. We were goin' out in full platoon strength then. Not like it be now. But even with all them dudes around I didn't feel safe. I mean, I'm a brother, man, and there are a shitload of white dudes out there and a shitload of wetbacks and a bunch of muffucks that don't like brothers, includin' the CO and most of them lifers. I can dig that. The first time we took fire I hit the fuckin' dirt and prayed that when I opened my eyes, I'd be back in Detroit. When the firin' stopped I opened my eyes and my ass wasn't in Detroit but my ass wasn't dead, neither.

"Then the activity quieted down in this area and goin' to the field wasn't no big deal. We started goin' out in smaller groups and we'd set up camp and just bullshit around. We knew them VC muthers was out there and they knew where we was there but we didn't fuck with 'em and they didn't fuck with us so everything was cool, man. Sometimes we'd have to fire some of 'em up if we caught 'em out in the open like we did today but, most of the time, things was cool, man.

"The first time I killed a dink I felt bad but then I realized he would'a killed my black ass. Besides, if you don't know 'em or have to look at their scraggly-assed faces, it ain't too hard, dude. With a rifle, man, you can kill 'em from a long way off. It ain't close up. You think them muthers that be droppin' bombs from planes worry about what they're doin'? Fuck no. They're just be passin' fuckin' time 'til they can land

18

an' light up a bigass joint. Them dudes who drop artillery shells don't give a shit neither. Them bastards never see what their badass shells do. The only ones killin' bothers is us shits ah have to look at 'em and then, after a while, your dumbass head gets to where it gets off on this shit, dude. Today when we fired up them fuckin' slopes it didn't halfass bother me none at all 'til I got down there close to 'em. Shit, man, nothin' bothered me until Jackson chopped off that dude's head. That really ripped my ass. That's why I been tryin' to find my nastyass dope."

Majewski seemed to sag a bit. He was wondering if he could adjust and evolve.

"You'll get fuckin' used to it somehow," Norris said as he lit up his marijuana cigarette. "It just takes some friggin' time."

"Yeah," sighed Majewski. "I suppose so."

"If ya don't, man, you'll go fuckin' nuts. Don't be worryin' about the dinks. Worry about them mines and booby traps them bastards build. That's where we lose most of our dudes in the field."

"Yeah," said Majewski softly, "I guess that's what I'd better do."

"Killin' the dinks ain't bad. It's watchin' your own dudes die that's a bitch. That really gets beaucoup shitty, man. Or dyin' y'self."

Norris left the hooch to smoke his dope in the latrine.

Majewski sat on the bed and rubbed his neck with his towel. Outside the monsoon rains began to fall again and Majewski felt chilled. Rain drops pinged on the tin roof and Majewski found himself alone with his thoughts.

Chapter 3

At precisely twenty-two hundred hours Captain Biondi and Staff Sergeant Jackson entered the hooch where the patrol had been assembled. The men stood at attention until Biondi began to speak.

"At ease men. Sergeant Jackson tells me that he had some problems today with a few of you. It seems that some of you weren't pleased with the actions he took regarding a dead gook. Well, men, let me say this. I came to Vietnam to do a job and that job is to kill as many VC and NVA bastards as I can. The more dinks killed by men in my command makes me look that much better and that makes it easier for me to be noticed by my superiors.

"I came to Vietnam to make rank and I will make it. You men are going to make me a Major and I will tolerate no insubordination whatsoever! When someone of higher rank tells you to do something, you'd better goddam' do it! If you don't there'll be hell to pay! Sergeant Jackson was doing his duty and any interference by anyone else will be dealt with severely! Sergeant Jackson did what he felt he had to do and, as long as he has rank over you, you'll not interfere. Is that clear?"

A collective but unenthusiastic "Yes, Sir" rose from the men.

"Good," smiled Biondi. "Let this be the first and last time a session like this is needed."

Burke raised his hand and said, "Sir, may I ask a question?"

"Ya."

"Well, Sir, we all know that the Vietnamese are goin' to find those dudes that we shot up if they haven't found 'em already and they're going to have the ass. That means they're goin' to start raisin' hell. It's been pretty quiet up here for the last few weeks and those of us who're short aren't lookin' forward to catchin' their shit. I think Sergeant Jackson made a big mistake choppin' off that gook's head and I just wonder what purpose it really served."

Captain Biondi's face flushed red with anger. "You just missed the point of what I just finished talkin' about! So what if they get pissed? Let 'em throw some shit at us! We'll throw it right back! You were sent here as a soldier, not as a Sunday school teacher. Soldiers come here to kill and you will kill at each and every opportunity. That's what this war is all about. I don't have time for men who are afraid to do their jobs! Sergeant Jackson did his today. He made 'em know that they weren't dealing with a soldier who plays silly-assed games. You men do the same or the shit will hit the fan. Is that clear?"

Again "Yes, Sir" was the response from the men.

"Good! Now no more bullshittin' around."

The men stood as Captain Biondi and Staff Sergeant Jackson left. When they were out of earshot the men began to talk to eachother.

"That fuckin' lifer," Burke said, "he's goin' to get us all killed! I'll bet money they hit us tonight or tomorrow night!"

"No takers," said Norris. "This is the fuckin' shits, man."

"I was talkin' to some other dudes about Biondi and Jackson today and they're really pissed about this

23

bullshit, too," interjected Davis. "Biondi talks pretty big for a muffuck who ain't never been out from behind his desk."

"Shit, that's 'cause he fuckin' knows if he ever got to the field, they'd bring him back wrapped in mutherfuckin' plastic," Norris said.

"Yeah, that might be the best solution all the way 'round," Burke said. "It would sure save us a lot of grief."

Majewski walked over and sat down next to Noland.

"Whada ya think, Ski?" asked Noland.

"I don't know," sighed Majewski. "It all seems so damn unreal. I don't remember hardly anything about today. It's mostly just a wet blur."

Noland leaned over close to Majewski and said, "you know, Burke and I spent two hours sittin' in the orderly room waiting to see the old man but he and Jackson were in his office bullshittin' around and drinkin' scotch. We finally left and went to the mess hall."

"I was in the shower washing off the blood. I just didn't think I could get it off well enough with rain water."

"Did you fire at them?" Noland asked.

"No. I shot the tree."

"I didn't even fire. I just closed my eyes and waited for the shooting to stop."

Majewski lowered his head and ran his fingers through his hair.

"Do you know what I remember most vividly?" Noland asked.

"Jackson chopping off the head."

"No. I remember when we were leaving I looked down and saw their rice was still cookin' and, I guess, nearly done. They weren't going to eat it and, for some reason, I wondered if rice prepared by men who were dead tasted the same."

Majewski shook his head. He walked back to his hooch, laid down on his bed and lit a cigarette. The pattern of his life had changed dramatically.

Noland and Norris entered the hooch, walked to Norris' AO and began rolling marijuana cigarettes and, when they had fashioned a number of joints, they walked to the door and opened it. The second they stepped outside the quiet night air around the Fire Base was shattered by a tremendous explosion and Majewski instinctively dropped to the floor and rolled under the bed.

"Incoming!" someone yelled.

"Claymore!" someone else screamed. "That was a goddam' Claymore!"

Noland and Norris had seen Biondi's hooch disintegrate.

"Someone fragged the CO!" yelled Norris. "Someone got the mother!"

Norris and Noland sprinted toward what was left of Biondi's hooch.

"Goddam'," gasped Noland, "what the hell happened?"

"Someone set off a Claymore mine," puffed Norris as they neared the hooch. "Someone fragged Biondi."

By the time Norris and Noland reached the hooch someone had run into the hooch, stopped, turned around and had run back out.

"Jesus," the soldier said as he shook his head, "someone got blowed clean away."

Noland noticed that the soldier was trying to shake something spongy and gray off his hand.

"I went through the door and when I tried to close it, I got this stuff all over my hand," stammered the soldier. "God, the whole side of the hooch is gone!"

A sergeant wearing a cowboy hat vaulted into the hooch and came out quickly. "There's two in there. Biondi and someone else."

Norris was overcome with excitement. He jumped up and down laughing, "It must be Jackson! It's gotta be Jackson! That jiveass mother!"

Soldiers, including Majewski, gathered around and a different sergeant pushed his way through the crowd and entered the barracks. He emerged a few minutes later carrying two sets of bent and bloodied dog tags.

"Men, Captain Biondi and Sergeant Jackson are both dead. I'm afraid there'll be an investigation. I don't imagine the man who did this would like to step forward and take the credit."

The crowd was silent.

27

"I guess there's not much we can do here tonight. I want all of you to go back to your hooches. I want everyone E-5 and above in the Orderly Room immediately. Dismissed."

The soldiers lingered for a while and then slowly made their way back to their respective hooches. Norris and Noland met Majewski outside the hooch.

"What happened?" asked Majewski.

"Some dude shitcanned the CO an' Jackson," giggled Norris. "One hundred percent pure dead, both of 'em!"

"Jesus," mumbled Majewski. "Jesus Christ."

"Ha," laughed Norris. "It's good trainin' for them jiveass mothers."

Majewski shrugged his shoulders and walked into the barracks. He hoped sleep would take him away.

Early the next morning a helicopter brought three Criminal Investigation Detachment agents to the Fire Base. The agents took photographs and began to question some of the men in the company. As Majewski, Noland and Norris waited to be questioned they watched three more helicopters land and unload majors and colonels.

"Apparently the brass is takin' this seriously." Noland said.

"I kinda figured they would," said Majewski.

"The brass," Norris spat on the sand, "is always where the action was. Let's go inside so we don't have to salute them bastards."

The three soldiers went into the hooch and sat on the bunks. Norris began to speak.

"I can't figure out what the big fuckin' deal is. I mean, man, look at it this way. Jackson killed dudes all the time, man. Biondi told him to. They were both dog-ass lifers. 'Nam gave 'em a chance to do what they both wanted. They wanted war, man. They knew there'd be beaucoup risks and they could die. Shit. What difference does it make if the dinks kill 'em or if we do?"

Makewski sat quietly and stared at the floor. He was trying to think of something to say.

Norris continued.

"I ain't sayin' what happened was right! I mean murder ain't right. All I'm doin' is sayin' what's done be done, man. Sure, the brass is goin' to want some friggin' answers. They're goin' to want to twist everything into a fuckin' cover-up. They really don't want to find out nothin. The las' thing them jiveass turkeys want is for this to hit the papers in the world, man. B'sides, can you honestly say you be sorry they be dead? They be gettin' what 'as comin' to 'em!"

Majewski shook his head. "I just got here. I didn't even know Biondi. I never even saw him 'till tonight. I don't know what he was like. Will his replacement be better? If they were killed because they were such hard asses it would surely be a bitch if we ended up with a couple of dudes who were worse."

"No shit. That would be a bitch." Norris said.

Early in the afternoon Majewski was summoned to his meeting with the CID agent. In a dimly lighted hooch Majewski sat down in front of an old wooden desk and removed his cap. Behind the desk the CID agent puffed on a cigarette as he read Majewski his rights. When he finished he turned his eyes to

Majewski and said, "Do you understand your rights under Article Thirty-one of the Uniform Code of Military Justice?"

"Yes, Sir" answered Majewski.

"Do you wish to answer questions?"

"Sure, Sir, but I don't know anything."

"You'd better let me be the judge of that. The lieutenant there is here for your protection," the CID agent said as he nodded to a spitshined second lieutenant who was sitting in the corner. "He's here to make sure you don't say anything that can be misconstrued or that I don't trick you somehow, or say that you said something you didn't say. Now, do you have any objections to the lieutenant's being here?"

"No, Sir."

"Okay, fine. Let's get started. State your name, rank and service number."

Majewski complied. "Majewski, Anton W., E-3, 664280331, Sir."

"Now, Private Majewski, I'd like to ask you a few questions about the incident that happened last night.

Can you tell me where you were when the Claymore was detonated?"

"Yes, Sir. I was lying on my bed smoking a cigarette."

"You were in your hooch then?"

"Yes, Sir."

"Are there any witnesses?"

"Yes, Sir. Noland and Norris were both there and saw me."

"Noland and Norris are both privates, aren't they?"

"Sir, Noland is. I don't remember what Norris is."

"And they were both in your AO?"

"Yes, Sir. Sort of. They walked through on their way out of the hooch."

"Oh, I see. They were outside when the explosion occurred."

"Sir, they were on the steps of the hooch."

"Are you sure?"

"Yes, Sir. Positive. I could see both of 'em."

"Did either of them have anything in his hands?"

"Sir, do you mean was either one carrying anything?"

"Yes."

"Not that I could see, Sir."

"Neither had the detonator for a Claymore? You know what a Claymore is, don't you? An antipersonnel weapon that shoots darts out after an electric detonation."

"I'm in the infantry, Sir. Of course I know what a Claymore is."

"Okay. Neither had the detonator for a Claymore."

"No, Sir. They weren't carrying anything that I could tell."

"Do you happen to know where they were going?"

"No, Sir."

"They didn't tell you?"

"No, Sir."

"I see. Now, Private Majewski, how long have you been in country?"

"Two and a half weeks, Sir."

"Two and a half weeks," the CID agent smiled. "You're getting short."

Majewski did not think the comment was funny but he tried to smile anyway. His smile was feeble and strained.

"Have you been to the field yet, Private?"

"Yes, Sir."

"You are a member of Sergeant Jackson's platoon?"

"Yes, Sir."

"I guess I probably should have said 'you were a member of Sergeant Jackson's platoon' shouldn't I since the good sergeant is no longer with us."

"I suppose that would be proper grammar, yes, Sir."

"Yes. We must treat this tragedy with proper English."

Majewski shifted positions.

"How many patrols were you on with Sergeant Jackson?"

"One, Sir."

"One? Can you tell me what transpired on that patrol?"

"Sir, we went out and found some soldiers by a stream and Sergeant Jackson ordered us to shoot them so they were shot and killed."

"By 'soldiers' I presume you mean enemy soldiers."

"Yes, Sir. That's what I was told."

"I see. And you took part in this shooting."

"Yes, Sir. I fired my rifle."

"I see. Did you hit any of them?"

"I don't know, sir. I may have. I may also have missed. Sometimes it's hard to tell."

"Okay. That's not really important. Can you tell me what happened next?"

"Sir, Sergeant Jackson and a bunch of us went down to check the bodies."

"Go on."

"Sir, I don't know if I want to."

"You have the right not to answer any more questions if you so choose but others have already told me what Jackson did."

"Then there's not really much point in me telling you again, Sir."

"Maybe and maybe not. I know that Jackson killed a wounded Vietnamese and then decapitated another one. Others have told me that the one he decapitated was dead already. Do you know that for a fact?"

"I think he was dead, Sir, but I wasn't too close and I'm not a doctor."

"Yeah, if you were a doctor you'd be an officer, wouldn't you?"

"I guess so, Sir."

The CID said, "when you saw him chopping off the soldier's head you and some others tried to stop him, didn't you?"

"Sir, I don't know what I was doing. I was near him, I do know that, but I don't consciously recall trying to do anything to stop him."

"And that's when Sergeant Jackson pushed you down, right?"

"You know about that, Sir?"

"Yes. You landed on a dead Vietnamese, didn't you?"

"Yes, Sir."

"And what was your reaction?"

"What do you mean, Sir?"

"What did you do?"

"I guess I went to the stream, Sir, to, you know, wash the blood off."

"And how did you feel about it?"

"About what, Sir?"

"About Sergeant Jackson."

"I don't know, Sir."

"Did you feel animosity toward him?"

"I don't know, Sir. I guess I didn't appreciate it much."

"He pushed you on top of a dead man and you got mad about it."

"Maybe. But I was mostly confused and more interested in getting the blood off, Sir."

"You said you were confused. How?"

"Are you kiddin' me, Sir? The whole situation was so grotesque and so repulsive I just couldn't believe it was happenin' to me."

"So you didn't like what Jackson did to you."

"No, Sir, I didn't. Would you?"

"This isn't about me, Private. It is about you. Did you dislike it enough to kill Jackson?"

"Sir, I was trying to forget what happened. War is new to me. The only dead people I've seen before have been laid out nicely in coffins. I've never fallen into a bloody corpse before. I didn't kill Jackson. There are witnesses to that. You know I didn't do it and I don't know who did. The fact that Jackson pushed me is immaterial. Jackson had a lot of guys mad at him so if you're looking for a motive, you won't have to look very far to find one, but don't look at me. I didn't do it."

"Okay. We're finished with you for now. We might want to talk to you again."

"I'll be around, Sir. I've got three hundred and forty some days left in country."

"Hopefully it won't take that long to clear this up. Tell me something, Majewski, off the record. Are you sorry that Jackson's dead?"

"Sir, I just got here. I don't know anything. Everything happened real quick. I wasn't sure what to expect but I never imagined anythin' like this."

The CID man stood up and stretched. He looked weary.

"You can go now, Private.

Majewski stood up.

"Good afternoon, Private."

"Good afternoon, Sir." Majewski said and turned to leave.

After Majewski left the lieutenant turned to the CID man and said "Do you think he did it?"

"No. He's a cherry," the CID man said. "He wouldn't have told the truth if he wasn't. We're looking for someone who's been here a while. Someone who'll either lie or evade the questions."

"I guess you're right," said the lieutenant. "Do you think we'll find the bastard who did it?"

"No," smiled the CID man. "We won't find him unless we're very, very lucky. If the guy brags about it we could get him. If he doesn't, we won't. He'll climb on the freedom bird and smirk all the way back to the States."

"I s'pose," the lieutenant said as he lit a cigarette.

"The kid was right about one thing," the CID man said softly.

"What?"

"War's new to damn near everyone here."

"I guess so."

The CID man sat down and picked up his pen. He arranged some papers in front of him and wrote a few words on the top sheet. He then looked up at the lieutenant and said "this is the shits."

The lieutenant nodded, looked at his watch and sat down. Shafts of sunlight angled across the room and a breeze rustled the canvas hanging across the window.

"Send the next man in. I want to get the hell out of here before nightfall."

"I don't blame you." the lieutenant said with a sigh. "I don't really want to be here at night."

"Lot's could happen. Two wars here. Us versus us and us versus them. This is the hard one. Ain't no winners here."

Chapter 4

In the days that followed the fragging of Captain Biondi and SSG Jackson events followed in quick succession. Captain Biondi was replaced by another Airborne officer, Captain Wyandotte, who promptly lined his hooch and office with sandbags and perforated steel plates. The new Commanding Officer did not want a repeat of the incident that had taken Biondi's and Jackson's lives.

A Lieutenant named Surrey from Quang Tri was brought in to be the new platoon leader. Sergeant Bible was promoted to platoon sergeant and the platoon went immediately to the field.

Rarely were the murders mentioned. Majewski honestly did not know or care who had killed Biondi and Jackson. There were more immediate concerns.

The platoon was in the field for ten days but made no contact with any real or imagined enemy. At night ambushes would be set up which, at first, made Majewski extremely uneasy to the point where his kidneys began to work quickly and he constantly felt the need to urinate.

After five nights with no contact Majewski began to relax. Sergeant Bible assigned him to work with Specialist Davis. Davis seldom spoke to anyone. He was quiet, reserved and coldly efficient in the bush. Majewski grew to depend on Davis' experience and on his military counsel. He learned a great deal about ambushes from Davis. Davis liked ambushes. An ambush allowed Davis to scheme. Davis took great care in setting out and camoflaging his Claymores, making sure they would provide a joyous, swift, deadly efficiency should the opportunity for detonation ripen and the need arise.

When Davis and Majewski set up an ambush Davis set the mines and Majewski kept him covered from a distance. They would then conceal themselves and wait, constantly watching for movement.

One night, after a week without any contact, Davis detected movement to the south of the ambush site. All Davis' senses became quietly alive and he moved with quick, quiet, deliberate intent. In an instant he was lying on his stomach searching for the source of the movement. Majewski laid quietly in the tall damp grass. It was Davis who first saw the enemy. He touched Majewski's shoulder and pointed at trees to the south. Majewski trained his eyes on the trees and then, by the pale moonlight, he saw people. First one man appeared walking cautiously and carrying a long rifle. Behind him five more Vietnamese appeared and carefully made their way across the flat land to the south of the Claymores.

"This is perfect," whispered Davis with a grin, "they're going to walk right into it."

Majewski didn't answer. His eyes remained on the Vietnamese that had bunched up and were walking close together.

"Two of them are chicks," whispered Davis.

Majewski confirmed Davis' observation with silence.

"You know, 'Ski, they might be mothers," Davis said softly as he picked up the detonators. "They could have kids at home…" The Vietnamese were slowly approaching the Claymores. "They could be pregnant

43

or have little babies waitin'…" The Vietnamese approached to within ten meters of the mines. "You know, if I kill 'em I could be makin' orphans out of their kids. I could be deprivin' their husbands of their services. Jesus, 'Ski, I don't really want to do this…" Davis let his whisper fade to silence and Majewski, who didn't really know if he wanted Davis to detonate the Claymores or not, held his breath.

"But," Davis sighed as the Vietnamese moved in front of the Claymores, "fuck 'em."

Instantly there was a flash of light and an explosion. The concussion shattered the still night air. In a fraction of a second Majewski saw the Vietnamese disintegrate and then, as the echo faded into the darkness, silence seeped in and filled the void.

Majewski waited and, as his eyes readjusted to the dark, he wondered what he should be thinking. He had just seen six people die and he wondered what was going through Davis' mind. Slowly he turned and looked at Davis. Davis still held the detonators in his hands and, when he saw that Majewski was looking at him, he smiled and said "Zap."

The explosion had been a novel change in the nightly routine and soon Sergeant Bible and Lieutenant Surrey appeared.

"You guys all right?" Bible whispered hoarsely.

"Ya," Davis answered. "We got at least six KIAs."

"Good," said Surrey, "we'll check 'em out in the morning. You got any more Claymores out?"

"No. They ate 'em both."

"Okay. I'll send a couple of guys out to replace you."

"Don't bother," Davis said. "I'll wait an' see what I got. 'Ski can go in if'n he wants."

Majewski thought for a moment and said "No. I'll wait, too."

"Okay," Bible said. "It'll be dawn soon anyway. Check out your count and get back inside the perimeter we have set up. You can catch a few z's before we move out."

"Okay."

"And," Bible added though he knew he didn't have to. "Stay alert. There could be more out there."

Davis patted his M-16 lovingly and winked at Bible. Bible knew Davis and Majewski would be all right so he tugged the lieutenant's sleeve and said "let's go."

Bible and Surrey disappeared into the darkness. Davis laid down on his stomach and said "that was beaucoup beautiful, wasn't it."

Majewski thought for a moment and then said "I think 'awesome' is the word."

"Ya," smiled Davis contentedly, "beautifully awesome."

At first light Majewski and Davis went down to check the bodies. The sight nearly made Majewski sick. Two of the bodies had been cut in half by the force of the darts. Appendages remained attached to torsos by sinewy strands of flesh and stringy red meat. Each body was lying in a different, grossly contorted position and was beyond recognition. Mouths, if they were still discernible, were hideously contorted and the flesh, in the early hours of death, was beginning to turn a bluish green.

Davis busied himself searching the victims. Majewski wondered if the dead had, indeed, left orphans at home.

Davis found nothing of interest on any of the Vietnamese. Another day was dawning and the Americans would spend it in the field. The population of Southeast Asia had been reduced by six. Six Asians never saw the new day dawn.

After five more nights without contact Lt. Surrey called the platoon together and offered them a plan.

"Men," he began, "I don't know about you guys but I sure as hell don't want to die here. I have too much to live for back in the world and I do intend to get back there alive, in one piece, and with all the parts and accessories I came over here with. Now we've been stomping around out here all day and sending out patrols at night and we haven't seen more than six dinks yet and Davis killed them. Now I have a couple of questions and a proposition for you. Please answer all questions with a show of hands.

"First, how many of you want to die here?

No one raised a hand.

47

"All right, how many of you want to get back to the States in one piece and alive?"

Every hand was raised.

"Okay, how many of you think you have a good chance of getting wasted on ambush or patrol?"

A majority of hands were raised.

"Okay. Now what I am about to suggest could get my ass into one hell of a big jam and could, theoretically, get your asses in a jam, too. So if you agree to it, you must also agree to keep your mouths shut. I'm going way out on a limb for you guys and for myself, too, so if you don't agree to this, I'll swear this conversation never took place.

"First, I'd like to see a show of hands if you agree to be cool with this and tie your throats shut about it."

Though confused and cautious, every hand was raised. It was difficult to anticipate what was coming but the talk about getting back to the States alive piqued everyone's desire for self-preservation.

"All right. I think most of you raised your hands. Now I'll give you my proposition. I propose to play a little game with the lifers called 'tell 'em we did but we really didn't' and the game will be played like this. When it comes time to send out ambush patrols we call back and give them the coordinates of where our ambush is supposed to be, according to what the old man wants. But, in actuality, there will be no one out there. We will instead set up a perimeter and post guards on shifts, put out the Claymores and just generally play it cool. If that sounds agreeable, may I see a show of hands?"

Every hand, even Bible's and Davis', was exuberantly raised and a few cheers rose from the sweating troops.

"Fine. However bear in mind that this can only be done when this platoon is out here alone. If they lay some company action on us, we'll have to play it their way and the same thing applies in the event that the CO starts feeling his oats and decides to come out here with us. So remember how it's done should the situation arise but, until it does, it won't."

So the platoon played the game. They moved through the countryside during the day and sent out ghost ambushes at night. When it was time to periodically leave the field for stand down and resupply, the men would go back to the Fire Base and rest up and relax with steaks and beer and cigarettes from America.

Majewski got drunk once on stand down. He passed out on the sand. He felt so bad the next day that he vowed not to drink again until his tour ended. From then on Majewski never did really participate in most of the stand down routines. He would eat a steak or two and drink a flat soda but he didn't like to lose control of his faculties. He dealt with the frustrations and tensions by replacing them with sleep and with the occasional letter home.

In Late February or Early March 1970

Dear Mom and Dad,

Things are fine here. I've got lots of new friends and we're safe and secure. This is a quiet area and we're not in danger. We are currently on stand down eating steaks and

relaxing so don't worry. Greet Aunt Janet and
Uncle Lou for me

Love, Anton

Noland, on the other hand, believed in marijuana
smoke. He and Norris would smoke whenever they
had an opportunity. When the patrol resupplied for
another trip to the field, Noland and Norris always left
room in their packs for a couple of cellophane twenty-
packs of marijuana cigarettes.

Majewski did not sit in judgment of either Norris
or Noland. Everyone had to deal with his mind in
some way or another. The pressures and uncertainties
of situations not of one's own making forced every
soldier to play games with is mind, emotions and
conscience. Incidents either affected a soldier
profoundly or not at all consciously and each soldier
dealt with war differently. No one Majewski knew
was fighting the war to win. Men were just trying to
stay alive. Majewski hoped he would live through his
tour but if something did come up and the possibility
of death did present itself, he wanted to be sober and

straight for it. Noland didn't. Noland seemed to want to be as screwed up as possible. Death may not have been inevitable in Vietnam but it was surely possible. Just the possibility of death made death something that had to be considered, even if one happened to be in the relative safety of the Fire Base or of a larger base like Quang Tri.

In the field Majewski was as cautious as possible. He watched where he stepped and where he slept. He was always aware of places that offered cover and concealment in the event he needed them. He was also well aware that the enemy could be using the same places for cover and concealment and that the VC or NVA could have boobytrapped likely places of cover. Eventually constant observation became tedious and exhausting and Majewski would grow weary late in the day. He would end up methodically trudging along putting his feet where the feet of the soldier in front of him had been hoping that he would not trigger a mine or booby trap and hoping that the platoon would soon make camp so he could rest. As time passed so did much of the paranoia Majewski had first encountered. Complacency was dangerous but probably inevitable.

Not all activity in the bush was handled by patrols or a platoon. Some activity consisted of company operations. Depending on the circumstances, large scale operations consisted of sweeping and securing a given area. An area would be cordoned off and methodically searched. Occasionally this would mean entering a village or hamlet and such operations presented their own problems and paranoias.

Entering a village was always undertaken with caution. Usually the operation would be planned so that the village would be entered at dawn. This would, in theory, trap the VC, NVA and VC sympathizers in the village before they had a chance to melt back into the countryside. Then, again in theory, they could be identified, apprehended, segregated, interrogated and detained. The information obtained could then be used to trap and destroy VC and NVA units. This would, again in theory, break the fighting spirit of the Viet Cong and the North Vietnamese and that would lead to capitulation. The Americans would win the war and go home. The South Vietnamese would find peace and security and would elect honest, qualified leaders in free and open elections and then they would settle down and enjoy their free lives while everyone in North Vietnam would be dead.

So much for theory.

In practice the VC were usually gone when the Americans arrived. Sometimes they had not been in the village at all because they also moved at night. If they didn't get out of the village in time, they hid in tunnels or behind false walls or in small compartments under trapdoors and, since very few Americans were inclined to search thoroughly for confirmation of expected or suspected VC, Majewski's platoon found very few VC. The suspected enemies the patrols did find were either turned over to the South Vietnamese or put on helicopters and sent back to the base camp for interrogation.

Every so often a prisoner would be pushed out of a helicopter either for effect or for fun and occasionally, if a suspected VC would exert himself or fail to show proper respect for his captors, he would be killed in much the same manner as Jackson had killed the wounded soldier on Majewski's first patrol.

Most of the time, however, the task of entering a village and checking the hooches was accomplished without incident. Majewski would preform his duty in a cautious and nervous way. He didn't want to kill anyone and he didn't want to die.

In a village the soldiers found themselves face to face with the Vietnamese and that seldom happened in the field. Entering a village, a soldier walked straight into Vietnamese life. Pregnant women, children and old people would gather around and stare at the American soldiers as if they were aliens who had just stepped off a spaceship. That made the soldiers feel uneasy. There was no way to tell which, if any, of those staring faces belonged to a VC or VC sympathizer.

Being a VC was often a psychological state fostered by any number of intangible inputs and reactions. There were no readily discernable indicators to help American soldiers identify the Viet Cong unless a suspected VC actually betrayed himself somehow. There was no way to strip off the outer stare, peer in and diagnose a VC mind. The quickest way to turn the average Vietnamese peasant into a VC was to act like an American soldier. If a group of soldiers came into a village and burned down a couple of hooches or dragged a couple daughters off into the weeds they created new VC.

Human nature responded in predictable ways. No Vietnamese responded positively to assaults on his or her home or family. No one, Vietnamese or American or anyone else, would embrace foreigners who came in and ravaged a village or its population.

The other side of the situation was that no one appreciated being shot at under any circumstances. If a platoon or company received fire from a village or its environs before they entered or while they were in the process of entering they would stop, call in artillery or gunship helicopters and wait until the village had been pulverized before moving in again. Then the villagers that were left would be brutalized because someone had fired on the Americans.

Noland and Majewski were usually assigned to guard the Vietnamese that had been herded into open areas near the village so they could be detained and interrogated by the interpretors. Going into hooches and ferreting out snipers and VC was left to those who liked to kill.

Watching the Vietnamese may have been unnerving to Majewski and Noland but it was better than entering Vietnamese shacks. On occasion both Noland and Majewski had been in Vietnamese hooches. Village homes were usually made of wood obtained from packing crates or plywood or pallets. Villages farther away from military installations were more traditional in that the hooches were made of reeds or strawlike material with bamboo pole braces and supports. Most often there was only one room where cooking was done over an open fire. Bamboo mats on the floor were for sleeping and water was generally procured from either a nearby stream that also served as a toilet or from a common well that either tapped an underground source or caught rainwater or collected seepage from a stream.

Coming from industrialized, convenience orientated America many soldiers looked upon Vietnamese living conditions with repulsion and disgust. The Vietnamese had found such conditions and accommodations adequate for hundreds of years but many Americans used their disgust to fuel their own prejudices and hatreds. Vietnamese homes burned well and, since there was nothing of perceived significant material value in them, they were often set on fire for no other reason than because they were there and flammable. No thought was given to the memories or the lives of those who lived there.

Villages have always been burned in war. Nothing was new. Such things had been happening for thousands of years. Vietnam was no different. It was simply immediate.

Chapter 5

In the first few months Majewski was in Vietnam there were many personnel changes. Sergeants Lewis and Burke finished their tours and returned to the States and, for a while, that made Majewski uneasy because both Lewis and Burke were conscientious, businesslike leaders who knew their jobs and took care of the men.

Specialist Davis made Sergeant and worked behind Bible. Sergeant Bible was cautious and worked closely with Lieutenant Surrey and Lieutenant Surrey took no chances at all.

Majewski and Noland were each promoted to the rank of Specialist Fourth Class.

Selective Service back in America eventually filled the platoon to full strength. Sometimes slots were filled by experienced infantrymen and sometimes slots were filled with brand new privates.

There were casualties, too. A second tour Staff Sergeant newly assigned to the platoon stepped on a booby trap and was blown apart.

In the first real firefight Majewski was involved in two new infantrymen got caught in the open and fell victim to a mortar round. It hadn't really been much of a firefight. The platoon had been instructed to enter a sector where Military Intelligence had determined that the NVA had hidden an ammunition dump. The area was cordoned off and the platoon began its sweep. As the platoon approached to within three hundred meters of the tree line, it began to receive small arms fire off to Majewski's left. Majewski and Noland, who were side by side and about five meters apart, hit the ground and flattened out.

"Where the hell's it comin' from?" yelled Majewski.

"I don't know! Over to the left, I think!"

Both Majewski and Noland kept low. The tall grass concealed them but offered no real cover. They could hear M-16s to their left return the fire and could hear Ortega call in air support. From somewhere to the right came the "woosh" of incoming mortar rounds. There were three muffled explosions. Somewhere fairly close someone was yelling. Within a very short time Majewski heard the sounds of helicopters overhead and then the report of machinegun fire and rockets. Majewski and Noland crawled to their left after they could no longer hear AK47 fire and got high enough above the grass to watch the gunships rain down firepower on the tree line. The gunships had no trouble spotting the pocket of NVA or VC soldiers and, within seconds, the soldiers were dead. The gunships then circled, looking for more VC to kill.

The tree line had begun to smoke and burn. Both Majewski and Noland were relieved that the firefight was over. From the left they saw Sergeant Bible approach. Blue gray smoke curled from the barrel of his M-16.

"You guys okay?" asked Bible.

"Ya," answered Noland. "we're okay."

From their right they heard Ortega scream into the transmitter.

"What's wrong?" yelled Bible.

61

"Cherries, man! Down there, man," Ortega yelled as he motioned to his right. "I jus' called a Medevac."

"Come on," Bible called and he, Noland and Majewski ran about sixty yards to where a group of soldiers had congregated. There, lying within three feet of eachother, were two dead American soldiers.

"Shit" Bible shouted. "What happened?"

A soldier was putting his first aid kit back into its pouch.

"Three rounds," the soldier said. "Mortars. The first about ten meters in front of them, the second right on top and the third out back there someplace. It was a one in a million shot."

"Dammit," said Bible, "how the hell many times to these dumb shits have to be told to keep five meters apart anyway!"

"I don't know," said the soldier. "One got his throat tore out by shrapnel and the other one caught it high on the back and low on the head. It was a one in a million shot."

"You already said that. Did anyone else get hit?" asked Bible.

Lt. Surrey had walked up to the group. "Yeah," he said meekly. "Sort of."

Bible turned around and saw that the lieutenant was holding his elbow and shaking his hand.

"What happened, Sir?"

"I hit my funnybone on something when we flattened out."

Bible shook his head. "Okay, men, let's secure a landing site for the Medevac."

Surrey was still shaking his hand. "Christ, I ought to put myself in for a Purple Heart."

Majewski and Noland looked at each other and shrugged. At their feet two American soldiers were lying dead in the tall grass. A couple of months ago they were probably trying to buy beer with fake I.D.s. Now they were making mud with their blood. Neither Noland nor Majewski even knew their names. Overhead the Medevac chopper circled until Bible popped a purple smoke grenade. The helicopter landed, picked up the bodies and flew off. When the helicopter left, Lt. Surrey called the men together.

"Okay, men, listen up. We've lost two men and the choppers say they got four. Let's check around for an ammo dump and get the hell outta here."

"Sir, may I say something?" asked Sergeant Bible.

"Sure."

"Okay, Now I don't know what the hell it's going to take to make you shitbirds get your shit together but if this doesn't do it, I'd hate to think what will. Two cherries got killed because they were too close together. It was stupid! It was senseless and it was unnecessary! Time and time again you've been told to keep five meters apart and now, by god, you're going to keep five meters apart! I don't want five yards! I want five meters! Even those extra few inches might save you or your buddy's life. Those two clowns are going to be the last men I lose out of stupidity! Is that clear!"

The men understood and most of them even believed.

"All right, let's find the ammo cache and get the hell out of here!"

The men in the platoon silently picked up their gear.

"Five meters, 'Ski," whispered Noland. "That's as close as I want to come to getting wasted."

Majewski nodded and then something Noland did startled him. Without hesitation Noland cooly and, in slow deliberation, did something Majewski never thought he'd see. Noland pulled back the charging handle on his M-16, released the bolt and chambered a round. Majewski stood still for a moment and then did the same thing.

"You know, 'Ski, we're sittin' ducks out here," Noland whispered. "Ever since I've been in the field I've been askin' myself where are they? Now I know. They're everywhere and they're watchin' us all the time."

Majewski's silence was agreement. The patrol moved out with a high degree of caution. Had the Vietnamese soldiers waited a few more minutes before triggering the ambush, many more Americans would have fallen victim to their fusilade and mortars. Each American knew that and each began playing a similar game as he moved out. In retrospect maybe the Vietnamese had been trying to frighten off the Americans. Perhaps they were trying to keep the Americans away from the ammo dump. Maybe they were trying to just hit and run. There may have been nothing to defend at all. Perhaps they were merely moving from one place to another. They could've been separated from their unit and, in attempting to get back, inadvertantly stumbled over the American patrol. They may have fired in fear or panic or they may have had an ambush set up for quite some time. Regardless of their motivation, they had succeeded in destroying two enemy soldiers before something they hadn't figured on, namely the helicopter gunships, ended their own lives in tearing, searing, mechanized screams.

Each American soldier on the ground found a great deal of comfort in the sound of helicopters overhead.

The platoon searched the area carefully. Every possible hiding place was checked out thoroughly but nothing was found. No weapons, no more Vietnamese soldiers and no ammunition dump. The only thing that indicated that soldiers had even been in the area was the empty, crumpled pack of Salem cigarettes that Ortega found.

Lieutenant Surrey took the pack and studied it more carefully than it deserved. He had lost two men and found a cigarette pack. He tossed the pack into the air and fired his M-16 at it. He missed. The pack fell to the ground unharmed and the patrol left for the Fire Base.

Back at the base Majewski took a shower and tried to think of pleasant things. It was difficult. To shower with the limited water supply one had to get wet, turn the water off, lather up, turn the water back on and rinse off. It was not particularly refreshing or effective but Majewski thought about the blood he couldn't wash off the day the late Sergeant Jackson had pushed him into the dead soldier. He smiled at the thought that, since that day, he had not had to wash off any more blood. He was so glad that he whistled as he dried himself. He wrapped his towel around his waist, put on his sandals and walked back to his hooch.

It was early evening and the sun had dropped toward the mountains to the west. Long shadows lay across the sand and the air was thick.

When he entered the hooch Noland was standing in front of a mirror adjusting his love beads. Majewski found a fairly clean uniform and, as he dressed, Noland opened his footlocker.

"Hey, 'Ski," Noland said hoarsely, "you wanna go out an' blow a little weed?"

"No. I never touch that shit. I'm going to grab a steak and hit the rack. I hear we're going out tomorrow."

"What?"

"We're going back out early with a couple more platoons."

"Shit," sighed Noland. "We're not going to try to find another phantom ammo dump are we?"

"I don't know. I heard Ortega say something about some gung-ho lifer and an intelligence report of troop movements near the A Shau."

"No shit?"

"Hey, my Spanish ain't too good but Ortega was jabberin' to someone and I think that's what he said."

"You sure?"

"You know Ortega. He can speak as well as anyone when he wants to. When he doesn't he lays a lot of cha-chas on ya and you can't understand a friggin' thing."

"Shit, the Valley of the Shadow of Death."

"We aren't going in," said Majewski. "We'll be on this side of the mountains. We'll stay to the east. The real nasty part is on the other side of that mountain range but we aren't crossin' it."

'That's better than going in."

"I hope Military Intelligence is as wrong about these troop movements as they were about that ammo dump."

"Have a little faith, 'Ski. Those spies could fuck up a wet dream."

"I'd sure hate for this to be the time they're got it right."

"You an' me both. You an' me both. But the night is young and I have shit to smoke before I sleep. Hey, 'shit to smoke before I sleep.' Ain't that from Frost?"

"No," sighed Majewski. "It ain't from Frost."

"Okay," said Noland. "See you later."

Majewski tossed his towel over the door and stretched. He was tired but he was clean. For the time being, that was enough.

Chapter 6

At four o'clock in the morning Majewski was awakened by a CQ runner and told to pack up and form up at the helicopter pad. He got up, dressed, shouldered his pack, picked up his M-16, checked out two bandoliers of ammunition and, in the predawn darkness, walked to the chopper pad.

The night air was crisp and fairly cool. Majewski inhaled deeply and then took off his pack and strapped the bandoliers across his chest. He allowed himself to briefly savor the early morning air. It smelled of gun oil and sweat.

Other soldiers walked slowly toward the chopper pad. They talked softly and complained about things soldiers complain about. Majewski lit a cigarette and watched the soldiers mill around the pad. There were lots of soldiers and Majewski soon realized that this operation would be more than a squad or platoon action. He wasn't sure if a big operation would be good or bad. The cliché about there being safety in numbers was overshadowed by the possibility that there could be large scale and heavy action. Majewski began to feel uneasy and then anxious. He was used to relatively small operations with a lot of sweat and dirt. Large operations were new and anticipation was bringing on its own anxiety.

Noland ambled across the sand dragging his pack, rifle and ammunition. He saw Majewski and walked over to him.

"Have you heard anything about this operation?" asked Majewski.

"Na," answered Noland as he let all his equipment fall to the ground.

"Nothin' more than you told me last night except there are goin' to be some big lifers along."

"Shit," said Majewski, "that means they'll probably expect to impress even bigger brass."

"Who needs it! This is really bullshit, 'Ski. Total bullshit. I'm tired and I've got one hell of a headache."

"Too much dope?"

"Not enough. There's a dope shortage around here. I couldn't find any more so I went back to my AO and," Noland's voice softened, "for some strange reason, cleaned my rifle. You were sleepin'."

"I was tired." Majewski said softly.

"I also did something else that was unusual."

"What?"

"I wrote my folks."

"You did? Why?"

"I don't know," Noland said softly. "I just felt the need."

"What did you write about?"

"I just told them I was all right. They worry, you know. Then I went to bed and had a weird dream."

"About what?"

"I don't remember."

"Did it have anything to do with the war or with being back in the States?"

"I don't know. It woke me up though and I was sweatin'. I mean I was sweatin' more'n usual."

Majewski didn't say anything. He took two cigarettes from his pocket and gave one to Noland.

73

Noland lit the cigarette, inhaled deeply, waited a few seconds and said "Thanks, 'Ski, but it ain't the same."

"It'll do for me." Majewski said.

Majewski and Noland smoked in silence. Other soldiers had arrived and, from the left, Ortega approached. He was not carrying his radio.

"Where's your radio, Peeedro?" Noland asked. "Ain't you humpin' the box today?"

"Yeah, man," Ortega grinned, "but that bitch gets beaucoup heavy. I don't wanna hump it any more'n I have to."

"I hear ya," Noland said.

"We're formin' up over by that revetment. We gonna fight the friggin' war from there an' you two're invited."

"You're a prick, Pedro," said Noland as he picked up his gear. "A little prick but a prick nonetheless."

"Si."

Majewski, Noland and Ortega went to the revetment and joined the rest of the squad. As the eastern sky began to lighten four officers moved to the center of the crowd and the men closed in around them. Lieutenant Surrey and the CO were joined by another captain and a lieutenant who stood behind the other officers. All the officers except the Commanding Officer carried rifles and supporting gear. The CO stepped forward and spoke to the men.

"Men, this is Captain Loomer. He is going to accompany you on this mission today and he'd like to say a few words."

The CO stepped back and Captain Loomer stepped forward. Loomer was thin and flat. His hair was cropped close to his head and his boots were spitshined. He was wearing a flak jacket.

"Thank you, Captain Wyandotte." Loomer said with a strong, firm and confident voice. "Men, our intelligence has reported enemy troop movements east of the A Shau Valley. We're going into that area to join with some ARVN units and see if we can find out what's going on out there. We're going to fly out when the ground fog burns off so relax and take it easy for a while. I want all squad leaders to come with me."

Loomer stepped back and the officers walked from the helicopter pad to a nearby hooch. Squad leaders followed. Soldiers began to talk among themselves.

"What do you think, 'Ski," asked Noland.

"I don't know."

"There's one good thing about this," Noland sighed. "We're flyin' in. Everyone from here to Hanoi'ill hear or see us comin'."

"God, I'm tired of this shit," Majewski said as he sat down on the ground. "I'm so tired of this."

"I wonder why that captain's comin' along," Noland said. "That can't be good."

"I don't know. Maybe he had to pad his fuckin' body count."

"I hope he doesn't pad it with my body," Noland said as he sat down next to Majewski. "I wish I had some dope."

Majewski said nothing. He just sat next to Noland and waited for something to happen. The ground was cool and damp. Majewski wanted to go back to sleep but the officers and squad leaders came back and everyone got up and walked slowly to the helicopters on the far side of the pad. In the east the sun broke the horizon and another Vietnamese day began.

Chapter 7

Majewski didn't really like or trust helicopters. They looked too awkward and clumsy. He had no understanding of the mechanics or the technology that provided flight and helicopters scared him. He didn't like being airborne in them and, most of all, he did not like the helicopters taking him to the field. The field was not where he wanted to be but, upon due consideration, helicopters were probably better than walking. He always hoped helicopters would alert a skittish enemy that would then prudently leave the area quickly and without incident.

Majewski didn't know how long the helicopter he was flying in had been airborne. It could have been five minutes or fifteen. All he knew what that he was glad when it touched down and even more glad when his feet did. Because he had a valid and intense fear of being decapitated by the blades, he kept low and moved quickly away from the helicopter. Then he began to orient himself. To the west bluegreen foothills rose to meet fogshrouded mountains and the scene before him was beautiful, awesome and mysterious.

To his left Noland was moving through the tall grass toward a group of soldiers so Majewski straightened his helmet and fell into step next to Noland.

"There are two things I don't like about this whole thing," huffed Noland.

"What?" asked Majewski.

"Long grass and no grass."

"Get used to it."

"Jeez," sighed Noland. "This is a bunch of shit."

"Yuh," Majewski mumbled as they joined up with other soldiers. Sergeant Bible and Lieutenant Surrey gathered the men around and Surrey began to speak.

"Men, I want to fill you in on the purpose of this mission. As you can see the platoon being led by Captain Loomer is on the other ridge." Surrey motioned to the platoon on the ridge across a shallow valley.

"We will parallel them taking this ridge and following it until we rejoin the other platoon. From this ridge we will have a good view and a good field of fire for a good mile and a half. Then our ridge joins the foothills and we'll cut across and join up with 'em. We will not, I repeat, not, head into the A Shau. We will bear east and continue with this mission. We are attempting to determine the extent of NVA and VC movement in this sector. I want all you men to keep alert and keep alive. I don't want any unnecessary noise. We're already big fuckin' targets up here on this ridge so let's not make things any easier for them.

"Sergeant Bible, you take point."

"Yes, Sir," Sergeant Bible said as he adjusted his pack. "I want the broken record between each of you and I want your steel pots on. No boonie hats as long as we have a big lifer along.

"Ortega, keep that radio workin'. If we take any shit I want you on it fast, is that clear?"

Ortega knew his job and was competent enough to resent being told what to do and when to do it so, instead of answering, he just silently stared back at Bible.

"Let's move out," said Surrey. "Five an' watch your step."

Sergeant Bible moved out slowly and was followed by Lieutenant Surrey. Four other soldiers followed and Majewski was next in line. He turned to Noland and said "Do you want to go first?"

"I don't give a shit," answered Noland as he slid a clip into his M-16.

Majewski waited until the man in front of him had covered five meters and then he followed. He soon realized the patrol was in an awkward position. It was true that they could see the surrounding area well but it was also true that they could be seen from the foothills above and to the right and from any place of cover or concealment on either side of the ridge. The tall grass provided excellent concealment and Majewski knew the patrol was easy prey for snipers. Small beads of sweat appeared on Majewski's brow and his hands began to tremble as he glaced quickly around. He saw no movement at all to his right but, in front of him, he saw something he didn't particularly like. The long grass he had been walking in gradually gave way to stones and flat rocks that could easily have been pried up, booby trapped and reset to be triggered by just such a patrol. It had happened before. Majewski become more cautious and more nervous. He felt closer to the possibility of death walking along the ridge than he had since he had been in Vietnam and he did not like the feeling at all.

Noland was unnerved, too. He stopped before Majewski did and took a step backward.

Sergeant Bible must have had the same feeling because he stopped the patrol, consulted briefly with Lieutenant Surrey and then sent word down the line for Ortega to come forward. Ortega moved past the men with deliberate caution and didn't speak until he was face to face with Bible and Surrey.

"Si?" Ortega said.

"Get Loomer on the horn," whispered Surrey. "I want to talk to him."

Ortega knelt and spoke softly into the radio microphone. Across the valley the other patrol stopped and Captain Loomer moved back toward his radio operator and took the microphone.

"Yankee May Two, this is Yankee May One, over."

Surrey took the microphone from Ortega.

"Yankee May One, this is Yankee May Two. Do you read me?"

"That's a roger, Yankee May Two. What's on your mind?"

"Yankee May One, we've got some problems over here, over."

"What's your problem, Two?"

"Yankee May One, we're stompin' over grass and flat rocks. Do you happen to know if Mike India {Military Intelligence} mentioned the possibility of Bravo Tangos {Booby Traps} over here? Over."

"Stand by, Two," Loomer said as he took a small notebook from his pocket. He paged through a dozen or so pages pausing occasionally and finally got back on the radio.

"Yankee May Two, this is Yankee May One, over."

"Go ahead, One. We read you."

"Mike India says 'beats the shit out of me' Two."

"Two to One. This ain't funny."

"One to Two. I know but what do you want me to do? Drive a herd of waterbuffaloes in front of you?"

"That would be nice, One."

"Listen, Two, you are to proceed under the assumption that there are Bravo Tangos and you are to complete this mission as assigned."

"One, this is Two. It's a dumb ass mission, Sir. Recon photos would've been better and safer."

"That's not for you to decide, Two. Just do what you're told or you will be in deep shit! Do I make myself clear?"

"Roger, One." Surrey said flatly.

"Roger, Two. This is One. Out."

Surrey handed the microphone back to Ortega and, knowing the microphone was not keyed, he said "that shit! If anyone gets hurt out here I'll smoke that bastard myself."

Bible stood silently next to Surrey for what seemed like a very long time. He took off his helmet, mopped sweat from his brow and finally said "there ain't much we can do is there, Sir."

"No, Sergeant," Surrey seemed to sag for a moment. "We'll just have to play this sillyassed game. We better keep moving."

Bible and Surrey motioned the platoon along the ridge line. Bible started out first again. He moved slowly and cautiously. Surrey followed him and the rest of the patrol fell in behind. Majewski felt awkward so he tried to adjust his pack. It didn't seem to help. He still felt like a very fat duck in a very small shooting gallery.

For twenty minutes the patrol moved along slowly and quietly without incident but with lots of sweat and lots of tension. The ridge line narrowed to a small path that crested the ridge for sixty or so meters and then spread out into the relatively flat area that led to the foothills.

Bible stopped the patrol when he got to the path. Surrey approached from behind and asked "What did you find?"

"I just don't like the look of this, Sir. Keep the rest of 'em here. I'm going ahead."

Surrey noticed that Bible's hands were shaking and that he had begun to sweat profusely.

"Slow and easy," Surrey said.

"Beaucoup slow and beaucoup fuckin' easy," mumbled Bible in a voice that cracked.

Surrey tried to think of something to say. He had a deep respect for Sergeant Bible and did not like being in the position of having to endanger Bible's life. Sergeant Bible was a professional. He spread himself out on the ground and crawled slowly along the path. Surrey watched him intently, hoping equally that he would find something and that he wouldn't find anything. About twenty meters down the path Bible found a trip wire. Slowly he reached into his web belt and pulled out a wirecutter. With slow, precise deliberation he moved the cutter toward the wire but the wire looked very strong and it was stretched tightly so close to the ground that the cutter wouldn't fit under it. Holding the cutter upright would mean the wire would have to be cut with the tips of the blades instead of with the meatier parts nearer the handles. Bible didn't trust his cutter so he laid on his stomach and considered his options. Trying to cut the wire could, theoretically, detonate whatever it was hooked to since getting the cutter placed properly could entail moving the wire. He pushed aside enough dirt and grass to see that the wire led back into the ground on each side so Bible did not know if the booby trap was to his right, to his left, directly underneath him or underneath someone else. A bead of sweat dropped from the tip of his noseand was quickly absorbed by the dirt below.

Bible crawled backward, turned around and slowly slithered back to Lieutenant Surrey.

"What did you find?" asked Surrey.

Bible took his canteen and tipped it to his lips. He swished the water around his mouth and, with a surprising loud gulp, swallowed.

"A trip wire, Sir."

Surrey shaded his eyes with his hand and peered down the path.

"Damnest thing I ever saw."

"Did you cut it?" Surrey asked.

"No, it was too tight and close to the ground. I didn't want to mess with it because I don't know where whatever it is wired to really is. It could be wired in a series. Who knows how many could go off at once. Usually they use trip wires in grass and pressure sensitive detonators in shit like this. I've got a feeling we've been stompin' through a minefield and it's just dumb luck we haven't set anything off."

The color seemed to drain from Surrey's face. Beads of sweat again popped out on his brow and mixed with existing sweat.

"If we go down that path, Sir," Bible said quietly. Battalion'll have to send out a big fuckin' sponge to soak us all up."

Surrey listened intently as he considered options.

Bible understood Surrey's predicament. Surrey disliked the situation and did not want to continue. He didn't want to die and he didn't want his men to die. Bible didn't like the situation either and seized the opportunity to further express that to Surrey.

"Lieutenant, they're smart. They've got us on this ridge between a rock and a hard place. It wouldn't surprise me if they were up in those foothills laughing their asses off right now."

"Yeah," Surrey mumbled, "but we ain't goin' to be here if I have anything to say about it. Ortega, bring the radio up here."

Ortega brought the radio and waited for instructions.

"Get me Loomer," Surrey said curtly, "I'm goin' to have a talk with him."

Ortega got Loomer on the radio and handed the microphone to Surrey.

"One, this is Two, over."

"Go ahead, Two. I read you."

"One, we found a Bravo Tango on the path in front of us and there are a lot more out there. We're sittin' on a time bomb here. Request permission to return to original Lima Zulu (Landing Zone), over."

The radio was silent for what seemed like a long time. Then it crackled with static and Loomer's voice came back on.

"Two, this is One. Request denied. Over."

"One, this is Two. Maybe you didn't understand me. I said we're walking into a trap. Over."

"This is One. I understand you. Now you understand me. We've got a mission out here and you're going to follow through with it! Over."

"This is Two. Again I request permission to return to the Lima Zulu.

Over."

"Permission denied. Look, Two, Battalion is probably monitoring us right now so this discussion is closed! Follow your orders! Over and out."

Blood vessels in Surrey's neck bulged.

"One, this is Two! Fuck Battalion! If they want this mission completed so bad let 'em come out here and do it themselves! I'm not about to sacrifice my men to this bullshit!"

"Two, this is One. Knock it off! You will continue with this mission! Over."

Surrey thought for a moment and then keyed the microphone.

"One, this is Two. We're going back. Over."

"Two, this is One. I don't care how in the hell you get there but you will rendezvous with us at the objective! Is that clear?"

"One, this is Two. Request permission to return to original Lima Zulu."

"No, goddam' it! I said get to the objective and you'd better be there! Is that finally clear? Over!"

Surrey remained quiet for a few seconds. He knew he was not going to win and concessions from Loomer so he mumbled "Roger," into the microphone.

"Two, this is One. What did you say?"

"One, this is Two. I said 'roger' goddammit! But we ain't takin' the goddam' path." Surrey tossed the microphone to Ortega and said, "shut the fuckin' thing off."

Bible had been listening to the conversation and knew what had happened but he said "any luck, Sir?" anyway.

"No," mumbled Surrey. "The son of a bitch won't budge. I guess we'll have to keep goin'."

"I was 'fraid of that." Bible mumbled. "This whole layout is textbook booby trap. Battalion should've realized it before they sent us here.

"I know," Surrey said as he tried to suppress his anger and bitterness, "but Battalion doesn't give a shit. If a couple of us get hit it makes it look like we're out there mixin' it up with the dinks every day."

"Sir," Bible said softly, "I've got a lot of respect for the dinks when it comes to shit like this. They do have their shit together. They can boobytrap anything an' they will an' there ain't no way I can know where them traps are. I was either very good to find that wire or I was set up. They may have wanted that wire found. There ain't no way to tell. I could probe with my knife but I think it's wired to blow a series of mines. I could trip it with something but who knows what else would happen. There could be mines every few feet. I could blow up who knows how many men."

"Can you probe it or try to trip it?"

"Sure."

"Okay, do what you have to do."

Bible crawled back down the path to the wire. He took his knife and pushed it slowly into the dirt. He found that the wire was propped up on the end of a small twig to elevate it above the ground but finding what the wire was really attached to was going to be nervewracking and difficult. Bible probed again and then again. He felt nothing. He moved his knife even further to the right and pressed slowly and gently. Finally the knife blade made contact with something unseen. There was resistance. Bible took a moment to gather his wits and then brushed away dirt around his knife. The wire, he found, was fastened to a stone. The stone was not fastened to anything so Bible followed the wire the other way and found another stone. He then cut the wire, secure in the knowledge that there was no booby trap attached. He then studied the area again and, feeling confident, he returned to Surrey.

"There was nothing there, Sir."

"Is that good or bad?"

"Beats the shit out of me, Sir."

Surrey thought for a moment and then presented a theory. Bible had just lit a cigarette when Surrey said, "do you think the dinks knew we'd come out here today?"

"Beats me. They ain't dumb. They've got agents runnin' around and ears everywhere. They know just about everythin' we do or plannin' on doin'!"

"I'll grant you that but is there really any way to tell if they knew we'd be here?"

"I think they prob'ly figured we'd get around here sooner or later. We've been fairly active in this area for the last couple of weeks and they had to know."

"Yeah, but why would they boobytrap this particular path? It would seem to me that they'd be taking a chance on blowing up their own men."

"Nah, they wouldn't use this path. All their men would either know it's boobytrapped or they'd avoid it because it's a perfect place for an ambush. They realize, Sir, that we're impatient. That makes us easier targets. Some of the soldiers on the other side of those hills walked all the way down here from North Vietnam. We flew a couple of miles in helicopters to get here and can't wait to fly right back. The gooks'll follow trails and paths and they know 'em a whole lot better'n we do."

"I suppose," sighed Surrey. "I'm sure anxious to get out of here."

"That could get us all killed, Sir. We have to be alert and cautious."

"Do you want to use the path?"

"Not 'specially. I can't shake the feelin' we're being set up."

"What do you think about getting around the path?"

"Well, Sir," Bible spoke hesitantly. "We'll probably have to go down the slope and get through near the bottom of this here hill. I don't wanna go that way but we should keep the other patrol in sight."

"Ya," Surrey said as he peered down the side of the hill, "it looks like it levels off a little bit before you get all the way to the bottom."

"There's somethin' still botherin' me."

"What?" asked Surrey.

"That trip wire. It made no real sense there. Maybe I was s'posed to find it all along and re-route us."

"That's a possibility, Surrey said. "We'll just have to find out."

"Yes, Sir."

Surrey motioned for Ortega and Ortega brought him the radio.

"I'll call Captain Shithead an' tell him," Surrey said.

"Okay, I'll tell the men what we're gonna do."

Surrey nodded and keyed the microphone.

"One, this is Two, over."

The voice of Loomer's radio operator came on. "Two, this is One. It's your dime."

"One, inform Oscar Three Lima (Captain Loomer) that we'll meet him at the objective but we'll be takin' a slight detour."

"Roger, Two. Will that be it?"

"Roger."

"Roger, Two. Out."

Surrey handed the microphone back to Ortega and walked over to Bible. Bible was talking to the men.

"Listen up. We've got a problem. I found a trip wire stretched across the path so we ain't gonna take the path. We're goin' down the side of the hill to see if we can get past the trouble but it's not gonna be easy. I want you bastards to stay alert and be careful. Watch for dry, dead grass and any old camoflage. Look for anything loose or out of place and, for chris'sake, keep five meters apart."

The cigarette Bible held was twitching because his hand was shaking. He noticed so he took a final drag, dropped the cigarette and crushed it with his boot.

"Remember, if you see anything at all, sing out."

Some of the soldiers nodded.

"All right," said Bible, "let's get goin'."

The men gathered their gear together and began to follow Sergeant Bible. Noland touched Majewski and, when Majewski turned to respond, Noland said "Does Bible seem nervous?"

"That's a stupid question," whispered Majewski.

97

"Shit," said Noland. "When he gets nervous I get nervous."

The patrol moved slowly down the slope taking great care not to detonate whatever may have been hidden under the grass and rocks. Bible led the platoon down through the long grass and stubby shrubs and, where the slope levelled out near the bottom of the hill, he turned and headed south. The sun had not risen high enough to light the entire area so the patrol moved through the shadow areas with extreme caution.

Bible and the reluctant Surrey were well out in front of the rest of the men probing, scanning, searching and suspecting anything and everything. The rest of the men followed, stepping where the man in front had stepped and staying alert and aware of the flanks. There was more to worry about than whatever happened to be directly in front so the soldiers followed Bible because they trusted his judgment and because Bible gave them time for their own self-preservation.

Bible and Surrey moved through the grass to a point where the terrain became more rocky and, since they wanted to explore any potentially dangerous area, they stopped the patrol and Bible crawled out to investigate.

From his vantage point inches above the ground, Bible surveyed and probed the rocks and dirt, looking for signs of looseness and tampering. All the rocks seemed to be firmly in place and appropriately and uniformly dusty. So, satisfied that there were no booby traps under the rocks, Bible turned his attention to the surrounding terrain. He studied approximately thirty meters of rocks and, beyond the rocks, there was another thirty meters of grass and shrubs and then a shallow climb that led to the flat area where they were to meet the other patrol. Bible resisted the temptation to believe that he was safe and the patrol was safe and home free. He knew there were still many variables so he exhaled loudly and looked toward the sky.

Above him all he could see was a vast expanse of cloudless, birdless blue and it relaxed him for a few seconds. He smelled the air and felt the warm sunlight on his bare arms. He savored the moment and then moved his eyes back to the ground around him. He resumed his reconnaissance. The slope above him was covered with rocks, low shrubs, weeds and grass. Below him the ground flattened out and was spotted with foliage and sand. Bible allowed his eyes to travel up the opposite slope. It was still shadowed and covered with rocks and shrubs. Bible could detect movement at the top of the other slope and, though he couldn't see from his vantage point, he knew the movement was the other patrol and that knowledge made him feel a little more secure. He stood up and motioned for the rest of the patrol to join him.

Surrey adjusted his helmet, waved back his complaince to Bible and signalled the men to follow him. The patrol moved out across the rocks and Bible moved out into the grass. He still had a job to do.

Majewski was now the fourth man in the patrol so, by the time he got to the rocks, Lt. Surrey was nearly to the grass. Majewski, like the rest of the men in the patrol, had been concerned about the rocks but now that Bible had indicated that he had found no booby traps, he and they relaxed a little. To Majewski the rocks were second base and the grass was third. He was rounding second and heading for third and he allowed himself to smile. It helped Majewski's state of mind to think of projects in terms of reachable goals and simple achievements. He was still a long way from safety so he returned his attention to the ground and watched very carefully where he stepped. He was concentrating very hard on what he was doing and all his senses were very much alive. He was stepping exactly where the man in front of him had stepped when he heard a rustling noise to his right. At the same instant his peripheral vision detected movement between two rocks. Majewski's head snapped to the right and he saw a clump of grass rise, pushed up by a human hand. Immediately Majewski knew what was happening. He could see a blackhaired head rising out of the spider hole and instinct moved him quickly. The soldier in the spider hole had pushed the trap door up with his left hand so he could keep his right hand ready on his rifle but the trapdoor hinged on the right so pushing across his body had cost the ambusher a fraction of a second and, in his haste to recover the element of surprise, he tried to rise too quickly and his rifle caught on the lip of the spider hole so he had to dip down quickly to free it.

Majewski saw the VC go back down into the hole and heard someone behind him yell "Hit it!" Majewski tried to dive into the bushes but his foot loosened a rock and he sprawled sideways half into the bushes and half out on the rocks.

The VC, having freed his rifle, raised it and fired. Noland had seen the VC and had shouted at Majewski but then, as he swung his rifle in the general direction of the VC, he was so surprised and shocked by the appearance of the ambusher that he froze and could not fire his weapon.

As the VC fired Noland heard a burst of gunfire behind him and to his left. Majewski, sprawling clumsily on his left side, saw the VC raise his rifle and fire. Near his feet puffs of dust and bits of rock flew into the air and, at the same instant, he saw the VC's body jerk and his shirt ripple as bullets passed through his body. The VC's body was propelled slightly upward by the force of the rounds as they passed through. The force of the bullets lifted the body and bent it over the back lip of the spider hole. As the VC was being torn apart his arm raised and, in convulsive defiance, he pulled the trigger of his rifle and fired the rest of his clip harmlessly into the air. Then, with his life and ammunition spent, his body slumped limply into death.

Majewski, still on the ground, struggled to rise but his left foot was numb and wouldn't support him. He crumbled back to the ground and furtively glanced at his ankle. It began to ache. Thinking he had been shot Majewski looked around for someone to help him. He saw Noland standing a few feet away. He was staring at the VC. Bible and Surrey had come back to see what had happened and were just reaching the spider hole.

Noland stared intently at the dead VC. He took a couple steps closer to the spider hole, raised his M-16 and fired four deliberate rounds into the dead VC.

Bible, seeing Noland fire, stopped immediately and stared at Noland. Noland shifted his gaze from the VC and saw Bible staring incongrously at him. Then he turned his eyes back to the VC and said "I thought I saw him move."

Bible looked down at the VC and said "he ain't gonna do much more movin'. Go see if anyone's hurt."

Noland flipped his safety on and moved down to where Majewski was lying.

"Are you all right?"

"I think I'm hit! My foot's achin'!"

Noland put down his rifle and looked at Majewski's feet. He couldn't see any place where a bullet might have entered so he asked Majewski which foot hurt.

Majewski was on his back, propped up on his elbows. "The left one. Jesus. It's startin' to hurt like a bitch."

"I can't see anything. No blood. Maybe he got you higher up."

A cold chill swept through Majewski's body and his eyes turned quickly to his crotch. There was no blood there and the pain was lower. Majewski was very relieved to know that whatever had happened had not happened to his groin.

Noland ran his hand up to Majewski's knee and then back down again. "I can't find anything, 'Ski. Maybe you just sprained your ankle."

Majewski tried to remember what had happened but the time sequence was blurred. He knew, however, that he hadn't dived as far as reflex and intention had dictated.

"Maybe I sprained it tryin' to get out of the fuckin' way."

"Yeah, let's get you up and see if you can stand."

Noland helped Majewski to his feet but Majewski couldn't put any weight on his leg.

"You okay?" asked Surrey.

"I think so. I may've sprained my ankle. I don't think I got shot."

"Loomer's patrol has the Medic. Can you wait until we reform?"

"Yeah, I think so," Majewski grimaced at Surrey.

Surrey and Noland helped Majewski toward the spider hole. Sergeant Bible, standing near the hole, said "This is the dude that tried to smoke you."

Majewski didn't say anything. He stood silently and watched Bible grab the dead VC by the hair and drag him slowly out of the spider hole. Majewski was surprised at how small the dead Vietnamese was. He couldn't have been taller than five feet and probably didn't weigh more than a hundred and ten pounds. He was wearing a pair of blue gym shorts and a ragged black shirt. When Bible pulled him completely out of the hole, Majewski was amazed at how young the VC seemed to be. The VC was barefooted and Bible had lifted him from the whole with one hand.

"All right, the rest of you shits keep alert," Sergeant Bible said. "There are bound to be more of these fuckers around here. You can bet this ain't the only gook in the woods."

Bible looked directly at Noland and said "Put 'Ski down and check out that spider hole."

"But Sarge," Noland protested. "I…"

"Just do it. It ain't boobytrapped. I'll keep you covered."

Noland helped Majewski lower himself to the ground and then handed Majewski his rifle.

"Hang on to this, 'Ski," Noland said and then he turned and approached the spider hole. He peered down into the hole and then looked up at Bible.

"Check it out," Bible said.

Noland laid down on his stomach and reached down into the hole. Sergeant Bible, angry at not having checked the rocks properly and upset at having led his men into an ambush, searched the dead VC.

Noland found two banana clips for the VC's AK47 and a pack of Salem cigarettes at the bottom of the hole. He showed them to Bible. Bible found an olive drab book of matches in the waistband of the VC's shorts.

"What did you find?" asked Surrey.

"Two clips. Some Salems an' a pack a ration matches."

"VC?"

"Yeah," Bible said as he took the pack of cigarettes from Noland and ripped off the tin foil on top of the pack. Surrey and Noland were surprised at what Bible found. Bible was not surprised. There was a twenty dollar U.S. Military Payment Certificate rolled up in what had been the covered part of the pack. Bible threw the pack down, unrolled the bill and held it up to Surrey and Noland.

"A double sawbuck," Surrey said.

"He's probably a VC with access to an American base, or at least to a place where G.I.'s spend money at. He didn't get this from Hanoi. If he is NVA he hasn't been here very long. He may have been trapped out here when the choppers came and may've got scared and panicked."

"He should've stayed where he was," Noland said, "we never wouldn've seen him."

"He's out here to kill us." Bible said as he took out an entrenching tool and caved in the walls of the spider hole. "Let's jus' hope he's the only one out here."

Surrey took a map from his pocket, checked the landmarks and made a mark with his pen. "We'll call in an air strike on this valley after we get the hell out of here."

Ortega had approached.

"Call Loomer and tell him what happened," said Surrey.

"I have, Sir." Ortega said. "Wan' me to call a Medevac for 'Ski?"

"Not yet. I don't want to bring a chopper down into this valley. It's pretty narrow. Wait 'till we get back up on the ridge."

"Si, Sir," Ortega said.

"What did Loomer say?"

"Not much, Sir. I thin' he tryin' to cover his ass."

"Probably," Surrey said. "The bastard."

"Si, Sir."

"Ortega, can you help Majewski alone? I don't want to tie up too many men."

Ortega didn't like the idea of dragging along both the radio and Majewski but he said "yes" anyway.

Chapter 8

Majewski struggled to his feet and waited for Bible to move the patrol out. Surrey was still folding up his map as he walked over to the rest of the men. He put the map in his pocket, held up the money and said, "Who smoked the gook?"

Davis smiled and said "I did."

Surrey handed Davis the money and said, "nice work."

Davis took the bill and stuffed it nonchalantly into his pocket. Then he winked at Surrey and said, "Thanks."

"All right," Bible said, "let's get the hell outta here."

The patrol began to form up again. Noland was adjusting his pack a few feet from Ortega and Majewski.

"Don't forget your rifle," Majewski said to Noland. "I can't carry it and it might come in handy."

"Yeah," Noland said as a look of bewilderment crept over his face. "Look, 'Ski, I was goin' to shoot him but Davis was quicker. I guess I'm not as used to this as he is."

"No sweat. Thanks for yellin'."

Noland smiled. "I guess that was important, too."

"Yep, I appreciated it."

Noland managed another smile. He knew he had not acted quickly enough. Majewski could have been dead because he had not been able to fire. The fact that Majewski was still alive made his indecisiveness a little easier to handle. He was thankful for Davis and thankful, too, that he hadn't had to kill. The VC had frightened him and, because the VC had come so close to shooting Majewski, Noland, in his frustration, had fired four rounds into the dead VC to belatedly satisfy pangs of guilt regarding duty and responsibility. There was anger, too, at the thought that the VC had put him in such a position.

The patrol got organized and moved out. Ortega and Majewski hobbled behind Noland. Majewski could put a bit of weight on his leg but not enough to prevent Ortega from having to be a support. Ortega was swearing in Spanish under his breath and Majewski, in English, was apologizing for inconveniencing Ortega. Majewski hopped along on his right foot and occasionally, when the terrain demanded, he would put his left foot down and limp painfully.

The pain in his ankle and the difficulty Majewski had crossing the rocks made it necessary for him to keep his eyes concentrated on the ground below and directly in front of him. He wanted his foot to quit hurting so he could get to the rendezvous point quickly. He did not like being near the bottom of the hill and wanted to know how close he was to the ridge so he looked up and, instead of seeing the ridge, he saw Noland's head snap back and explode in a red mist. At the same instant Majewski heard the hollow clap of an AK-47 and the loud splat of Noland's head as it disintegrated. Majewski and Ortega were splattered with blood and tissue as Noland's steel helmet spiraled high into the air.

Majewski went numb with the realization that Noland had been shot. Ortega realized it quicker and, as he dropped to the ground, he pushed Majewski and sent him sprawling across the rocks and into the bushes. Bullets from the AK whizzed harmlessly over the prone Ortega and the flailing Majewski. Farther up the path the rest of the men scattered for cover. Sergeant Bible, who was well ahead, dropped to the ground and tried to determine where the shots were coming from. He thought they came from across the valley but he wasn't sure so he looked back at Davis.

Davis was flat on the ground firing at a clump of bushes next to a boulder on the opposite slope of the valley. Bible could see the bushes move and dust fly from Davis' bullets as they ricocheted off the rock. From Bible's position he could not see anyone because whoever was firing was on the other side of the rock. He could hear the AK fire back so he knew that Davis had not hit the sniper. Instantly Bible scrambled to his feet and charged down the hill. Surrey, seeing Bible move, began firing at the rock. Bible was aware of the covering fire he was getting when he reached the bottom of the slope and started across the sandy valley floor but the VC, in order to avoid the increased fire from Davis and Surrey, had moved behind the rock and around to the other side. It was then that the VC saw Bible running toward him and his reaction was instantaneous. He raised his rifle and fired. Sergeant Bible's left leg kicked high into the air behind him and his body pitched forward and sprawled on the ground. His helmet flew off and his rifle sprang from his hands and stuck, barrel first, in the sand.

Surrey, seeing Bible fall, switched his fire to the other side of the rock and kept the Vietnamese from getting another shot at Bible.

While Davis and Surrey kept the VC pinned down, Ortega got on the radio and tried to contact Loomer.

"Where the hell are you guys, man?" Ortega screamed into the microphone. "We're takin' shit, man!"

"We're at the rendezvous point," answered Loomer's radio operator. "Sit tight. We'll get some support back to you."

"Hurry up, man. Shit!" screamed Ortega.

Surrey's covering fire was close enough to force the VC back around the rock and Davis, sensing the movement, fired short, concentrated bursts into the brush. Soldiers farther down found cover and began to fire at the VC's position. Since the VC was positioned so well behind the rock a direct shot was impossible so fire was directed low into the bushes and at the base of the rock with the hope that the bullets would ricochet and find the elusive target.

The concentrated fire allowed one of the GIs to slip down the hill to the flat ground. The soldier positioned himself behind a bush and waited for a clear shot at the Vietnamese. He kept his eyes trained on the sniper's position and, when he saw some movement, he fired. His bullet hit whatever he had seen and he saw his target rise up and then fall out of sight behind the bushes. The soldier fired again because he did not know if the initial wound had been fatal so he yelled "I hit him! I hit him! I don't know if he's dead but I hit him!"

Davis, hearing the soldier yell, held up his hand and yelled for everyone to cease fire. Immediately the firing stopped and the only sounds in the valley were the agonizing groans and grunts being made by Bible as he tried to crawl to cover.

Davis, anxious to help Bible but unsure of the status of the ambusher, turned and looked to Surrey for guidance. Surrey looked back and shrugged.

"Who said they hit him?" Davis asked Surrey.

"I don't know. I think it was Lansing. He's down there in the sand behind that bush."

Davis craned to see Lansing's position but Lansing was concealed so he yelled "Lansing!" Davis saw the bush move and Lansing slowly raised his hand. Davis, with a darting motion of his arm, motioned for Lansing to head across the valley. Then he pointed to himself and repeated the motion to indicate that he would cross the valley, too.

Lansing nodded his head and began to move across the flat ground.

Davis turned to Surrey and said "I'm goin' across directly in front of that rock. Keep your eyes on the right side because that's the side I'm goin' around. If you see the son of a bitch before I get around, shoot him."

Surrey nodded and Davis and Lansing moved out. Davis moved quickly down the hill and started across the sand. His feet kicked up puffs of dust. Davis was moving so quickly that, when he got to the rock, he had to wait for Lansing to get high enough up the other slope so Lansing could provide cover. While Davis waited for Lansing he looked over at Bible. Bible's face was contorted with pain. Bible tried to drag himself across the stones and sand. Davis knew he could do nothing for Bible so he put his finger to his mouth to indicated to Bible that Bible should remain still and quiet. Bible nodded and lowered his head to the sand. For an instant Davis thought Bible had died but then realized that Bible must have been exhausted and was using the opportunity to rest and play dead.

Davis turned his attention from Bible to Surrey's position and, when he was satisfied that Surrey was covering him, he turned and looked for Lansing. Lansing had moved across the sand and up the hill far enough to be out of Davis' field of vision so Davis returned his attention to Surrey. Surrey indicated with gestures that Lansing was above and to Davis' left.

Davis inserted a full clip into his M-16, released the charging mechanism and flipped the selector switch to automatic. He then inhaled deeply, crouched and began to move slowly around the rock. He knew the Vietnamese would be somewhere behind and to the far side of the rock so, when he was nearly around, he crouched low and sprang out away from the rock. His eyes caught a glimpse of the VC lying on the ground and he immediately fired. His bullets shook the VC's body and kicked up dirt and pieces of rock. Davis didn't know if the VC had been dead or not when he came around the rock but he did know that, by the time he had emptied his clip, the VC was surely dead.

To make sure, Davis inserted another clip and approached the body cautiously. The VC was lying on his stomach and Davis' fire had been concentrated on the torso so, when he rolled the body over, he saw that huge chunks of flesh and bloody organs had splattered the ground.

Lansing scrambled down to the rock and, by the time he got to Davis, Davis had let the body fall back to its original position.

"You hit 'im in the ass," Davis said as he pointed to the body. "I couldn't have got 'im there. You either killed him or paralyzed him because, when I came around the rock, I don't think he moved."

Lansing stared at the motionless body and then quivered slightly. He was fairly new to war and death was less familiar to him than it was to Davis.

"You done lookin'?" asked Davis.

Lansing nodded.

"C'mon, let's go help Bible."

By the time Davis and Lansing got to Bible Surrey was already there. Bible was on his back, propped up on his elbows. He was watching Surrey as Surrey inspected his wound.

The bullet had hit Bible midway on his left thigh and exited through the back of his leg a couple of inches above his knee. The exit wound was bleeding profusely and it was evident to everyone that a Medevac helicopter would have to be called in immediately. Surrey yelled for Ortega to call in a chopper.

Ortega, spattered with blood and bits of Noland's brain, appreared and called on the Medevac frequency. He handed the radio to Surrey.

"We've got one Kilo India Alpha and two Whiskey India Alphas (one killed in action and two wounded in action). Over," Surrey said.

A voice answered with a crackling "Roger. One Kilo India and two Whiskey India Alphas. Are these Uniform Sierra (U.S.) personnel or Victor November (Vietnamese)? Over."

"Uniform Sierra."

"Roger. Echo Tango Alpha (estimated time of arrival) six mikes (six minutes). Over."

"Roger."

Majewski didn't know what had happened or what was now happening. The last thing he clearly remembered was seeing Noland's head explode. From then on events were blurred in his memory. He could remember hurtling through the air and landing in the bushes and he knew that many shots had been fired but the pain in his leg and his desire for cover blotted out any recollection of subsequent events. Hearing Surrey say that one man was dead and two were wounded jarred Majewski enough to make him realize that the wetness he felt on his face and chest had been, just minutes before, inside Noland's head. That realization must have pumped adrenaline through his system because, in spite of the pain in his leg, he struggled and freed himself from the bushes and crawled over to Noland.

Noland was lying awkwardly on his back with his right arm resting across his body just below his chin. Majewski was horrified to see that there was a small bloody hole between Noland's left eye and the bridge of his nose. The pool of blood under Noland's head was expanding and Majewski noted that the peace sign tattoo on Noland's arm was resting less than five inches from the entrance wound.

The realization that Noland was dead drained all the strength from Majewski's body. He sat down on the ground and buried his head in his hands. He was aware that Ortega was standing close to him but didn't acknowledge it until Ortega tapped him on the shoulder. Majewski looked up and saw that Ortega's outstretched hand was holding an olive drab handkerchief.

"Wipe your face, Man. Chopper comin'. We got to get down to the sand, man."

"What about him?" Majewski asked.

"They'll take him, too, man."

"But…"

"Shit. There ain't nothin' more you can do, man."

Majewski rubbed the handkerchief across his face. Blood and debris collected and, when Majewski tried to hand the handkerchief back to Ortega, Ortega refused to take it.

"Take the goddam' thing," Majewski shouted, "I don't want it anymore!"

Ortega took the handkerchief timidly between his index finger and his thumb and dropped it into the bushes. He turned back to Majewski and said "C'mon, man, let's go."

"Help me up."

Ortega helped Majewski down to where Bible was lying and two other soldiers followed with Noland's body.

Majewski, remembering that he had heard someone say two men had been injured, tried to figure out who else besides Bible had been hurt and, after seeing that everyone else was all right, he realized he was the other injured man.

Ortega helped Majewski sit down next to Bible and then went and covered Noland's upper body with a poncho liner.

"You okay," asked Bible. His voice was strained and timid.

"Yeah. How 'bout you?"

"The bastard got me in the friggin' leg."

"Noland's dead."

Bible propped himself up on his elbows and watched Ortega spread out the poncho liner. Noland's tattooed arm was left uncovered either by accident or design and, seeing the peace sign, Bible lowered himself and said nothing.

Majewski heard a commotion behind him. Captain Loomer and three of his men were coming down the embankment. Surrey watched as Loomer and his men stopped to look at the dead VC and, when they stopped, Surrey muttered something under his breath and ran toward the rock. When he got to Loomer, Loomer was still staring at the body.

"You satisfied!" Surrey yelled.

Loomer, thinking Surrey was talking about the dead VC said "Yes, you did a fine job."

"That's not what I mean, you stupid shit! You cost me three men!"

"What're you talkin' about?"

"I asked you repeatedly for permission to return to the LZ and you wouldn't give it. You sent us down here against our better judgment and now you're responsible!"

"Lieutenant, you were given a mission to carry out and that's that! Casualties are part of the game."

"Game!" screamed Surrey. "Game! You come down and tell that to those three men and when you get to the one that's laid out like a Thanksgiving turkey, you'd better shout loud 'cause he's goin' to have a tough time hearin' ya!"

"Lieutenant, I'm sorry about your men."

"Sorry! Where the hell were you when we were getting shot at? You were supposed to be on that fuckin' ridge!"

"Lieutenant, I don't have to put up with this! I was completing my mission."

"Completing your mission! Your mission was to cover us and you sure fucked up!"

"Lieutenant, you are addressing a superior officer…"

"No! I'm addressing a shithead!"

"I don't have to take this," Loomer said and turned to walk away. Surrey grabbed him by the shoulder and spun him around.

"Don't you walk away from me! This isn't over yet!"

"I say it's over!" Loomer shouted.

"You do, huh? Well you can go fuck yourself!"

"All right, that's it. We'll see what Battalion has to say about this."

A sly smile crept across Surrey's face. Loomer had just said what Surrey wanted him to say.

"That sounds like a good idea, Sir. Let's go see Battalion."

Loomer, realizing that he had been goaded into the suggestion said, "we'll see when we get back."

"Okay, Sir, but just remember there'll be a debriefing sometime and your name will definitely come up."

"Lieutenant, don't threaten me. I've dealt with punks like you before."

Lieutenant Surrey smiled sarcastically at Loomer. "Sir, I'd love to stay here and chat with you but the Medevac's coming in and I have to load up your casualties."

Loomer let the remark pass. He was beginning to worry about what Surrey might say back at the base. He wasn't overly enthusiastic about the coming showdown so he reformed his men and moved back up the ridge. Surrey moved down the hill and arrived at the helicopter just as the medics were loading the body bag containing Noland. Bible and Majewski were already inside the helicopter. Surrey picked up Noland's rifle and handed it to Majewski.

"Hang on to this, 'Ski. Turn it in when you get back to camp."

Majewski reached for the rifle and Surrey said, "Be careful. It's loaded."

Majewski took the rifle and pulled it inside the helicopter. The M-16 was hot and dust mixed with Noland's blood had caked on the stock and barrel. Majewski unloaded the rifle and cleared the chamber. Noland had fired his rifle only to sight it in and then again, just moments ago, as an outlet for his churning anxiety and frustration. Majewski handed both rifles back to Surrey. Surrey accepted them without comment.

The helicopter rose slowly and loudly. When Majewski felt the helicopter leave the ground he turned his attention to the Medic.

The Medic was hunched over in front of Bible wrapping Bible's leg with pressure bandages.

"We've got to get this bleeding stopped, Sarge," mumbled the Medic, "or you'll end up like you buddy."

Bible winced and groaned.

"Do you want something for the pain?"

"No! Just get me to the fuckin' hospital!"

"We'll be there in a couple minutes. We're taking you to Eighty-fifth Evac in Phu Bai."

"Why not Quang Tri?"

"What's the difference, Sarge," grunted the Medic. "You'll be in Japan soon anyway."

A strange quiet look came over Bible's face and he appeared to smile. The thought of Japan made the pain easier to bear. The Medic continued to wrap bandages around Bible's leg.

Majewski turned his attention to the body bag on the floor. Its surface was shiny and smooth and there were mounds and valleys all along its length. It didn't look as if it held the body of his friend. For an instant Majewski doubted that Noland was even in the bag so he reached out to touch it. Though the bag looked shiny and wet it was warm and dry.

Majewski's fingers pressed on a firm lump that he could not identify so he moved his hand to the left and pressed down with the tips of his fingers. The new lump gave a little and there was a squishing sound like someone stepping softly on a wet sponge. Majewski pulled his hand back in horror. He realized instantly that he had just pressed on Noland's head. Immediately his stomach began to churn and his chest heaved and he knew he was going to vomit. He crawled along the floor and stuck his head out the door. He closed his eyes, held on tight to whatever was available and sprayed everything in his stomach all over the Vietnamese countryside.

From the far side of the chopper Majewski heard the Medic say "Attaboy, kid, bomb the bastards with puke."

Chapter 9

Eighty-fifth Evac Hospital at Phu Bai was a dismal gray complex where smells of sweat and antiseptic fused. The helicopter landed on the eastern pad and Bible was carried into the hospital. So was Noland. Anton Majewski was nauseous, hurt and confused but he was in better shape than either Bible or Noland. He limped into the hospital and waited for his eyes to adjust to being inside.

Bible was carefully examined by a doctor. Majewski watched as the doctor probed and poked at Bible's left leg. The bandaging was removed slowly and deliberately.

"We've got both an entrance and exit here," the doctor said to the assisting corpsman. "Let's get a picture and see what that bone looks like."

The corpsman nodded.

"Don't waste any time. Get him on the table."

The corpsman nodded and wheeled Bible away. The doctor straightened up and turned his attention to Majewski.

"What happened to you?" he asked.

"It's my left ankle," Majewski mumbled. "I think I sprained it."

"Were you in the same firefight as the sergeant?"

"Yes, and the same one he was," Majewski said at he nodded toward Noland's body bag.

"Cut this man's boot off," the doctor said to another corpsman.

While the corpsman was cutting Majewski's boot the doctor picked up a clipboard and walked over to the body bag. He knelt down and opened it slowly. Majewski imagined that opening body bags was a very unpleasant task for doctors. There was never anything pleasant inside.

Noland's clothes were cut away and his body was examined. The doctor noted the entrance wound and then turned Noland's head to the right and observed the exit wound. He wrote on a chart fastened to his clipboard and then turned to Majewski.

"So he was a friend of yours, huh?"

"Yes," answered Majewski. "We went through a lot together."

"If it is any consolation your friend went quickly," the doctor said softly.

"He didn't suffer. He was dead before he hit the ground. A wound like that is pretty merciful."

"I wonder," mumbled Majewski. "A few inches either way and the bullet would've miss him."

"That's the way it is sometimes," said the doctor as he began a new chart for Majewski. He turned to the corpsman and said "Get him to x-ray and, if it's not broken, have someone wrap it and send him back to his unit with a profile."

The corpsman helped Majewski into a wheelchair and pushed him down the hall. At the door of x-ray Majewski met Bible as Bible was being wheeled out. Majewski was shocked by how pale Bible looked. Bible's eyes were drooping and glassy and his face looked as if someone had coated it with flour. Majewski touched the arm of Bible's attending corpsman and said "is he going to be okay?"

"I'm not a doctor," the corpsman said, "but I've seen worse. He'll probably be fine but it'll take a while and a lot of time and effort."

Bible's eyes had closed and his breathing was irregular. He looked as if he was dying.

"When he comes to," Majewski said to Bible's Corpsman, "tell him I'm sorry."

The corpsman nodded and wheeled Bible away. Majewski was placed on the x-ray table and the technician began to position his foot. The technician twisted Majewski's foot with such a brusque movement that pain shot up Majewski's leg and caused him to scream. He began to sweat and hovered precariously between being sick to his stomach again and passing out because of the pain.

It took a long time for Majewski to regain his composure. X-rays were taken and the corpsman wheeled him to a treatment area. Another doctor arrived, studied the x-rays and wrapped Majewski's ankle.

Majewski, while his ankle was being wrapped, began to look around the room. When he initially entered the room he had been aware of the presence of other people but his concerns were immediately his own. Now he could afford the time and the curiosity to study the people around him. He actually heard the man to his left before he saw him. The man was screaming and Majewski soon learned why. The soldier was lying on his right side and two men wearing white coats were standing facing his back. Their movements were smooth and then jerky. They were pulling jagged pieces of shrapnel from the soldier's back and dropping them into a metal pan. The shrapnel hitting the pan made a pinging sound.

The sight made beads of sweat pop out on Majewski's brow. He turned his eyes from that soldier only to see an even more disturbing sight on the far side of the room. There, near the far wall, a heavyset soldier with black hair was on his back propped up on his elbows. He was watching two corpsmen slip a plastic bag over the lower half of his body. The soldier was quiet and seemed unemotional. The lower half of his body looked like ground beef.

Majewski began to feel lightheaded. He closed his eyes and waited for the doctor to finish wrapping his ankle.

The hospital proved to be an enlightening experience for Majewski.

Noland was dead. Bible's leg had been shattered and Majewski found he had some time to reflect.

Everything had happened so quickly. One second Noland had been alive and then he was dead literally in the blink of an eye. Part of Noland's brain and a fair amount of Noland's blood had been splattered all over Ortega and Majewski. The tall grass had been flattened by the bodies of soldiers seeking concealment and nourished by the blood that had been spilled. The grass kept growing. Noland didn't.

Majewski's transportation back to the Fire Base was a truck carrying supplies. The ride gave him a chance to see the Vietnamese countryside without being overly close to it or overly far above it. The land was beautiful. Vibrant greens mixed with blue sky and distant hazy mountains to form a soft, quiet and peaceful landscape. Rice farmers and waterbuffalo toiled in the paddies as they had for hundreds of years and there was a natural order that was easy to feel. Majewski allowed himself to relax and to savor.

When the truck arrived at the Fire Base Majewski limped to the hooch that served as the Orderly Room. A Specialist named McGill ran the Orderly Room and, when Majewski appeared at the door, McGill rose from his desk and helped him to a chair.

"How ya feelin'?" McGill asked with a genuine tone of concern.

"Like homemade shit," said Majewski.

"I was real sorry to hear about Noland and Bible," McGill said as he retrieved Majewski's M-16 from the corner of the room. "They were both good guys."

"Yeah."

"Did you see Bible or hear how he is?"

"Someone said he was goin' to be sent to Japan. The wound may be serious enough to get him sent back to the States."

"Hummmmmm," McGill muttered. "I don't know if that's good news or bad."

"Bible will be breathing when he goes back," Majewski said. "Noland won't."

"Bummer. I heard Noland caught it in the head."

"Right in the eye," Majewski said softly.

"Jeezus. That's really sad. I liked Noland."

"The doctor said he didn't suffer but how would anyone know?"

"I don't know," McGill shivered and shook his head. "I don't want to find out."

Majewski looked over McGill's shoulder at the Commanding Officer's office. The door was open but the office was empty.

"Where are they? Surrey must be back because my rifle's here."

"About an hour ago the CO and Surrey and Loomer hopped into a chopper and headed for Battalion."

"Did they say anything?" asked Majewski.

"No, but Loomer looked scared and the CO looked pissed. Surrey sauntered out of here wearing a shiteatin' grin."

"That sounds encouraging."

"Maybe, but you know the fuckin' Army. The lifers will band together and stick the ole green weenie to Surrey. I've seen it happen a hundred times."

"You're probably right," sighed Majewski. "Surrey's not really Army."

"We'll find out sometime. Do you want a cigarette?"

"Yeah, I ran out at the hospital."

McGill took a pack of Marlboros from his pocket and slid them across the desk with his lighter.

"Marlboros?" Majewski looked fairly puzzled. "Where the hell do you get Marlboros?"

"I've got a friend who works at the PX in DaNang. He sends me twenty cartons a month. I sell 'em for beaucoup bucks."

"Shit. I haven't seen anything but Salems since I got to I Corps."

"Keep 'em. I've got plenty."

Majewski slipped the cigarette between his lips, picked up McGill's lighter and lit it. Savoring the taste of an unmentholated filter cigarette Majewski happened to notice some engraving on McGill's Zippo. He read it.

YEA THO I WALK

THRU THE VALLEY OF

THE SHADOW OF DEATH

I WILL FEAR NO EVIL

FOR I AM THE EVILEST

SON OF A BITCH

IN THE VALLEY

It seemed to be a pretty presumptuous statement for an Orderly Room clerk whose contribution to the war effort was blackmarketing cigarettes.

Majewski handed the lighter back to McGill. Then he reached into his pocket and pulled out a piece of paper.

"I have a profile about my foot."

McGill took the paper and glanced at it.

"This should keep you out of the boonies for a while. You can ghost for a couple of days and then pull some company detail. You'll have it dicked for a few days."

"Where are the rest of 'em?" asked Majewski.

"Oh, I was going to tell you," McGill said. "They formed up with that Vietnamese unit and ended up out on an ambush."

"What? We were just supposed to check out the area!"

"I don't know about that but, after Noland and Bible got hit, someone decided they should stay out and waste a few VC tonight."

"Who decided?"

"I don't know for sure," McGill said. "Loomer probably. Then he came back here and probably left one of his lieutenants in charge. He wanted to get to the CO and Battalion before Surrey could."

"Figures."

"Yeah, with everyone except Surrey out in the boondocks it's Loomer's word against Surrey's."

"What about the CO? Does he know what happened?"

"I doubt it. He's probably just goin' to sit back an' see which side wins. He's so afraid that someone's goin' to frag him he probably won't say anything. Besides, Loomer has more pull with the brass than the CO does."

"Too bad Ortega didn't come in. He knew everying that went on."

"That puts you in a bad position, 'Ski."

"How?"

"You were out there. You know what happened."

"I don't know shit about what happened. I was way back in the line. Surrey and Bible were out front."

"Someone in Battalion may talk to you about what happened."

"They won't get much but I will side with Surrey. The path was mined."

"I guess it really don't matter much," sighed McGill. "What's done is done."

"Oh, it matters to Bible and Noland. This is a day they'll remember."

"Bible won't forget," McGill said. "What about you?"

141

"Mac, I'll never forget it."

McGill sat at his desk and shuffled some loose papers. When the papers were nicely stacked he looked up at Majewski and said "I'll take care of Noland's rifle."

Majewski nodded. He was feeling very tired.

"I'm going back to my AO and rest my foot."

McGill nodded. "See ya later."

"Yeah. You will. It's a small war."

"Oh, 'Ski, wanna hear something weird?"

"What?"

"I sent a letter of Noland's out this morning on the chopper."

Majewski said nothing. He turned and left the hooch. The sun was still high and it was hot and humid. He limped slowly back to his hooch.

Once inside the hooch Majewski hobbled into Noland's AO. The AO was small, hot, dark and cluttered. There was no moving air. On the floor lay a pair of unpolished jungle boots and a towel. The bed was rumpled and Noland's blanket was draped across his padlocked footlocker like a flag across a coffin.

Majewski sat down on Noland's bed and pushed the blanket away from the lock. He pulled on the lock but it held tight. He did not know the combination. He had wanted to open the footlocker so he could get rid of any dope Noland left behind but then he remembered Noland had said something about being out of dope so Majewski decided to leave the footlocker alone. Someone would eventually cut the lock and check the contents.

Majewski then picked up Noland's pillow and squeezed it a couple of times. It was better than his own.

At some point in time Noland would be replaced. His AO would belong to someone else. Until that happened the AO and everything in it would still be Noland's except for his pillow and his small electric fan. Majewski commandeered both to make himself more comfortable. Majewski left Noland's AO and returned to his own. He rolled up his own blanket and placed it at the foot of his bed. He plugged Noland's fan into an outlet, turned it on and laid down on the bed. His head was propped up by the luxury of a second pillow. Noland's fan hummed distinctively and, in the late afternoon quiet, Majewski felt very hollow inside and his mind turned to thoughts of death. He had wondered about death often and each time someone he knew died, he became more confused. Accepting death must be, he thought, a strange maturing process. In his youth death had been explained by adults as "God has taken someone to His Kingdom because that someone's allotted time on earth was up and it was God's will that that someone be brought home to God's Kingdom." The red flag on the cosmic parking meter has popped up. That would mean old age, traffic accidents, regular fatal accidents, heart attacks, cancers, fatal diseases, crimes, murders and even wars were all God's instruments and even God's will. Could such explanations be possible? Majewski did not know. He speculated about the existence of Heaven and Hell. Where were they? Heaven was up and Hell was down but they apparently existed in a spiritual dimension that man, unless he died, could not experience. Man could speculate and perceive but he could not, on this earth, really know.

What did one do in Heaven? What did one do in Hell? Was life after death some mental gymnastic pursued only by man? Was life after death an evolved concept or a contrived religious convention? Majewski was not a scholar. Did mankind build the concept of life after death because mankind was too egotistical to believe that mortal life was all there is for such a special and unique species? Did the spiritual separate from the physical and move on?

Where was Noland now? In Heaven? In Hell? All Majewski knew for sure was that Noland's body was in a plastic bag at 85th Evac Hospital in Phu Bai.

The day had been terrifying. Noland was dead and nothing could change that or anything else that had happened.

Majewski buried Noland by lighting up a Marlboro and by silently vowing not to die in Vietnam. He closed his eyes and felt the quiet. He allowed himself to drift. Sleep followed. He did not know how long he slept. He was awakened in the early evening by the sounds of someone in his AO. He awoke startled. Lieutenant Surrey was standing near his bed.

S. R. Larson

Majewski, prompted by the reflex of military courtesy, attempted to get up. Surrey held out his hand and said "Don't bother."

Majewski grimaced as he eased himself back down onto the bed. The sudden movement had jarred his foot and pain had shot up his leg.

"How's the foot?" Surrey asked.

"It hurts, Sir."

"I guess you won't be able to use it much for a while."

"I guess not. At least that's what the doc said."

The expression on Surrey's face became sullen and it appreared to Majewski that Surrey was laboring over what he wanted to say. Majewski waited quietly until Surrey spoke.

"'Ski, I got my ass chewed by Battalion for smartassin' Loomer out there in the field. They said I was wrong."

"I'm sorry to hear that, Sir," Majewski said. "I think you were right. You had our best interests at heart."

146

"Best interests. The Army doesn't give a shit about best interests. It just wants to maintain the status quo."

"Yuh," sighed Majewski.

"We're nothin' to them. They don't give a goddam' about us. The only thing they look at is the casualty reports. We got two of them and it only cost us one. Bible's not dead. He's just out of service for a while. It's like he's on R&R. They just shuffle some papers and everything's all right."

"Will he be okay?" Majewski asked.

"I guess so but I haven't heard for sure. I tried to look after you guys and get my job done at the same time but I couldn't do it. Two of my men get shot and you get wracked up. Noland's dead and Bible's all busted up and they call me in and chew me out for calling Loomer an asshole."

"What?" Majewski was genuinely puzzled. "They chewed your ass for that? That sucks."

"Do you want to know what else they did to me, 'Ski?"

"What?"

147

"Can you keep what I'm going to tell you confidential? Can you keep it under your hat?"

"Sure," said Majewski.

"This is really rich. You'll like this. They told me that they weren't going to court martial me but, as a punishment for the disrespect I showed to Loomer, they were going to pull me out of the field, put me in the rear and bar me from reenlistment."

"You're shitting me!"

"No, I'm not."

"Jesus."

"Yes, they said they didn't want someone like me commandin' troops in the field."

Majewski looked around to see if anyone could possibly hear what he was about to say. When he was satisfied that he and Surrey were, indeed, totally alone he whispered "Did they know about the ghost ambushes?"

"No and I didn't tell 'em. There's all kinds of that shit goin' on out in the field. What the brass doesn't know might save a few lives. At any rate, tellin' 'em would've made it worse for me and everyone else."

"I suppose so."

"Ya, well, that brings me to what I wanted to talk to you about. McGill says you took Noland's death pretty hard."

"Yeah, I did. We'd been through a lot together. His brains are on that shirt on the floor."

Surrey looked down at the shirt. Then he looked at Majewski and said "You can limp around the base for a few days and then we'll assign you as a bunker rat. You can work Green Line for a while. I can at least do that."

"That would be great, Sir," Majewski said.

"You've got to keep your shit together, though. Stay awake and alert and I don't want you smokin' dope up there. There are enough shitbirds and smokejumpers on Green Line. I want you up there to keep things straight."

"I don't smoke dope, Sir."

"Fine. Get your foot in shape." Surrey took a small metal flask from his pocket, unscrewed the cap and poured some of the flask's contents into the cap.

Then he handed the cap to Majewski and raised the flask.

"Let's drink to it," Surrey said. "To bullshit. Good old B.S. Can I live without it?"

"I sure can," Majewski said. He then drank the contents of the flask cap. It was whiskey. It burned all the way down and caused him to cough slightly. His eyes closed and he allowed his head to sink into the pillow.

"I'll leave this with you," Surrey said as he handed the flask to Majewski. "I have a bigger bottle in my hooch. This has been a day I'll remember so I'm going to try to forget."

Majewski opened his eyes and looked at the flask.

"I can't take this, Sir."

"Don't worry about it. Keep it under your pillow. I'll pick it up in the morning."

Majewski wrapped his hand around the flask and was amazed at how good it felt. He didn't really want to drink any more but he knew that he might change his mind. There was something reassuring about the flask and the liquid it held.

"I'll see you tomorrow," Surrey said, "take it easy."

Surrey left the hooch and Majewski clasped the flask to his chest. He was tired and spent. He closed his eyes and savored the momentary quiet of the night. Sadly he acknowledged that Noland had been dead for just about half a day. Majewski allowed his mind to recall what Noland had looked like in life and how he had appeared shortly after death.

The hooch was quiet. Off in the distance the electric generator hummed and he could hear voices. He heard the pop of a flare and perceived a faint change of light. Noland no longer existed. For the first time in Noland's life he was dead so Majewski raised the flask and whispered "Adios, Freak." It was time to say goodbye.

Chapter 10

Majewski laid around for two entire days and pretended that his foot hurt more than it really did. Convalescing gave him a chance to catch up on his sleep. The strain of staying alert and alive in the field had dictated that he spend most of his hours awake. In the relative safety of the Fire Base Majewski relished the replenishment and relaxation of sleep. He knew that soon he would have to be alert again. His mind occasionally wandered back to Noland and he remembered Noland had said that, the night before that last fateful patrol, he had written a letter to his parents. Majewski began to feel that the act of writing had been an omen and, instead of writing to his parents, he wrote to this aunt and uncle.

Dear Aunt Janet and Uncle Lou,

A few days ago my best friend died out in the field. The night before he wrote to his folks. I thought this over and decided it would be best if I didn't write to mom and dad until things change.

It would be tempting fate.

Please tell them this. I hope they understand.

Love, Anton

When his ankle had healed enough to permit limited use he was assigned to Staff Sergeant Elmore. Elmore was in charge of detailing men to perform certain unpleasant but necessary tasks around the Fire Base. Majewski limped through a couple of days' worth of clerk and CQ duties and then found himself holding a shovel and standing in the middle of a bunch of other misfits and "soldiers of injury."

Sergeant Elmore addressed the men.

"The Commanding Officer walked by the Bunker Nine Piss Tube this mornin' and sunk a couple uh inches into some soggy muck. He informed me that the Bunker Nine Piss Tube has overflowed. We are goin' to unoverflow it."

A multitude of groans rose from the assembled detail. A piss tube was just that. It was a pipe that emptied into a buried fifty-five gallon drum. Above ground all that could be seen was the open end of the pipe. A piece of wire mesh screen kept unauthorized material out of the tube and a semicircular piece of corrugated drainage tin was mounted between two poles and placed near enough the piss tube to provide either a semblance of privacy or a white knuckled brace for soldiers who had returned from their Rest and Relaxation visit to Bangkok. The Bunker Nine Piss Tube had overflowed because more than fifty-five gallons of urine had been deposited in it, making it one of the world's largest specimen bottles. It was Elmore's responsibility to see that the situation was quickly remedied.

"You men are gonna dig up that there drum an' replant it over by bunker thirteen."

"We don't have to," someone in the crowd yelled. "It's unsanitary and we don't have to pull any detail that's a health hazard!"

Elmore did not answer politely. "A health hazard! Hell, boy, you got two choices! You can either replant the drum or pound the bush. It's up to you. Which do you think is the bigger health hazard?"

The soldier that had voiced the objection reached over and took the shovel out of Majewski's hand. Then he held up the shovel and grinned at Sergeant Elmore.

"Good," Elmore grinned back, "now use it!"

Elmore stepped back and the detail milled around for a few minutes and then slowly began to dig. Majewski walked up to Elmore and, from his pocket, produced the piece of paper that detailed his duty limitations. Elmore read it thoroughly.

"So, Majalawski, you're still ghosting with that foot, aren't you?"

"It's Majewski, Sergeant. The 'W' is silent."

"Ya," mumbled Elmore, "whatever."

"The fact remains, Sergeant, that my profile relieves me from this type of detail."

"Well, Maja…"

"Majewski."

"We'll just have to find something else for you to do. Come with me."

Majewski followed Elmore with his most exaggerated limp. He had no desire to dig out the drum.

Elmore stopped briefly and glanced over his shoulder. Some of the men in the detail were not as yet digging.

"I want to see some action from you dickheads! If there ain't considerable progress by the time I get back a lot of you shits are goin' to be humpin' the boonies!"

Those who had not been digging began to dig and Elmore proceeded to the Orderly Room with Majewski following at a distance and pace appropriate for an invalid.

Once inside the Orderly Room Elmore went in to talk to the Commanding Officer and Majewski got a cup of coffee and spoke with McGill.

"What's Elmore got goin' on today?" McGill asked.

"He's got a bunch of potheads and shitbirds diggin' up the Bunker Nine Piss Tube."

"Oh, my god," moaned McGill, "that's funny!"

"Not if you're doin' it."

"I can't believe that!" laughed McGill. "What did you do in the war, daddy? Well, son, I dug up piss tubes."

"Oh, yeah, there are a bunch of 'em out there with shovels diggin' up old Number Nine. I showed him my profile and got out of it."

"I don't blame you. How's your foot anyway?"

"As long as they're doing that," Majewski said as he motioned in the general direction of the piss tube, "my foot's goin' to hurt real bad."

"How is it really?"

"Oh, it still gives me trouble. I can't put a lot of weight on it and I can't move very fast. It's still prone to turning whenever I'm on uneven ground."

"Good. It'll keep you down for a few more days."

"I hope to hell so."

The door to the CO's office opened and Elmore emerged.

"Come on, Alphabet, we'll have you supervise."

157

Majewski put down his coffee cup and mumbled "shit" softly under his breath.

Just as Elmore was about to leave the Orderly Room McGill called to him.

"Sergeant Elmore, I've got some papers for you."

Elmore looked puzzled as he approached the desk. Apparently he wasn't used to receiving papers.

"What are they?"

"Rosters."

"Rosters?"

"Yeah," said McGill. "That one's for the men assigned to your detail and the other one is a list of Fahnoogees {fuckin' new guys} they're sending up from Phu Bai. They may need some in-country trainin'."

Elmore ran his eyes slowly down the papers to see if there happened to be any names he recognized. Then he turned and, still reading, walked out the door. Majewski began to follow but McGill called him back.

"You forgot your coffee."

Majewski hesitated for a moment and then, figuring he could handle a hot cup of coffee since he was no longer using his crutches, picked up the cup and followed Elmore.

The detail had made progress. They had widened the hole considerably but every time they removed a shovelful of mud, the space vacated quickly filled with rancid, putrid urine. Now, instead of a muddy ring around the piss tube, there was a twelve foot circular lake that widened with the action of each shovel.

Intent on finishing the detail as quickly as possible the potheads were digging furiously and no one saw Elmore approach and no one knew he wasn't watching where he was walking.

Staff Sergeant Elmore had walked from the Orderly Room to the Bunker Nine Piss Tube countless times in the past but he had never done so while reading. Majewski wasn't paying much attention either. Carrying hot coffee was difficult even if one didn't have a sprained ankle so, when he did look up at Elmore, his surprise was immediate. Majewski looked up in time to see impending disaster but not in time to yell a warning to Elmore. Majewski heard Elmore scream and saw him disappear into Piss Lake.

Everyone's reaction was immediate. There was an explosion of laughter. Uproarious, sidesplitting, falling on the ground convulsive, hysterical laughter. In spite of the hot coffee that spilled and burned his wrist, Majewski laughed as loudly as anyone. Seeing Elmore's arms flail and hearing his highpitched, absurd scream blotted all the misery from Majewski's mind and he collapsed into his own hot coffee and doubled up with pure, honest, wholesome laughter. It was the best thing that had happened to Majewski since he got drafted.

Everyone except Elmore laughed. Elmore gaged, hissed, struggled and panicked at the thought of drowning in piss. The shock of falling in gave way to the frustration of not being able to get out. When Vietnamese mud is mixed with water and American urine it has a tendency to become very slick and difficult to maneuver in.

Elmore yelled for help time and time again but no one was able to help him. Everyone was laughing too hard and, finally, when someone did manage to control himself enough to extend a shovel to the stranded sergeant, the sight of Elmore struggling in piss up to his chin must have been too much for the soldier to bear. He collapsed again in laughter and dropped the shovel.

Elmore sank. He eventually grabbed the tube and pushed his head above the surface of the muck. He screamed loud enough and long enough to attract the attention of a couple of passing cooks who, since they hadn't been around for the initial splash, were able to summon enough presence of mind to extend the handle of a shovel and pull Elmore out before they, too, found themselves overtaken by laughter.

Staggering to his feet drenched and dripping, Elmore's first reaction was a torrent of curses. Vulgar and obscene phrases cascaded from his moist lips and his face turned beet red. That fostered another round of raucous laughter and Elmore, spurred on by his rage, broke into a superhuman sprint for the shower room. He ran under a spigot, twisted the handle and one drop of water fell and hit him directly in the middle of his forehead. Elmore did not know there was no water and that there wouldn't be any until late afternoon or early evening.

Elmore spent a fair amount of the morning rubbing dry sand over his naked body. He spent a fair amount of the evening under the shower with shampoo and soap and, when he was finished, he put on clean fatigues and burned the pair he had gone swimming in.

The next day Elmore went to the supply room and tried to turn in his jungle boots and cap.

"Was the damage due directly to combat?" the supply sergeant asked as he surveyed the boots and cap Elmore had place on the counter.

"Yes," answered Elmore.

"Gee, they look all right to me, Sarge. What's wrong with 'em?"

"They got wet."

"Shit, that ain't goin' ta hurt 'em none. They was designed to handle wet."

"Well I can't wear 'em anymore."

"I don't see no real damage that'd make 'em unusable. Maybe if you told me what happened to 'em I could do somethin'."

"Nothin'," said Elmore. "Never mind. They just got wet." He gathered up his boots and cap and left the supply room. As he trudged away he could hear the supply sergeant break into laughter. That left a bad taste in Elmore's mouth.

Elmore set his boots outside his hooch and let them stay there. No one ever considered stealing them. He also bought McGill's spare cap for twelve dollars. When it came to selling his spare cap to Elmore McGill was in full control. It was clearly a seller's market and supply and demand nested in McGill's pocket. McGill would not accept Elmore's trade-in, either.

Chapter 11

Remembering Elmore's swim made Majewski laugh countless times for the next week. During that week his patrol came in, resupplied and returned to the field. Majewski felt left out in a strangely satisfying way. He admired and liked everyone he had been in the field with but he couldn't help feeling happy about not being with them. They had all been glad to see him and they were concerned about his welfare. Majewski didn't tell any of them that he was going to be working for Surrey on Green Line. They'd find out soon enough anyway. Sometimes, Majewski thought, it was good to just leave well enough alone.

Majewski continued to pull company detail and the pain in his foot lessened. One day McGill came to his hooch and said "Surrey wants to see you in the Orderly Room."

Surrey was sitting on the edge of McGill's desk drinking a cup of coffee and, when Majewski entered, Surrey motioned for him to sit down in a nearby chair.

"How's the foot?" Surrey asked.

"Still hurts, Sir," Majewski answered with a look of pain. "but I am being careful."

"Good. What I talked to you about still stands. I want you on Green Line tomorrow night."

"Okay, Sir. Will that be all?"

"Not quite," Surrey said softly, "something's up. I don't know what's going on but a ten ton just pulled in loaded with mortar rounds and artillery shells. I'm afraid I'm going to have to ask you to help Elmore's crew load some of them into that conex."

Surrey pointed out the door so Majewski turned and looked. From McGill's desk Majewski could look out and see the truck, the conex {a large metal cube that the Army used for storage} and Elmore's crew as it milled around waiting for direction. He could also see Elmore coming toward the Orderly Room.

"Elmore's comin'. Do you want me to go with him, Sir?"

"Yeah, but this time watch where he walks."

Majewski and Surrey waited for Sergeant Elmore. When Elmore entered Surrey smiled and said "Hi, El. How's the old Australian crawl comin'?"

Elmore glared at Surrey. He was not amused. With a sneer he said "Fuck you, Sir."

Surrey smiled and motioned for Majewski to get up.

"Here's your man, Sergeant."

Elmore looked at Majewski. "Okay, Alphabet, get out there and help them dickheads unload that truck and don't even show me no goddam' profile."

"Okay, Sergeant."

"And keep them lousy bastards workin'. They can put in a good hour's work before the mess tent opens."

Majewski nodded and left the office. He walked out across the sand to the truck. The sun was high and there was very little breeze. Majewski wasn't looking forward to this particular detail. Not only did it seem to be too hot to work but the thought of unloading live ammunition didn't sit well with him, either. The fact the truck had made it all the way to the Fire Base without blowing or being blown up was of little consolation. It could have just been luck and luck, Majewski believed, was not constant or consistent. But then if the mortar rounds were to be used to keep the VC and NVA away and, therefore, keep him alive, it might be worth the effort to unload the truck. So, resigned to the fact that he would have to help, Majewski positioned himself in the line and passed mortar rounds from the soldier on his right to the soldier on his left.

There were four men working with Majewski. One on the truck, two others plus himself on the ground and one in the conex. Majewski knew the four vaguely as the camp incorrigibles. The shitbirds. The fuckups. The dickheads. They were eager and nearly constant consumers of alcohol and marijuana and were also disciplinary problems. The shitbirds were not good soldiers. Noland had known them better than did Majewski. The company was prudently reluctant to put them into the field, fearing they would jeopardize the other men, so they were kept in the company area under Elmore's control and they embraced that situation.

Loading ammunition was more enjoyable for them than being shot by it so they strained and swore and laughed and sang and complained as they loaded mortar rounds into the conex. Majewski had a difficult time keeping up with them. He was glad when the mess tent opened and, instead of eating, he spent an hour resting in his AO in front of the fan.

When it was time to return to work, Majewski walked to the truck and waited for the rest of the crew to return. He sat on the truck bed for fifteen or twenty minutes then moved inside the cab and waited another half hour until Elmore showed up with the four ammo handlers.

"I thought I told you to keep an eye on these bastards!"

"I didn't eat with 'em, Sergeant."

"They didn't eat. They smoked shit!"

Majewski looked at the four men. Their eyes were glassy and they were staring off into the distance unconcerned about Elmore, Majewski, or the mortar rounds. Majewski had seen enough smokejumpers to know that his four companions were, indeed, stoned.

"Goddam' potheads," Elmore mumbled. "I don't know why I even fuck with 'em! They ain't good for nothin' in this man's Army."

Majewski suppressed a smile as Elmore turned to the potheads.

"All right," Elmore screamed, "I want you fuckin' jerks to get this fuckin' truck unloaded and I want it unloaded right fuckin' now! If you don't get your shit together, you'll all be stompin' the boondocks! Now get your stupid asses to work!"

Majewski climbed down from the cab and the others seemed to come out of their organic stupor long enough to position themselves approximately where they had been before breaking for lunch.

Four or five artillery rounds were passed down the line and placed in the nearly full conex. Then, from the truckbed, Majewski heard the word "Catch" and turned in time to see the smokejumper on the truck toss an artillery round to the first man on the ground. The first man caught it and pitched it to the second man who, in turn, tossed it to Majewski. Majewski caught it and held it firmly.

"What in the hell are you doin'?" yelled Majewski. "Are you nuts?"

The soldier on the truck smiled his silliest smile. "Don't sweat it, man," he cooed. "It won't go off. Everything's cool."

"I said knock it off," Majewski shouted as he handed the round to the man in the conex. "And I mean it!"

The pothead on the truck smiled and shrugged his shoulders.

"Whatever you say, pollack."

Majewski stared intently at the grinning soldier. "I meant what I said. If you throw one more round I'll come up there and kick your ass!"

The smokejumper picked up a round and stared at Majewski. Majewski stared back until the smokejumper leaned over and handed the round to the man on the ground. He smiled at Majewski and asked, "Is that better?"

Majewski didn't say anything. He took the round when it was handed to him and handed it to the man in the conex. He wiped his sweating palms on his pant legs and waited for the next round to be placed in his hands.

Working with potheads made Majewski nervous. Unloading ammo was nervewracking enough without the added risk of marijuana. Majewski wished he still had his profile but really didn't need it because he heard McGill call his name and, when he looked up, McGill was standing halfway between the truck and the Orderly Room motioning for him to come over.

Majewski left the line and trotted toward McGill. He was glad to be away from the shitbirds. So glad, in fact, that he didn't look back to see if they were throwing artillery rounds even though he suspected they were. When he reached McGill he stopped running.

"What's up?" Majewski asked.

"I have to talk to you," McGill said as he turned and walked to the Orderly Room.

"What about?"

"It has to do with that incident in the bush when Noland and Bible got hit."

Majewski figured he was getting into the middle of some type of Army investigation so, when they got inside the Orderly Room, he slumped down into the chair and expected the worst.

"Battalion found out that you're eligible for a Purple Heart, 'Ski, and they want you to take it."

Majewski was torn between relief and rage.

"A Purple Heart!" Majewski blurted. "I dont want a Purple Heart!"

"I didn't think you did," McGill said. "I told the old man that but he said to call you in anyway."

"Where is he?"

"Talkin' to Elmore in his office."

"Well, I don't want it and I won't take it!"

"Hey, 'Ski," McGill said apologetically, "there's no need to jump in my shit. I'm just doing what I was told."

"Ya, Mac, I know and I'm sorry. It's just that it really gives me the ass!

Noland got his head blown off and Bible got his leg mangled and they want to give me a Purple Heart! All I did was fall on my ass and sprain my ankle."

"They're gettin' 'em, too."

"They deserve 'em!"

"Hey, look, 'Ski, don't get pissed at me…"

"I'm not pissed at you," Majewski said as he got to his feet, "I just…"

Majewski never finished the sentence. He was interrupted by a brilliant flash of light and a tremendous explosion that peeled the roof off the Orderly Room and pitched Majewski across the desk. He landed on top of McGill.

The Orderly Room disintegrated and collapsed around Majewski and the sound was deafening. All the air had been sucked out of the building and then forced back in by a flash of orange and gold light. Majewski's ears rang and he kept hearing either echoes of the explosion or the violent concussions of subsequent blasts.

From his position on top of McGill Majewski was sure of nothing. His mind and senses were totally confused and they refused to even try to figure out what had happened. It was irrelevant. Instinctively he folded into the fetal position that protected his crotch.

He covered his head with his arms and prepared to die as pieces of metal smashed through the walls and debris crashed and dirt sifted down around him. Underneath Majewski McGill squirmed to free himself from his overturned desk and from Majewski. Behind and to the left Elmore staggered out of what had been the CO's office.

"Someone help!" Elmore groaned. "For chrissake someone help!"

Majewski and McGill slowly managed to get to their feet. They climbed over boards and tin and timbers to where Elmore was standing.

"Are you all right?" yelled McGill.

"Help the CO! He's trapped in his office!" Elmore was bleeding from a gash on his head. He was holding his left forearm with his right hand and his eyes had glazed over.

"You're bleedin' bad," Majewski blurted.

"Don't worry about me! Help the CO!"

McGill and Majewski pushed their way into the CO's office and looked around for him. Dust was swirling and they found the CO when they heard him groan and saw his feet.

The CO had apparently been sitting with his feet propped up on his desk when the explosion occurred. The blast pushed him back just like it had pushed McGill but, instead of depositing a person on top of him like it had done to McGill, the blast brought down a support plank and pushed the desk toward the CO so he was trapped flat on his back, or rather on his head, with his butt on top of the overturned chair. His feet rested on the corner of the desk and a support beam laid across his chest just below his chin.

"Jesus, let's get him out!" McGill yelled. "He'll die under there!"

Majewski didn't believe that the CO would die but he didn't feel he should waste time debating the possibility. He moved over the debris and lifted the support beam. McGill pulled the CO out from under the beam and all four men staggered outside. They did not have to use the office door. They walked through what had been the wall of the CO's office.

Once outside Majewski saw that Elmore was holding his forehead with his right hand and blood was oozing between Elmore's fingers, trickling down his arm and dripping off his elbow.

"How bad're you hurt?" Majewski asked.

"Don't worry about me! How bad's the CO?"

Majewski turned and saw that Captain Wyandotte was inhaling deeply with breaths that arched his back and pointed his chin upward. When he tried to talk he was very hoarse and his hands were moving up and down his chest as he was apparently feeling for any outward indication of injury.

"I'm okay," the CO gasped. "What the fuck happened?"

Majewski turned and looked at the ammo conex. It was gone. A gnarled, twisted, burning chunk of metal was all that was left of the truck. Off to the right a row of hooches lay in ruins and two were burning. To the left roofs were peeled back on a row of hooches and one hooch had collapsed. From his vantage point Majewski couldn't see his own hooch so he broke from the group and ran across the sand.

The roof on the far side of the building had peeled slightly but the section over his AO was intact. Majewski entered the hooch cautiously. He didn't know how safe it was and he didn't want to fall through the floor or dislodge any debris. The hooch was dark and strangely quiet. Curious shafts of light from holes in the roof held particles of dust in suspension and Majewski noticed no sound except the ringing in his ears. The hooch had managed to stay upright through an explosion violent enough to crumple a ten ton truck like it was a piece of waste paper. Buildings had been shattered and Majewski did not know what had happened. Was the base under attack? Did a bomb fall from a plane? Majewski explored war possibilities and then came to a chilling realization. The blast had come from behind him, from where the potheads had been unloading the ammunition truck. Had someone been wrong in assuming that tossed ammunition would not explode? What had the explosion done to the men that had probably caused it? What had happened to the men Majewski had been working with up until a moment or two before the explosion? They were certainly dead but Majewski was not. The knowledge that he had escaped death drained all the strength from his body. His knees buckled and deposited him on his bed in a sitting position.

He broke out in a cold sweat and extended his hands to brace himself. As soon as his left hand contacted the bed his reflexes jerked it back. He had put his hand on something jagged and hot. Instantly he was on his feet inspecting his bed. A jagged piece of shrapnel had crashed through the roof or wall and imbedded itself in the middle of his mattress where it was now smoldering in the mattress stuffing. Majewski noted uneasily that, had he been lying in the bed, he would now be crotchless.

Majewski used a towel to protect his hand as he pulled the shrapnel out of the mattress. He then pried the smoldering stuffing out with a bayonet. When he was convinced that the mattress was no longer smoldering he dragged it into Noland's AO and dragged Noland's undamaged mattress back to his bed.

Then he went back in to Noland's AO and put his damaged mattress on Noland's bedframe.

"You won't be needin' a good mattress," Majewski said to Noland's bed. "I hope you don't mind if I borrow this."

Majewski picked up the shrapnel, took it out into the sunlight and looked at it. It was a thick piece of metal about two and a half inches long and a little over an inch wide at its narrowest, least jagged point. It could have been part of the conex or a piece of perforated steel plate or a casing or any number of other things that explosions can make lethal. It did not really matter much to Majewski what it was. All he knew was that it could have killed or maimed him. It was bigger than a bullet or the shrapnel from a grenade and yet, by its insignificance, it was terribly significant. Soldiers got killed by such insignifance.

That was the way with war. Majewski felt strangely despondent and the fragment he held in his hand became a symbol of futility. He took the piece of metal back into his hooch and locked it in his footlocker. He had decided to keep it as a souvenir.

No one ever knew which of the four potheads dropped a round or even if a round had been dropped. Perhaps the explosion had some other cause. Specialists were sent in and a few lesser brass from Battalion showed up and put together a hasty and cursory investigation. The only trace ever found of the four ammo handlers was a short section of someone's spinal column. It was charred black with red sinewy fiber clinging to its curious nobs and the medic holding it cradled it in a towel as if it were a premature baby.

"Nasty shit," the medic said as he held out the piece of spine for Majewski's inspection. "From what I hear this could've been part of you."

Majewski turned away. He didn't want to look at the fragment because he was all too well aware that the bone could have been his. It seemed ironic to Majewski that his life had been saved by a Purple Heart he refused to accept.

Majewski didn't care about the smokejumpers that had died and he didn't particularly care about the injuries to Elmore or the CO or to any of the other soldiers that had been injured in the explosion. All he cared about was the ringing in his ears. When the ringing eventually stopped the entire incident died and was buried somewhere in the back of his mind. He concentrated on his new assignment on Green Line.

The soldiers who manned Green Line where a special breed. They were slovenly and irresponsible misfits who camouflaged their boredom and discontent with either marijuana smoke or, when it was available, alcohol. They were brash and rude when sober and mellow and smiling when they were not sober. Most of the time they were mellow and, Majewski guessed, it was easier for them that way because the bunkers and towers around the fire base were pitifully depressing places.

Two towers had been destroyed by the explosion. They were not rebuilt. The bunkers were primarily composed of sandbags that attracted an impressive and notable array of rats and cockroaches. Sometimes rain water accumulated and mildew was inevitable. The bunkers stank. The soldiers stank. Green Line was for the shitbirds, the dickheads, the fuck-ups and for soldiers that were recovering from life in the field.

181

The bunkers were places where one could be alone with one's thoughts or where one could share the company of others of like inclination. There were occasional cockroach races and bullshit sessions and dope and liquor and rifles and ammunition and flares and the random, frantic mad minute where thousands of rounds were propelled into the surrounding countryside. In the most recent count, no Vietnamese, NVA or Viet Cong had been killed but the shitbirds had managed to kill a number of trees that, of course, did not stand a chance. Trees were unable to find either concealment or cover. Tombstones and shrines also took a rather complete beating. Small temples were not unusual in the area. For hundreds of years life and death had run their various courses and the Vietnamese, being primarily Buddhist, built memorials and shrines and tombs of family significance out of respect for their ancestors and in line with the tenets of their religion. The tombs and shrines were targets if they were in range. They were landmarks if they were out of range or distinctive enough.

Majewski adjusted quickly to life on Green Line. He let his hair grow and shaved every third day. Polish eluded his boots and a boonie hat occasionally replaced his regular Army cap. His steel pot was worn only rarely.

Infantry patrols continued to venture into the countryside and occasionally the enemy was engaged.

The Orderly Room was rebuilt as were most of the damaged hooches.

Majewski did not succumb to the lure of drugs and alcohol. He figured someone on Green Line should be sober and responsible.

Green Line provided him with a great deal of solitude. He became quite intrigued by flares and by the Starlight Scope he was occasionally permitted to use. He did not know how the Scope worked but, looking into it, whatever he looked at was presented in the color green and heat was depicted in a light, almost white, green. Anything alive or moving that threw off heat could be seen clearly. Movement was easily distinguishable as images showed up clearly and, on a number of occasions, Majewski watched helicopter gunships fire on targets off in the distant hills. Explosions could be seen with the Starlight Scope that could not be seen with the naked eye. It was quite an impressive tool in the arsenal of Green Line. Potheads loved the Scope. It provided them with hours of bizarre visual amusement.

Flares flew and drifted each and every night. Occasionally movement would be detected and fire would be directed. The next morning a patrol of misfits and potheads would go out and inspect areas that had drawn fire but they rarely found any evidence of enemy activity. Every so often, though, the VC would fire rockets or mortars at the Fire Base just to let the Americans know they were, indeed, around. Such attacks rarely caused damage or injury as the rockets were not particularly accurate and the range of mortar rounds had to be adjusted so, by the time the VC found the proper range, they were usaully out of mortar rounds. Much more damage had been caused to the Fire Base by the explosion of the ammunition conex than had been caused by the VC or NVA.

The VC and NVA would have been more interested in the Fire Base if the artillery units had been more active. Artillery was comforting if it was outgoing. It was very disturbing if it was incoming. The situation was explained by an artillery officer when the shitbirds actually did complain that artillery fire was keeping them awake.

"We can kill our enemies in thousands of ways. We can stab 'em and strangle 'em and shoot 'em and drop bombs on 'em from planes. We can send in missiles from air, land or sea and we can let fly with artillery rounds. We can fire a round twenty miles and drop it in your pocket and we do that to protect American lives so don't bitch about the noise. You want quiet, die."

Amen.

Artillery rounds periodically whistled through the air on their violent rush toward unseen targets. Whether or not the rounds hit anything depended on the reporting source. Majewski did not really care. The sound alone should have been enough to frighten any potential enemy. The power and the lethal potential of artillery should have been enough to discourage even the most ardent enemy.

The enemy adjusted creatively and cleverly to American military power. Adjustments are the products of conflict and determination. The Vietnamese were very good at making adjustments. Green Line adjusted, too, in its way. The shitbirds, potheads and misfits came and went. So did the artillery. The howitzers were removed in April and the nights became less noisy. The base, which had not been much of a target, became even less so.

Majewski also made adjustments. In the high moon hours of night the world belonged to desolate, hollow souls where either solitude echoed serenely or where the sharp talons of loneliness swooped to gouge out the last dismal remnants of hope.

Nights were for souls that needed darkness for both liberty and bondage and for souls that solemnly recognized both the insignificance and the incredible potential of life.

Nights were for souls that reached out alone to grasp a moment's peace and beauty because all else had ceased to exist. Nights were for souls that twisted and weaved all the feelings and thoughts and emotions that made human beings so wonderfully complex. Nights were for souls that were troubled by guilt and frustration, that were tormented by anger and rage and nights were for souls that needed time to adjust by being alone. Majewski needed the nights. He adjusted and embraced them as an affirmation of life. After his time in the field Green Line was time he could have for himself alone but time was a private affair that depended on the cooperation of others. Majewski could be alone in the middle of a crowd but he could not be comfortable or serene and serenity depended, to a large extent, on freedom from others.

The bunkers and towers of Green Line became Majewski's world; his home; his life; his mental fortress. Day flowed into night and night drifted back into day and days slipped into weeks and weeks evolved into months and Majewski liked Green Line because Green Line kept him out of the field.

There were three deaths on Green Line early in Majewski's bunker tour. Two occupants of a particularly boring bunker died of drug overdoses and one former cook died of alcohol poisoning. The deaths were not really much of a surprise. Two junkies and a drunk. Maybe the VC were content to just let the Americans poison themselves. Maybe the VC figured if they waited long enough drugs and alcohol would weaken American forces and American morale enough to cause a weakening of American will. They may have been right. They may also have been wrong. Many Americans had nothing to do with drugs or alcohol. Many American soldiers did not engage in such activities, nor did they embrace the erotic or exotic pleasures of sex in the orient. "Gettin' out alive" was a highly embraceable and purposeful pursuit and many soldiers followed the dictates of acceptable, moral and prudent behavior.

Staying awake was a problem on Green Line. Not everyone was good at it. Majewski would fill his canteen with coffee and that would keep him awake. Most of the soldiers on Green Line preferred to sleep.

One night fairly early in his Green Line tour Majewski partnered with a Specialist named Stanton who seemed to be quite levelheaded and businesslike when it came to bunker duty. He was fairly alert, didn't smell like marijuana, didn't smell like liquor or beer and was even fairly clean.

Talk in the bunker would center around past lives in the States. Education, women, expectations, achievements and underachievements were frequent topics of conversation. The war was also an occasional topic.

"I don't give a shit about this war," Stanton said one particularly quiet night. "I don't care if it is right or wrong or what. If this war wants me it will come and get me. I ain't gonna help it and I ain't gonna run from it. It's here and so am I."

"I'm leaning toward that," Majewski said in response, "But I'm not there yet. I still think I can make sense of all this."

"You prob'ly can. It's jus' that if you can reconcile all this it probably won't mean anything to anyone else. I mean to agree with whatever your stand is a person would have to think like you and that ain't likely."

"You're probably right."

Discussions of morality or honor did not often take place between Stanton and Majewski because, as Stanton was fond of declaring, "When you're here, you're here."

Discussions of the state of Green Line were far more relevant and frequent. Neither man appreciated the fact that the base was being guarded and protected by shitbirds.

"I'm tired of these dumbass potheads," Stanton said one particularly boring night. "They're all fucked up and we're vulnerable! I'm gonna do somethin' about 'em right now."

"What?"

"You'll see. Cover for me," Stanton said. "I've got something to do."

Stanton left the bunker for eight minutes and his return was an unpleasant surprise to Majewski. Stanton entered the bunker with a huge snake draped over his shoulders.

"What the hell is that!" yelled Majewski. "Get that fuckin' snake outta here!"

"He won't hurt ya," Stanton said as he stroked the snake. "He's harmless."

"Harmless my ass!"

"It's a Burmese python. His name is Grasp. I named him after my ex- wife."

"I don't give a shit what he is or who he's named after. I don't want him in here!"

"Keep cool, 'Ski. He'll control the bunker rats. Both the rat rats and the human rats that're stuck out here."

"If that son of a bitch comes anywhere near me I'll shoot it!"

"Relax. He'll behave."

"Where the hell did you get it?"

"I bought him from a rice farmer for eight roots of evil. I got a good deal."

"Oh, you'll think so right up 'til the time he eats you and turns you into snake shit."

"Ah, he's just a baby. He's only five 'er six feet long. He won't eat me. If he wants people he'll eat a kid."

S. R. Larson

"Oh, yeah, I used to work with a guy back in the world who was on Fiji during World War Two and the natives came over one day and got him and a couple of other guys and took them out to a clearing and showed him a snake that'd started to swallow a waterbuffalo but the snake started from the back and, when it got to the head, the horns were there and he couldn't go any farther and couldn't puke up what he'd swallowed so they killed the snake while it was lyin' there with a waterbuffalo in its mouth. He said the snake was nearly ten yards long."

"That could be," Stanton said. "They're amazin' animals."

"That's going to be a dead amazin' animal if it ever comes near me."

"Just calm down. Don't you see what can happen?"

"No. What?"

"Word'll get around and the shitbirds on the line will hear about this snake or we'll show it to some of 'em and then, every so often, we'll put out the word that the snake has disappeared and it might be in the towers or the bunkers and that'll keep the shitbirds awake."

Majewski shook his head. The idea had merit but there were plenty of people around that didn't like snakes and there was plenty of ammunition. If Grasp ever did pose a threat Grasp's life would be short.

Stanton took the snake from his shoulders and put in on the floor of the bunker. It took a certain effort as even a small Burmese python is heavy.

Grasp didn't move much. Majewski broke out in a significant sweat.

"He's checkin' things out," Stanton said. "He's just checkin'. Flickin' his tongue and tastin' the air."

"He better not be checkin' me out. I'll shoot him."

"Ah, he's fine. You're fine."

"How am I s'posed to keep watch out there if I'm always looking for that fuckin' snake? I mean I'd be afraid to turn my back on it!"

"Ah, you worry too much."

"Where do you keep him?"

"In my AO. I got a bamboo cage. He likes it."

"Is it strong enough? I mean what's to protect you if you're asleep and he gets hungry. A hungry snake ain't even got no conscience."

"You'd be surprised how strong bamboo is, Ski. Besides, why would he want to get out? He's got a place to sleep and I feed him."

"What?"

"I'll buy a live chicken from a farmer and toss it in the cage when Grasp gets hungry. That works."

"I'm glad you thought this out so well."

"Hey, he'll be fine. Look at him. He's one of us."

Grasp became one of the bunker fixtures. Sundown would find Stanton walking toward his assigned tower or bunker with Grasp draped over his shoulders. Majewski would follow as he did not want to turn his back on the snake. The rat population of the bunkers decreased noticeably and the human bunker rats would stay awake if the idea of a snake on the loose was planted sincerely enough.

"Stanton's snake got away," Majewski used to say to bunkers under napping suspicion. "Keep an eye out for it. It's probably hungry."

Grasp would spend the nights doing quiet snake things and once, when Grasp did escape from his bamboo cage, it took three full days to find him. Sergeant Elmore, sporting a scar of honor from the conex explosion, walked in to the shower room early one evening and ran out very quickly. Grasp was wrapped around a shower pipe.

Stanton was summoned and retrieved, with considerable effort, Grasp.

"How in the hell can a snake that fuckin' big get halfway across the fuckin' compound without anybody seein' it? Don't anyone notice nothin' around here?" Elmore was quite upset. "I mean, Jeez, I coulda been killed!"

Had Elmore been armed Grasp would have been shot. Elmore filed a complaint and demanded that Stanton rid the camp of Grasp. Stanton refused and the Green Line shitbirds, potheads and drunks banded together in support of Grasp and Stanton. Grasp remained in the bunker with Stanton and Majewski. Elmore asked for a transfer but the transfer was denied.

While Stanton, Majewski and Grasp shared a bunker the United States invaded Cambodia.

Majewski's unit was too far north to be involved in the invasion as they were much closer to Laos than to Cambodia.

Kent State brought varied reactions and both Majewski and Stanton were stunned that students had been shot.

"Shit, a year ago I was a student," Stanton said. "Zoology major. I flunked out."

"I graduated last May," Majewski said. "Just in time to get drafted."

"Maybe that's why the artillery got pulled outta here," Stanton speculated. "They probably needed it for Cambodia."

"I think there are plenty of artillery pieces lying around for them to use."

"Well, I'm glad we're up here. I don't want to invade any other country. You never know what you're gettin' into. I was talkin' to a dude from Quang Tri a few weeks ago and he said they ran into a gook patrol and there was a huge guy that charged them and it took sixteen shots from an M-16 to drop him. He just kept comin'.   They figure he was Mongolian or Chinese or some type of Cossack or somethin'."

"Bullshit," said Majewski.

"No, I believe him. They loaded him up and took him somewhere for an autopsy and even the doctors were spooked. They had no idea where he had come from.   Northern China somewhere they eventually figured.   Just a giant of some sort.   He didn't have fillings in his teeth."

Majewski was skeptical but remained all the more alert. Invasions and possible giants were worth added vigilance and concentration.

No one ever asked Grasp's opinion on anything.

Chapter 12

Majewski and Stanton shared bunker duty for two months until Stanton's tour was up and he returned to the United States. Grasp was released into a rice paddy a considerable distance outside the camp and was not seen again. Majewski missed Stanton and even Grasp as he had grown grudgingly fond of the snake over the weeks the three of them shared the bunker. He admired Grasp's ability to keep people awake and alert. The real rat population of the bunker increased after Grasp's departure.

After eight months in country Majewski got an R&R leave in Hawaii. He enjoyed the workable showers and the hot water and the food and the clean sheets but missed Vietnam and was oddly pleased to get back. He felt very out of place in Hawaii as he just did not seem to fit. Hawaii felt foreign to him. Vietnam felt like home.

When he got back to the Fire Base Lt. Surrey was the first person he saw.

"How was Hawaii?"

"Okay. It was a bit too clean."

"You've come to that, huh."

"Yeah. How were things around here?"

"Nothin' happened. Just the same old shit. We got a new sergeant and four new guys today and it's been quiet all week."

"Good," said Majewski.

"How 'bout you? Did you have a good time? Did you get laid?"

"Nah, I was sittin' in a hotel bar and some bimbo sat down next to me and started talkin'. She knew I was in the Army because she was waitin' for her husband to come in the next day. She got sort of friendly and set me up because, when I got real interested in her, she asked me how many babies I had murdered and called me an asshole. Then she got up and went and hustled some other guy. Imagine that. Her old man's comin' in the next day and she spends the night with some other guy."

"That shit happens."

"I don't understand women. Anyway, it's kinda good to be back. I missed Asia."

"Could be. I'd like it here if the situation was different," Surrey said.

As Surrey and Majewski were talking the new sergeant walked up and saluted Surrey.

"Sergeant Lark," Surrey said. "This is Specialist Majewski. He's just back from R and R. He's my main man on Green Line."

Lark nodded at Majewski and turned to Surrey.

"Whadda ya want us to do, Sir?"

"Nothing. Just find a place and settle in for now."

"Request permission to take the new men out on a short patrol, Sir. You know, just to kinda get their feet wet."

"No, Sergeant. Just kick back and take it easy. You'll get out into the field soon enough."

"But, Sir, I jus' thought…"

"Look, Sergeant," Surrey said firmly. "The war's winding down. Grunts aren't doin' much at all anymore. They're sittin' back and playing it cool. No one wants to be the last person to die over here."

"The war ain't dyin' down," Lark said firmly, "It's jus' we done forgot how to fight it."

"Maybe," said Surrey. "But then again maybe everyone's getting tired of it."

"Not me," said Lark. "I volunteered for another tour. This's my second."

"I volunteered for Italy," said Majewski.

Lark smiled. "You didn't make it, did you?"

"Nope."

The three soldiers stood in silence for a moment and then Surrey said "That will be all, Sergeant. Quarter your men."

Lark saluted, turned and walked briskly toward the replacements.

Surrey turned his attention back to Majewski. He whispered "Lifer."

Majewski smiled.

"Listen, 'Ski," Surrey said softly but seriously. "I've got a bad feeling about things. Something just doesn't feel right. I've had the creeps all day. Did you notice anything comin' in on the chopper?"

"I wasn't paying much attention," Majewski said as he turned his attention to the perimeter.

"Something just ain't right."

Majewski trusted Surrey's feelings.

"I did notice that it was getting foggy in the valleys," Majewski said. "But that's not so unusual. It often gets foggy at sundown."

"It rained here most of the day. There's goin' to be all kinds of fog tonight. Maybe that's what's botherin' me."

Majewski felt uneasy. Fog made tower duty difficult. Starlight Scopes helped tremendously but there were only four for the entire Green Line. Fog swallowed the light from the flares and offered concealment that quiet movement would not betray. If a bunker or tower guard did not want to do his duty or if he happened to be intentionally chemically impaired, the fog offered him a relaxing, cozy comforter under which he could sleep. Majewski knew the bunker rats well enough to know that most of them would sleep, especially since the threat of Grasp was no longer a crushing concern.

"Sir," Majewski said reluctantly, "if you want me to I can pull duty tonight."

Surrey said nothing. He appeared lost in his thoughts. Majewski understood and waited silently for the Lieutenant to speak.

"No, 'Ski," Surrey finally said, "you look tired. I'll just go put my foot in some asses."

"Thanks. I'm really beat."

"Yeah, I know you are. Thanks for offering, though."

"If you really need me…"

"No. Get some sleep. I've got the new guys. This'll be good for 'em."

Surrey walked toward the perimeter and Majewski walked to the recently rebuilt Orderly Room to sign back into the company.

"Welcome back, 'Ski," McGill said. "How was Hawaii?"

"Okay."

"Did you get laid?"

"No," Majewski said quietly. "I didn't get laid. I did call my folks, though. They were glad to hear from me."

Majewski signed back in to the company and then looked at McGill.

"I need my rifle and a bandolier."

McGill walked over to a footlocker, opened it and removed Majewski's rifle. He opened another footlocker and removed two bandoliers and an ammo box.

"Goin' huntin'?" asked McGill.

"I hope not," Majewski said. Talking to Surrey had made him cautious. Lieutenant Surrey did not like visiting the Commanding Officer because he did not particularly like the Commanding Officer. Usually when they met it meant that Surrey was going to get his ass chewed but Surrey considered the fog a serious enough problem to confront the CO. He walked briskly up to the Captain Wyandotte's hooch and knocked on the door.

"Yes, who is it?" The voice inside the hooch sounded distant and muffled.

"It's me, Sir. Lieutenant Surrey."

"Okay, come in."

Surrey had to push hard to get the door to swing open. The CO, still fearing a fragging, kept his hooch lined with perforated steel plates and sandbags. The door was backed with steel.

"Sorry to bother you, Sir," Surrey said as he walked into the stifling hot room, "but there's something I'd like you to be aware of."

The CO was lying on his bed in his underwear. He was flanked on each side by a footlocker and on each footlocker a fan blew air on him. Gray sandbags formed the walls and the CO had driven wooden stakes between some of the sandbags to form hangers. Within arm's reach of the bed the CO had hung an M-16 with an inserted clip, two bandoliers of ammunition and a pistol belt containing a bayonet and a loaded .45.

"What's the problem, Lieutenant?"

"It's the fog, Sir."

"Fog? What fog?"

"The fog is rolling in, Sir. Lots of it."

"So? We've had fog before."

"Yes, Sir, I know, but this is going to be bad."

The CO leaned over and took a cigarette from the pack on the footlocker. He lit it with a silver lighter.

"You think they'll use the fog for cover and hit us tonight?"

"Yes. From their point of view it would sure be a dandy time to send us some shit."

"What does Military Intelligence say?"

"I haven't been in touch with them."

"Don't you think you should be?"

"Sir, if I couldn't figure out how to pour sand out of my boot and called M.I. and asked 'em, it would take a good three hours for them to come up with an answer."

"Do the VC and NVA have good weather reporting capabilities, Lieutanant?"

"Huh?"

"I mean with all our equipment and knowledge don't you think we're far more capable of figuring out if and when we're goin' to have fog?"

"It's their country, Sir. They're used to weather patterns and how the fog comes in and how it goes out. We're playing an away game here."

"I personally think you're full of shit, Lieutenant, but there hasn't been much action around here lately."

"I've got a feeling, Sir, that we're about due. We're undermanned, you know. Second platoon is on stand down in Quang Tri and first platoon is out in the boondocks with the ARVNs. That leaves us one platoon and Green Line and some cooks and a mechanic and the five new men who just came in."

"We got five new men?" the CO said with genuine surprise. "I sure wish someone would tell me these things. It's nice to know what's going on especially if you're in command."

"Majewski's back from R&R, too, so that gives us six."

The CO nodded, got up and started to dress.

"When do you post the guard and make your first rounds?"

"In about half an hour."

"Pick me up. I'll go with you."

"I figured, Sir, that we'd have everyone on the base draw weapons and we'd take additional ammo and flares out to the bunkers and let the shitbirds shoot it up."

"If nothing else," the CO said, "it'll keep a couple of 'em awake."

"Maybe we should pull that platoon back in, too."

"No, They'd be better off stayin' where they are."

"Okay," Surrey said as he walked toward the door.

"We'll have to make do with what we've got. Besides, there's really no indication that they'll hit tonight."

"Yes, Sir."

"Who's the sergeant in charge tonight?"

"Elmore."

"Okay. Grab him and meet me in the Orderly Room in half an hour."

Surrey walked outside and took a deep breath. The air was thick, wet and heavy. He walked slowly to the perimeter and looked out over the countryside. Fog was filling the hollows and depressions and creeping toward the fence. He turned and looked at the Fire Base. It was not much of a fortress.

The next half hour brought the fog completely up from the hollows. It covered and wrapped the base. Surrey made sure all the gates were secure and the guards were properly armed and posted. He warned the shitbirds that the CO would soon inspect them in person and then he walked through the fog to the Orderly Room. He got a cup of coffee and sat down on one of McGill's ammunition or cigarette footlockers. Sergeant Elmore sat with his feet propped up on McGill's desk. He rubbed his eyes. He was patiently waiting for the CO.

"Do you really think they'll hit us tonight, Lieutenant?" Elmore asked just before he yawned.

"Do you want the truth?"

"I don't know. What is it?"

Surrey took a drink of coffee and put the cup down on the footlocker next to him.

"They've got cover and concealment. We're undermanned, tired and lazy. Choppers aren't going to do us any good tonight and things have just been too damn' quiet around here. All and all I'd say it's pretty probable."

"I hope you're wrong," Elmore said as he stood up. "I hope you're real wrong."

Elmore picked up his pistol belt and put it on. He removed the .45 from its holster, inserted a clip and reholstered the pistol. He sat down just in time to have to stand again as the CO entered the room.

"Gentlemen," the CO said with dry determination. "Let's take a walk."

Elmore and Surrey followed the CO. The fog swallowed them. It was thick and heavy and it tasted gritty.

"Lieutenant," the CO said in a hoarse whisper, "you know where we're going so lead the way."

"Yes, Sir," Surrey said as he moved passed the CO and made his way cautiously toward the perimeter. "I sure hope I do but it would sure be a lot easier if I was a bat."

The three men moved toward the wire slowly, feeling the ground cautiously with each step and moving their free hands from side to side in front of them in an effort to locate both fixed, upright objects and each other.

"Jeez," said Elmore. "This is the worst I've ever seen."

"That's why were not letting you lead," said Surrey. "the Captain and I don't want to go swimmin'."

When the three men got to the base of the first tower Lieutenant Surrey knocked twice on the pole.

A voice from above shouted "Halt! Who sets forth tracks?"

The CO turned slowly to Surrey and, with a look of exasperation, asked "Who the hell is that and what's he on?"

"Hey, California," Surrey rasped in what was either a loud whisper or subdued command, "Come down here."

"Is that you, Lieutenant?" a voice asked from the fog above.

"No, it's Ho Chi Minh. Get your ass down here."

Someone from the tower came down the ladder and, on seeing the CO, came to a position of attention and saluted.

"At ease, Private," the CO said without saluting, "the Lieutenant wants a word with you."

"Yes, Sir," the Private said.

"I want you to go to the Orderly Room and get more flares and ammunition for your tower." Surrey said in a voice quiet enough to mask his nervousness. "Find McGill. He knows you're coming and'll give you what you'll need. When you get back I want you to start poppin' flares and every few minutes I want you to throw a few rounds down into the wire around the base of the tower. Is that clear?"

"Yes, Sir."

"Good. Do you have any Claymores out?"

"Yes, Sir. Two."

"Okay. Get two more and set 'em up here at the base of the tower. Fan one that way and one that way but don't blow them unless something happens and you absolutely have to."

"Yes, Sir." The Private was getting more nervous.

"Are there tracer rounds in your clips?"

"Yes, Sir. Every fifth round."

"Okay. When you're reloading clips make it every third and when you set off those flares, set them off low over the wire. Don't be tryin' to set any altitude records."

"Yes, Sir."

"One more thing. Keep your eyes and ears open. No one sleeps tonight. If I catch anyone sleeping I will personally put a bullet in his ear. Is that clear?"

"Yes, Sir! No, Sir! I mean no sleeping, Sir."

"Okay. Get your shit."

The Private started off in the general direction of the Orderly Room and was quickly engulfed by the fog. Surrey, Elmore and the CO moved on toward the next bunker but Surrey stopped them by extending both hands. He turned slowly toward the wire and, since the fog was so think, listened intently.

"They're out there," Surrey said softly, "I can feel 'em. I know they're there."

Elmore's hand tightened on his pistol and the Commanding Officer stepped back in an effort to put more fog between himself and the wire.

"Where do you think they'll try to hit us?" the CO whispered.

"Near the chopper pad," Elmore answered.

"Yeah," said Surrey.

"We'd better try to reinforce that area," the CO whispered.

"With what?" asked Surrey.

"We've got those new guys," Elmore offered.

"I don't know. I'd hate to use cherries. They'd end up shootin' themselves and Majewski's asleep on his feet."

"That new sergeant is already out on the perimeter somewhere," Elmore said. "He came in and checked out a weapon before you two got to the Orderly Room."

"Find him," said Surrey, "and have him round up the new guys and keep them all together. He can get them through this. Get them down to the chopper pad.

The CO and I can take the rounds. Meet me at the chopper pad when you're done."

"Okay, Sir," Elmore said as he turned and left the perimeter.

"Oh, and Sergeant," Surrey called softly after him. "watch where you walk. Don't fall in the piss pit."

Elmore mumbled something and disappeared into the fog. Surrey and Captain Wyandotte moved from tower to bunker to tower telling each man the same things they had told the Private in the first tower. When they had made a complete circle of the base, the CO went back and locked himself in his AO. Surrey was very apprehensive as he went to meet Elmore at the helicopter pad. He hoped that the bunker rats were ready for whatever might possibly happen.

Near the pad Surrey stopped and again peered into the fog. He could see nothing but fog and he felt very uneasy.

Majewski's M-16, though dusty, seemed to be in working order. Neither its barrel or firing mechanism seemed to be corroded and Majewski took care of the dust by taking a green towel from his footlocker and rubbing it across the rifle. When his rifle was sufficiently clean he moved his mattress away from the wall, placed the rifle between the bed spring nearest the frame and the frame and pushed the mattress back so the rifle stock stuck up in the air and the barrel pointed down. He put the towel and ammunition bandoliers into his footlocker and locked it with his padlock. For a moment he looked at the footlocker. Then he unlocked the padlock and took out the bandoliers. He closed the footlocker and placed the. bandoliers on its lid within easy reach of his bed. He took off his boots and laid down.

The bed slowly began to feel familiar. Majewski stretched and yawned and felt his muscles loosen. He closed his eyes in anticipation of sleep. With his eyes closed he began to relax. He concentrated on the little blue and yellow dots that seemed to be swirling like amoeba on his eyelids. He became fascinated by the way the dots moved to the corners of his perception only to fade away into an expanse that was not really black and yet not really a color either. When all the dots faded he opened and closed his eyes quickly, then rubbed his eyelids to make more dots. Concentrating on the dots he slipped into a solitary milky way universe where shapes and images floated through his perception and made him feel both finite and infinite. He felt as if he were standing on a high hill while all the simple, pleasant, quiet beauty of shapeless serenity moved slowly past and through him. He was alive and experiencing a soaring of the spirit. He was free and his soul was expanding into a boundless realm which he was creating by himself and for himself alone. He felt refreshed and refortified but he knew that, if he began to think or to reason or to concentrate, his universe would fade and shrink and become something like the fog which seemed to be limitless in its essense but which really wasn't. If he could drift he could sustain his universe. Thought and concentration would limit and eventually destroy it and yet he knew that he could not live behind his eyelids. Reluctantly he opened his eyes and greeted the light. He was disappointed. He got up, turned off the light and went back to bed.

Majewski slept well and deeply while, on the perimeter, M-16 fire increased. He did not know how long he had been asleep when something woke him. Some sound that was unfamiliar caused him to stir. Sleep can be accomplished in spite of considerable noise providing the noise is familiar. The mind will listen and sort and interpret sounds which are in keeping with things that are expected and will jar one awake when a sound is new or different or out of place. Majewski had heard an unfamiliar explosion, a new noise in the night. There soon followed other explosions and shouts from the perimeter and, almost immediately, sounds of debris sprinkling down on the corrugated tin roofs. There were more shouts and sounds of people running and the hollow popping of M-16 fire. Someone a long way off in the fog yelled "Sappers! They're through the friggin' wire!"

Another explosion shattered the air. Sounds of splintering, creaking and cracking of thick wooden poles were followed by the tremendous, agonizing crash of a tower as it hit the ground.

Majewski lept from his bed, stumbled over his footlocker and sprawled, face down, on the floor. Instantly there was another explosion and he could feel the concussion and displacement of air and he could hear pieces of shrapnel pierce the walls of his hooch. Somewhere close something had caught fire and shafts of light crossed Majewski's AO and, in the light, fog was suspended. That gave the hooch a very eerie appearance as if the fog were dissolving and then reforming in the shimmering light. Majewski spread his arms out to his side. The floor felt of sand and the light danced with the dense and heavy air.

Outside M-16s fired and Claymore mines exploded.

AK-47 fire could be heard off in the distance and explosions resounded close by. Men were shouting and running and Majewski heard bullets fly through his hooch. He heard a splattering sound and a thud and then a rasping sound and another explosion so he scrambled to his feet, dove out the door and landed on the wet sand. Someone jumped over him and ran off to his left. He heard gunshots and a muffled moan and the thud of a body hitting the sand. Two soldiers ran past and another, from the fog above, yelled "You okay?"

"Yeah," Majewski said instinctively.

The man ran off into the fog.

Majewski was awake but very confused. He looked to his right and saw that one of the hooches was on fire. In front of him he could see the faint outline of another hooch and of the main gate. To his left there were figures in the fog that he could not identify and, when he looked behind him, he saw his hooch was still standing.

"Jeezus!" He yelled to himself, "Sappers!"

Majewski pushed himself to his feet and ran back inside his hooch. He groped in the dark for his rifle and finally found it. He found his bandoliers, loaded his rifle, threw the bandoliers over his shoulder and ran outside. He took five or six steps before he realized he had no idea where he was going so he stopped, looked around and decided to return to the hooch.

Death could take any shape in the fog. He did not want to be shot by his fellow Americans and he didn't want to be shot or exploded by the Vietnamese wherever they were. He strategically withdrew to the steps of his hooch.

The explosions stopped as did the AK-47 fire. He could hear American voices from his left. His eyes were quickly becoming adjusted to the foggy night and to the haze and smoke from his right. The air was thick and foul with the smells of fire and gunsmoke and dust. In front of him on the bunker line he could hear moaning and shouting and there was a short burst of M-16 fire and then, for a few seconds, there was quiet except for the crackling of the fires.

"I got one," someone shouted.

"There's a dead one over here, too," someone else shouted.

"What the fuck happened?" shouted a voice from the dark.

Majewski could hear and see figures moving toward him from the left. He tensed and felt his finger find his rifle trigger.

"Are you all right, Ski?" It was Lieutenant Surrey.

Majewski sighed.

"You okay?" Surrey shouted again.

"Yes, Sir," said Majewski with considerable relief.

"Okay, get your gear on and get to the bunker line. They blew one of the towers and we've got at least two holes in the wire. We think we got all the sappers but you never know with those bastards. We'll check everywhere when the sun comes up. We've still got a long night ahead of us."

"What time is it, Sir," asked Majewski.

Surrey appeared to be stunned and annoyed by the question.

"I don't know! About two I guess. What the hell difference does it make?"

"Shit, None I guess," said Majewski. Dawn was still hours away and who knew what was out beyond the perimeter.

Majewski returned to his hooch and got his steel pot, a flak jacket and a flashlight. He walked slowly and deliberately to the bunker line. Men were milling around and someone was groaning in obvious pain. Light from the fires cast bizarre shadows and fog swallowed the smoke and the night seemed to shimmer.

Surrey was standing near a large gap in the wire.

"Check the tower poles, 'Ski. We've lost one tower already."

Majewski moved toward the poles.

Surrey looked up at the tower, cupped his hands to direct his voice and yelled "You! In the tower! Are you okay?"

"Yeah. Are there any charges on my poles?"

"We're checking. Pop a flare."

Majewski waited for the flare. From above came the sound of a hollow pop and finally the unfolding of white light which was quickly swallowed by the fog.

Majewski checked the tower base and found nothing that did not belong. He looked up into the fog and, again, there was nothing unusual. He turned and began to walk back toward Surrey but saw Surrey crouch and fire his M-16 low into the gap in the wire.

"The son of a bitch is out there," Surrey yelled. "but I think he's dead."

Surrey made sure by firing a new clip into the same area.

"You got any ammo up there?" Surrey yelled at the tower.

"Yeah."

"Fire up everything from the perimeter out. Let 'em know we're still here."

"Okay, but is my tower all right?"

Surrey looked at Majewski and Majewski nodded.

"It's okay!" Surrey yelled. "Keep an eye on the hole in the wire. If anything moves blow it away!"

Surrey turned his attention back to the gap in the wire.

"They're still out there," He said to Majewski as he removed the empty clip from his rifle. "You got any extra ammo?"

Majewski took one of the bandoliers from his shoulder and handed it to Surrey. Surrey inserted a new clip and chambered a round.

"C'mon, let's check the damage. The tower southeast of the chopper pad got hit. It went down."

Majewski nodded and, when he and Surrey got to the pad, they saw the Commanding Officer. He was standing in his olive drab underwear wearing his steel pot, flak jacket and shower sandals. He was holding a pistol.

"What's the damage, Sir," asked Surrey.

"I don't know for sure," Wyandotte answered. "I guess there were three of 'em."

"There may have been four," Surrey said. "I think I fired up one in the gap a few minutes ago."

"I was wonderin' about that," the Commanding Officer said. He looked at Majewski and said "got a cigarette."

Majewski took three cigarettes from his pack and gave one to the CO, one to Surrey and he kept one for himself. They all lit up from the same match.

"What about casualties?" Surrey asked as he exhaled. The smoke became part of the fog.

"I don't know," the CO answered. "I know someone got fucked up pretty bad when the tower fell."

"How bad?" asked Surrey.

"Come on, I'll show you," the CO said.

Surrey and Majewski followed the CO. The CO's sandals clomped and flopped loudly on the perforated steel plates that made up part of the chopper pad. Majewski found it odd that sounds of war should be followed by the sounds of shower sandals on steel.

The Commanding Officer led the way to a beam of light from a flashlight that someone was directing over a soldier on the ground. Majewski recognized the injured soldier as the kid from California. He could also see that the Californian's thigh bone was sticking through a tear in his pants. Blood was flowing freely from the gash in his leg.

"Oh Jesus God," the kid cried, "I don't want to die! Christ, let me live!"

A corpsman arrived and began cutting the kid's pantleg with a bayonet.

"Don't cut off my leg!" the kid screamed and tried to raise himself, "Oh, Christ, I can't even move! God it hurts so bad!"

"I'm not cutting off your leg!" the corpsman said in a voice that was brusque and curt initially. Then his voice softened as he said "Just take it easy and play it cool. You'll be all right."

The corpsman removed the pantleg and began to gag. He pushed himself to his feet and staggered over to the CO.

"Jesus, Sir," the corpsman gasped as he tried to regain his composure "We've got to get him out of here quick or he'll bleed to death. I'll apply a tourniquet but he'll need more than I can give."

"Okay," said the CO. "Do what you can."

The CO then took the flashlight from the soldier that had been holding it and said "Get over to the commo bunker and tell whoever is there to get a Medevac here ten minutes ago!"

The soldier scrambled to his feet and ran off into the fog. The corpsman returned to the Californian and applied a pressure bandage and tourniquet.

Surrey finished his cigarette and crushed it with his heel. He turned to Majewski and motioned for Majewski to follow. Majewski did and they walked a few feet to the fallen tower. One of the poles had been shattered by an explosive charge and the tower holding the Californian had fallen quickly.

Off to the right a soldier was standing swaying slowly from side to side. As Surrey and Majewski approached the soldier smiled and said "far out, man, that was really cool." The soldiers eyes were dull and seemed to be looking at where the tower had been.

"A fuckin' pothead," Surrey said in disgust.

The soldier continued to grin.

"Are you all right?" asked Majewski.

"Yeah, man. Far out."

The sound of someone running across the perforated steel plates caused both Surrey and Majewski to turn.

"That must be what's-his-name who went to call the Medevac," Surrey said and he and Majewski walked back to the CO.

"Sir," the soldier gasped as he approached the Commanding Officer. "They say they're fogged in and can't fly unless it's absolutely critical."

"What!" screamed the CO. "Did you tell them that we've been hit and this is an emergency?"

"Yes, Sir, I…"

"Well, go back and tell 'em to get their asses out here or, when this fog lifts, I'll come in and shoot every one of them fuckers myself."

"Yes, Sir…"

"Never mind! the CO yelled. "I'll tell 'em myself."

The CO and the soldier disappeared quickly. Majewski looked at Surrey and said "now what?"

"I don't know," Surrey sighed. "I knew they were comin'. I told everyone to stay alert. What the hell happened?"

"They're slick," Majewski said. "Those sappers can crawl up a gnat's ass without hittin' the sides."

"Yeah but, Jesus, you'd think somone would see or hear something."

"It's tough. Especially with all that tall grass."

"I know. That's gonna get burned off as soon as it's light," Surrey said softly. "I guess it should've been done today. I just wasn't thinkin' ahead."

Majewski nodded, lit another cigarette and looked at Surrey. It seemed to him as if Surrey was beginning to absorb the responsibility for the sapper attack even though his competence and expertise had probably kept damage to a minimum. Somehow it just didn't seem fair for Surrey to blame himself but there was nothing fair about war and, ultimately, someone must bear the responsibility.

Surrey looked very sad as he walked toward the corpsman and the corpsman, seeing Surrey approach, rose and walked toward Surrey. He wanted to get as far away as reasonable from the Californian before he talked to Surrey.

"How's he doing?" Surrey whispered with genuine concern.

"I don't know. I've done all I can with what I have."

"Well…"

"We've got to get him out of here as soon as possible. He severed an artery."

Surrey stood quietly for a moment and then glanced over his shoulder in the general direction of the communications bunker.

"I wonder what the CO found out," Surrey said mostly to himself.

"I hope they're comin'," the corpsman said as he wiped his brow with the palm of his bloody hand. "He'll die without help."

"Was he the only one wounded?" Surrey asked.

"No. One of the bunkers took a satchel charge but the guys got out so they didn't get hurt bad."

"Where are they?" asked Surrey.

"Sergeant Elmore's gettin'em. He's bringing 'em over."

Surrey looked over his shoulder and saw Elmore and another soldier helping a wounded man across the sand. The wounded man was swearing.

Surrey and the corpsman walked to where Elmore had placed the wounded soldier. The wounded man was lying face down on the perforated steel plates and there was blood on his back and shoulder. The corpsman knelt and ripped the shirt off the wounded man. The wounded man's back was covered with small holes that oozed blood. Majewski was fascinated by the way the blood seeped and trickled out of the man's body. The wounded man continued to swear.

The corpsman mopped up most of the blood with the injured man's ripped shirt.

"You're gonna be all right," the corpsman said. "They're just superficial."

"They should be," the wounded man groaned. "We ran like hell when that charge flew in."

"We sure did," the other soldier said.

"It's good you did," said Elmore. "That fuckin' charge blew the bunker away. There's a shitload a sand all over."

Elmore began to pat one of the soldiers on the back but quickly pulled his hand away and exclaimed "what the fuck! I cut myself!"

The corpsman stood up, looked at the soldier and said "turn around."

The soldier complied. The corpsman was surprised to see a long jagged piece of shrapnel protruding from the shoulder blade.

"You've been wounded, too, buddy," the corpsman said. "There's a piece of metal in your back and you're bleeding."

"No shit! I thought I was jus' sweatin'."

"You're sweatin' bright red blood," the corpsman said.

"I was wonderin' why my shirt was rippin' every time I moved my arm."

"Can you feel the shrapnel?" the corpsman asked.

"Not really. It's jus' kinda numb but, now that you mention it, I can feel somethin' ain't right."

"Sit down next to your buddy," the Corpsman said as he saw Captain Wyandotte approach. "It'll start hurtin' now."

"Gather 'round," the Commanding Officer said as he tried to catch his breath. "The chopper will try to make it through. They said ten, maybe fifteen minutes at the most. They want us to pop four white flares, one at each corner of the pad, as soon as we hear their engines. Then they want the whole landing zone lit up with everything we've got. Headlights, flashlights, lighters and anything else tha'll work."

The CO paused to catch his breath. He was not in the best of physical condition.

"They ain't gonna be here long! It's gonna to be quick! In and out! They're takin' a hell of a chance the way it is especially if the dinks have been monitoring the radio frequency and know what's gonna happen. That's why we need headlights so fire up the trucks and get them on each side of the LZ so the headlights point toward the middle."

The CO paused again and Surrey filled the huffing silence by shouting "All right, you heard the man! Get your asses in gear! Majewski, get the Jeep. Elmore, grab some men and get the trucks rollin'!"

There were three two and a half ton trucks on the Fire Base. One was parked near the conexes south of the helicopter pad and the other two were near the communications bunker. The Jeep was usually parked west of the helicopter pad but Majewski had trouble finding it. He was swearing under his breath and looking back to the south in the general direction of the single truck when he saw a flash of light and heard an explosion. The truck disintegrated and chunks of metal clanked and bounced noisily across the PSP.

Majewski ran back to where the CO, Surrey and the wounded men had been. All were lying on the PSP and the CO and Surrey were peering into the fog. Majewski turned in time to see Elmore stagger through the fog. Majewski was surprised at how beautiful a sight it was seeing Elmore silhouetted against the diffused light of the burning truck.

"Jesus Christ," Elmore gasped as he reached Surrey and the CO, "the son of a bitch blew up!"

Elmore turned and stared at the burning truck with eyes that seemed as big as silver dollars. For some reason Surrey began to laugh. Knowing that Elmore wasn't hurt made laughing easier. Surrey turned to the Commanding Officer and said, "There's some light for you, Sir."

The CO looked at Surrey incredulously. Then he turned his attention back to the fire and said, "Burn, baby, burn! They must've tossed one with a delayed fuse in there."

Surrey laughed even more.

The CO turned toward the communications bunker, cupped his hands and yelled, "Check those trucks for satchel charges!"

From off in the fog a muffled, resigned voice shouted "Now he fucking tells us!"

The Commanding Officer dropped his hands and shrugged. He turned to Majewski and said "What are you waitin' for?"

"I can't find the Jeep," Majewski said.

"It's up by my office. Get some flares as long as you're up there."

"Yes, Sir," Majewski said as he turned to leave.

"Get some more men down here," the CO shouted.

"Yes, Sir," Majewski said and, as he trotted off in the general direction of the CO's office, he could still hear Surrey laughing.

Majewski found the Jeep, loaded it with flares and drove it slowly back to the helicopter pad. He parked it on the southeast corner of the pad, shut off the engine but left the headlights on. The burning truck gave off a bizarre and eerie light and Majewski sat in silence for a few seconds and watched the fire attack the fog. He then gathered up as many flares as he could carry and took them to Surrey.

Surrey was surrounded by half a dozen men and was giving instructions on how to load the wounded. He wanted the helicopter loaded quickly and properly when it did arrive and back in the air as soon as the wounded men were properly loaded. When Surrey saw Majewski he said "You help with California. He's top priority."

Majewski nodded and moved over to the Californian. The kid wasn't screaming anymore. He was crying. Majewski felt very sad and struggled to think of something to say. Nothing he thought of seemed remotely appropriate so he knelt down next to the corpsman hoping that just his closeness would comfort the kid. He did not know if it did or not because when he looked at the kid's horribly injured leg, he became dizzy and had to steady himself by dropping his left hand to the PSP. He was surprised to find that the PSP was very cold and clammy. The moisture and the act of bracing himself took his mind off California. Majewski's hands were dirty so he moved his fingers along the contours of the PSP and rubbed away some of the grit and dirt. Some of the moisture on the PSP was the kid's blood.

Majewski heard the helicopter about the time the CO began yelling.

"Fire the goddam' flares!" the CO screamed. "Show 'em where we are."

Simultaneously eight flares were fired and, in a matter of seconds, burst into light and outlined a shape that dangled clumsily in the eastern sky. The helicopter seemed to be rocking slowly as it approached the pad and, when the pilot was sure of his bearings, the helicopter lunged forward quickly and hovered just north of the men. Slowly it began to descent and Majewski thought it was going to land directly on top of him.

"Keep your heads down!" Surrey yelled as he crouched next to the kid. "When I give the word we all lift at once and move fast!"

Majewski nodded and the helicopter touched down with a thud that shook the PSP.

"Now!" someone yelled from the helicopter.

"Let's move!" Surrey shouted.

"All at once!" the corpsman ordered and the attending soldiers lifted the kid simultaneously and scurried him to the open helicopter door.

Two men inside helped ease the Californian into the helicopter.

"He's hurt bad," Surrey yelled. "Turn on the sirens and run the stoplights."

"How many more?" someone in the helicopter shouted.

"Just these," Surrey yelled as the other wounded men approached and were loaded into the helicopter. "You guys are the greatest! Thanks."

"Well send you the bill," shouted someone in the helicopter.

Everyone on the ground kept low and backed away from the helicopter. From an area outside the wire came the sounds of AK-47 fire but no one paid much attention. The bullets were probably aimed at the helicopter or at least at the activity inside the camp. The helicopter revved its engine and lifted into the fog.

The Commanding Officer walked up and stood next to Surrey.

"Do you want to say it now?" the CO asked.

"Say what?"

"You told me so."

Surrey stood quietly for a few seconds and then said, "No."

"Meet me in my office in, oh, an hour. I want to talk to you and all the NCOs."

"Yes, Sir," Surrey said softly. "In an hour."

The CO walked away as Surrey checked his watch.

"Ski," Surrey said. "Go shut off the Jeep lights."

"Okay," Majewski answered.

"Oh, and do you think you could do me a favor?"

"What?"

"Fill in on the bunker line until dawn."

"Yeah," Majewski said quietly.

"Shut off the lights and we'll get some coffee."

"You buyin', Lieutenant?"

"Yeah, I'll buy. Call it a welcome home present."

Majewski disappeared into the fog.

Chapter 13

The Commanding Officer lit a cigarette and inhaled deeply. He was in full uniform and his boots were shined to a brilliant black. Lieutenant Surrey and a number of NCOs were in his office and the meeting the CO called was about to begin.

"Now, men," the CO said as smoke seeped from the corners of his mouth. "let's talk about tonight."

Surrey shifted positions and waited to receive the blame.

"Tonight was no one's fault," the CO said to Surrey's relief and surprise.

"We just got what we decided to expect. Lieutenant Surrey was correct and I praise him for that but now it's over. I think we all know what has to be done as soon as the sun comes up. We'll have to do some chopping and burning in the kill zone to get it back to where it should've been all along. Lt. Surrey'll be in charge of that."

Surrey nodded.

241

"Sergeant Elmore, give the Lieutenant a hand. You, too, Lark. I got ahold of Sergeant Bertram's patrol and, on the way back, he's going to check things out west of the camp. I'm sure he and his men are well-rested and won't mind helping out since they haven't done jack shit all night.

"Now, as soon as the sun has been up for a while and they figure it's safe, the lifers will arrive and there'll be more birdshit and scrambled eggs around here than you can shake a stick at. Unfortunately they're going to want answers and we're the ones who'll have to come up with them. I'll take all the big birds but I want to brief you on what we have so far, just in case some of the little birds want answers, too. We'll have another meeting before they get here just in case anything new shows up with the sun.

"Incidentally, Lieutenant Surrey, you did get a sapper in the wire. That was confirmed about ten minutes ago."

Surrey didn't say anything. The CO picked up a sheet of paper from his desk and began to read.

"Apparently four sappers came through the wire east of the helicopter pad, blew the tower, destroyed the bunker and tossed either a delayed fuse charge or a defective satchel charge into the bed of a two and a half ton truck. "Three of the sappers were killed in the vicinity of the helicopter pad. The other one got tangled in the wire and was subsequently killed. His body is still in the wire and will be retrieved at the earliest safe opportunity.

"The bodies of the other three sappers are on display on the southeast corner of the helicopter pad. Whether the fourth sapper, the one killed in the wire, had a charge or not has not, as yet, been determined but it would appear at this time that two charges were used to destroy the tower."

"One, Sir," said Surrey. "Only one of the poles was destroyed."

"Whatever," said the CO. "There could conceivably be one or two more charges lying around the camp. I would suggest that a search be made of the hooches at first light."

The men nodded.

"Casualties were insignificant," the CO stated as he laid the paper back on his desk.

"So much for my prepared statement. When the men get off bunker duty they will be divided up into three groups," the CO said firmly. "One group will go with Lieutenant Surrey and Sergeant Elmore to burn or chop or somehow extend the kill zone. The second group will go with Sergeant Lark. Welcome to the neighborhood, Lark. Sergeant Lark has graciously volunteered to lead this hardy band in a thorough sweep of the area before Lieutenant Surrey's group leaves the camp. Isn't that right, Sergeant?"

"Yes, Sir," Lark snapped to attention.

"The third group will sleep from seven until noon and then take the place of one of the other groups and we'll work out the rest of the details later."

The CO stood and asked if there were any questions. No one said anything so the meeting was adjourned.

Majewski spent the rest of the night on the bunker line. He could occasionally hear movement but did not have a Starlight Scope so he could not see through the fog. When dawn did arrive it arrived slowly. The fog lingered and then retreated cautiously as if it did not want to relinquish its power and its majesty.

Daylight brought new responsibilities for the soldiers on and around the Fire Base. Sergeant Lark and his men left camp while the fog was still in the hollows. Lark's men displayed an unusual alertness considering what misfits Lark had so quickly accumulated. They moved with deliberate assurance and showed a surprisingly high degree of competence and skill. The previous night's actions affected everyone on the base. The war had become personal.

The dead sapper in the wire was extracted by three of Lark's men. He was carried into the base and dropped next to his dead comrades. The VC were stripped and their clothing was searched and Majewski realized that one of the sappers had leaped over him as he laid in the sand.

The sappers had only been wearing gym shorts and T-shirts. No information and nothing of importance was apparent and the sappers had died namelessly.

Outside the base Lark's patrol found trails of blood and places where the tall grass had been matted and crushed. No other bodies were found indicating that if another sapper had been present, he had been wounded and had crawled away and perhaps died in one of the foggy hollows. In places there was a lot of blood.

Lark's men were very careful. Anything and everything was suspicious and changes in the terrain were explored with caution and respect. One of Lark's men, working an area west of the others, felt the ground give ever so slightly under his foot. He stopped, held up his rifle and yelled, "Over here! I found somethin'!"

Lark moved cautiously toward the man.

"This here ground's softer'n it were over there," the soldier said. "My foot done sunk in. I'm feared to move."

Lark handed his rifle to the motionless soldier and got down on the ground. He probed with his stubby fingers.

"It ain't no booby trap," Lark rasped. "Get offen it. I found a seam."

The soldier stepped quickly to what he hoped would be solid ground.

"Get the CO an' Surrey," Lark ordered. "An' bring back a shitload of grenades. Frag an' 'cussions."

The soldier nodded and ran toward the base. Other soldiers gathered around Lark.

"You guys spread out an' find the other end of this friggin' thing," Lark said. "It'll prob'ly be farther down the hill where it can't be spotted by no towers. Check all them depressions an' little valleys. I wan' three men here with me to cover this here tunnel when I open it."

Three soldiers spread out and readied their M-16s.

"We'll wait an' pop this when they find the other end an' when the CO's here."

Lark didn't have to wait long. Surrey and the CO arrived quickly.

"What'd you find?" the CO asked.

"A tunnel, Sir," Lark answered. "My men's tryin' uh find the other end. I sent for grenades."

A soldier appeared with two boxes of grenades and, from a considerable distance away, another soldier waved his rifle and pointed to the ground. He had apparently found the other end of the tunnel.

"Give me some of them frags," Lark said. The CO and Surrey each took grenades, too.

"All right, men," the CO said in his most authoritative voice. "When I give the word the show begins."

Everyone was ready. Lark knelt by the seam, put three handgrenades on the ground and nodded at the CO.

The CO nodded back and yelled "Now!"

Lark yanked the lid off the tunnel with one quick motion and grenades from the CO and Surrey dropped down the hole. Lark grabbed his grenades, pulled the pin from the first one and dropped it into the hole. Then the three men pulled their heads back out of the way and waited for the explosions. In rapid succession there were three very loud concussions and dirt sprang from the opening. At the other end of the tunnel the grass shimmered and twitched.

Three more concussion grenades were tossed down the shaft and each exploded with earsplitting ferocity.

Fragmentation grenades were dropped down the hole. They exploded and sent puffs of dust and dirt back out the opening.

The CO held out his hand.

"Wait an' see what we've got," the CO said as Surrey turned and walked down to the other end of the tunnel. A trapdoor was partially ajar. Soldiers were standing around with M-16s at the ready.

"Do you want me to crawl in there?" one of the soldiers asked.

"Fuck no," Surrey answered as he nudged the trapdoor open with his foot. "Toss a couple grenades in."

Two grenades were thrown into the tunnel. They exploded and sent clouds of dust back out the opening.

Surrey turned and walked back to the CO.

"That's how they got so close," Surrey said. "They used this tunnel. It's been here a long time. Let's get the deuce and a halfs over here and collapse it."

"How do we know there ain't more of 'em?" the CO asked.

"We don't. I would suggest that we drive all over everything out here and then burn all this out."

"Okay," said the CO. He turned to Sergeant Lark and said "have someone drive those trucks all over out here. We should be able to cave in the tunnel with enough weight."

Eventually the two and a half ton trucks showed up. Slowly they drove over the tunnel and collapsed it, leaving a long trench. Each truck got stuck and had to be pushed by sweating, swearing soldiers. Gasoline, diesel fuel and kerosene were spread over the kill zone and ignited. The flames leapt high into the air and the smoke brought visits by curious helicopters.

No other tunnels were found. If there were any others they were well hidden and deep enough to be unaffected by the trucks. The kill zone was expanded and Claymore mines were again deployed. Two fifty caliber machine guns were sighted in on the trench and Claymore mines were set along its length with their fields overlapped. Sandbags were filled and the damaged bunker was repaired and reinforced. The tower was dismantled and its space given over to a new bunker with wide fields of fire.

The concertina wire was repaired and the hole in the fence mended. Everything that could be salvaged from the burned hooch was saved and the rest of the hooch was ignited and allowed to burn to the ground. The burned out deuce and a half was allowed to stay where it had died. For an infantry unit they had been hard on trucks.

Soldiers worked hard at repairing the camp and they did not rest until everything that could reasonably be done was done. By the time the fog burned off entirely the men were exhausted.

It was nearly noon when Surrey and the CO walked to the helicopter pad to meet the incoming senior officers. A colonel, a major and a captain were escorted into the CO's office. The CO's uniform, once so proper with its creases and starch, was wrinkled and covered with dust. Somehow he had torn his pants and the bill of his cap was bent. He contrasted sharply with the spitshined rear echelon officers. Surrey looked far worse. He still had blood on his uniform.

"Come in, gentlemen, and sit down," the CO smiled politely. The officers entered his office and took their seats. Surrey entered last and sat on a footlocker in the corner.

"Here, gentlemen, are copies of my report," the CO said as he passed out carbon copies of the typed report he had hastily written and read earlier. The report had been expanded and clarified and rewritten and neatly typed by McGill.

"Please read this carefully because I am going to expand on it."

The CO sat down as his desk and waited until the officers finished reading the report.

"Gentlemen, you have before you my initial report. I would now like to add that no additional explosive charges have been found. This morning a tunnel was found and subsequently destroyed. There are four dead sappers on display on the corner of the chopper pad. You may have noticed them when you arrived. We have taken steps to extend our kill zone but, gentlemen, we are just pissing into the wind."

The CO paused expecting a reaction. There was none visible from any officer.

The CO reached under his desk and picked up an object wrapped in black plastic. He put it on his desk and slowly undid the fastening twine. He paused for a few seconds and then unwrapped the object. It was a small, thin arm.

"We found this outside our kill zone. The four bodies we have all have their arms. This means that there are more VC out there and they're active.

"We did the best we could last night with the fog and bein' undermanned. Here it's our job to kill people. We're here to kill. The owner of this arm was a killer, too. He was dedicated to what he believed in and took steps to inflict as much damage on his enemy as he could. I don't know how many men this guy killed before we blew his arm off but I imagine if he did kill, he killed us."

The CO paused. He cleared his throat and pushed the arm across his desk toward the nearest officer.

"We're out here in the middle of nowhere. We're not strategic. We control nothing and probably don't

253

make any difference to anyone at all. We're sitting here in this long grass and I can't figure out why. If the VC or NVA really gave a shit they'd have overrun us last night. We've got no artillery pieces here. You pulled out the artillery unit and it's just us grunts sitting up here with our asses hangin' out. What's going on?"

"I can assure you, Captain," the highest ranking officer said, "we're aware of your problems but there are certain plans..." The Colonel paused, looked around the room and then continued.

"There are certain operations in the planning stages that I am not at liberty to discuss at this time but, suffice it to say, there will be a number of changes you will benefit from and understand down the road. I am not authorized to discuss anything until everything has been formulated, finalized and passed down to me from higher headquarters. At that time, and it should be in the very near future, you'll be informed and all appropriate steps will be taken to implement whatever programs are applicable to your situation. Until then, Captain, I suggest you just grin and bear it."

Captain Wyandotte sat for a moment and stared at the Colonel. Then he leaned forward, smiled and said "horseshit, Sir."

"I can assure you, Captain, that you'll understand all of this in due time."

"Really? Can you get me some replacements?"

"Probably not. They're needed elsewhere."

"I need more men."

"I understand your position, Captain, but we can't spare any now."

"Why not?"

"Captain, you're pushing your luck and my patience."

"Then we should consider ourselves expendable."

"If that's what it takes then, yes, consider yourself expendable."

The Colonel rose and the other two officers rose, too.

"Would you like to inspect the damage, Colonel?" the CO said as he, too, stood up.

"No. We saw it when we flew in."

"We saw it from down here on the ground. Close up."

"Look, Captain," the Colonel said quietly. "We know you got hit last night. We know you're fairly unprotected out here but this is a war. Some sacrifices do have to be made. From what I can see your casualties were far fewer than they could've been. You'll know what's going on eventually and everything will fall into place."

"I hope so," the CO said. "I certainly hope so."

The Colonel, the Major and the Captain turned and left the CO's office. On the way out the Major turned to the CO and said, "Your wounded man, the one that was Medevaced, died shortly after arriving. He bled to death."

Neither the CO nor Surrey responded with words. They both felt stunned, cold and empty. The CO stepped forward and slammed the office door with as much ferocity as he could muster. The walls emitted puffs of dust. The CO turned and walked slowly to his desk. He sat down and put his head in his hands.

Surrey lit a cigarette and held it out toward the CO. The CO looked up and accepted it.

"Thank you, Lieutenant," the CO said. Surrey nodded and lit a cigarette for himself. He sat down on the footlocker and shook his head as if he were trying to shake the Major's words out of his memory.

"I wonder what's going to happen," the CO said softly. "What I expect is the sapper attack last night was just the beginnin'. Who knows how many of 'em are out there? They could have a thousand men waitin' to swoop down on us and there's nothin' we can do about it that we haven't already done."

Surrey nodded in agreement.

"We've got to come up with something or we'll all end up dead."

There was a knock on the door. The CO looked at the door but said nothing. There was a louder knock and the CO said "Yes."

"It's me, Sir. McGill."

"Whadda ya want?"

"We need you out here, Sir. There's a papasan here from the village."

S. R. Larson

Wyandotte and Surrey rose and walked out into the bright sunlight. They walked silently to the perimeter where a very old Vietnamese man was standing near the gate with his hands raised. Standing nearby and staring at the man was a soldier wearing fatigue pants, a T-shirt and a boonie hat. The soldier looked at the Commanding Officer.

"He's from the village, Sir. He walked across the kill zone with his hands up." The soldier was older than the average man on the base but didn't appear to be much brighter as he gave the impression of being a total and complete drug burnout.

"Do you speak Vietnamese?" the CO asked.

"Yeah, a little. I speak German, too, but there ain't much call for it here."

"Who is he and what does he want?"

"He says he's from the village. He came here because last night someone shot his waterbuffalo. He says it was us."

"How the hell could we kill his waterbuffalo? The village is, what, four or fives from here," the CO said.

258

"I don't know.   Maybe our patrol got it or a helicopter."

The CO stood quietly for a moment as if he were lost in thought.

"Tell him we'll let him in but he must be searched," the CO finally said.

The gate opened and the old man stepped cautiously and tentatively inside the perimeter.   He kept his arms raised and submitted to a frisk search. The soldier motioned for the old man to lower his arms. The old man complied and then began to speak. The soldier listened and soon put up his hand.

"He wants us to pay him for his waterbuffalo," the interpreter said.

"Tell him to eat my shorts," the CO said and turned to leave.   Then he stopped, turned back to the interpreter and said "How much are we paying for waterbuffaloes these days?"

"Seven hundred and fifty dollars, Sir." the interpreter said.

"How much for Vietnamese civilians?"

"Six hundred, Sir."

"Wouldn't it be cheaper just to shoot him?"

"Probably but we'd still have to pay for the waterbuffalo."

The CO was silent for a moment. Something was occurring to him and he wanted to play all possible consequences in his mind before he spoke.

"Tell him," the CO said to the interpreter, "that there was a lot of shooting around here last night and ask him how he knows we shot his cow. It could have been the VC."

The interpreter talked to the old man and the old man talked to the interpreter and the interpreter talked to the CO.

"He says last night his waterbuffalo was shot. We had rifles. The VC only had one bomb."

"Ask him how he knows that."

The old man became uncomfortable and eventually talked to the interpreter.

"He says he just knows. He says GI rifles make a different noise."

The CO took a number of steps backward and motioned for Surrey and the interpreter to move away from the old man. They joined the CO for a few moments of whispered conversation and then returned to the old man.

"Ask him how many VC there are in the village."

The answer came back as none.

"How about around in the countryside?"

"He says he doesn't know and he doesn't care. He just wants his money."

The CO nodded to Surrey and Surrey stepped forward and talked to the interpreter.

"Tell him it will take a few days to get his money. We want him to come back every day and give us information and he'll get his money when we're sure he is telling the truth."

The translation brought a look of bewilderment to the old face. The old man talked softly in a resigned and quiet way and the interpreter listened intently. When the Vietnamese finished talking the interpreter turned to Surrey and the CO.

"He says there aren't any VC in the village but there are some in the countryside."

"How many?" asked the CO.

"He says maybe thirty. Maybe forty. He says they come into the village every three nights to take rice. One of them comes in every night because he makes babies with one of the village girls."

"Ask him how they come into the village."

The interpreter talked to the old man and the old man knelt and began drawing in the sand with his bony finger. He talked as he drew and the interpreter relayed the information.

"They hide in the trees on the other side of the water. There must be a stream of some sort near the village."

"Yes," said Surrey.

"They hide in the trees and there's a tunnel under the water that leads into the village. That's how they get in."

The old man said something that the interpreter didn't fully understand so the old man took a couple steps back and snorted a few times and drew circles with his fingers.

The interpreter closed his eyes and seemed to be concentrating. The old man continued to snort and then interpreter finally opened his eyes and smiled.

"He says the tunnel comes up in a pig pen. I was having trouble understanding what he was talking about but the tunnel runs from the trees under the stream and ends in a pig pen. That's how loverboy gets in to screw the village girl."

"Through the pig pen!" said the CO. "How romantic."

"He says when lots of VC come they don't come through the tunnel."

"Ask him if he'll show us where the tunnel is."

The translation caused the old man to tremble and shake his head.

"No," the interpreter said. "He won't show us anything. He says if the VC find out he's talking to us they'll beaucoup kill him."

"All right," said Surrey. "Ask him when the VC will be back."

"He said they came last night. They won't come tonight or tomorrow night but the next night except for the one who comes to the girl. He'll be there tonight."

The CO pulled Surrey aside.

"I'm not going to worry much about our pigpen romeo but if I can splatter a few the day after tomorrow I'd sure feel a lot better."

Surrey nodded.

"Ask him how long they've been coming into the village."

"He says two or three years.

"What time to they come in?"

"Between two and three. Never before two and never after three."

"Okay," Surrey said. "Thank him for us."

The interpreter and the Vietnamese talked for a few seconds.

"He wants to know when he'll get his money."

"Tell him soon. Tell him to keep comin' back and we'll talk some more."

The old man bowed, turned and left the camp. He walked slowly and cautiously.

Surrey looked at the CO.

"Do you believe him, Lieutenant?" Captain Wyandotte asked.

"Not for a second, Sir."

"Think he's VC?"

"Sure," said Surrey. "He got sent up here to check the damage. He glanced at the trench a time or two while we were talking. I wouldn't believe much of what he said."

"Let's get his money and hold it but not set up an ambush right away. Let's let 'em get comfortable and let's see if he brings us anything. When Bertram gets in we'll talk things over with him. He'll come up with something."

Early in the afternoon the men in Sergeant Bertram's platoon returned to camp. They looked tired and were sweaty, dirty and unkempt so they looked as they usually did and no one paid much attention to them.

Bertram looked fairly refreshed. Once inside the perimeter he sat down on a pile of sandbags and lit a cigarette.

"What happened?" Bertram said to no one in particular. "Did y'all have a party while we was gone?"

Someone on the bunker said "yep."

Bertram smoked his cigarette silently. He looked around the camp and took note of the damage. He was studying the wire when McGill approached.

"CO wants to see you," McGill said.

Bertram said nothing. He finished his cigarette, wiped his brow and slowly got to his feet. He nodded at McGill and they walked slowly to the CO's office.

"What's he want?" Bertram asked.

"Beats me. I just work here."

Bertram walked into the CO's office. Surrey and the CO were waiting for him.

"Sit down, Sergeant," the CO said.

Everyone sat down.

"How was the field?"

"Okay, Sir. No big deal either way. Look's like y'all took some shit, though."

"A little."

"Anybody get killed?"

"One."

"You're lucky."

"Listen, Sergeant," the CO said. "An old guy came in here a little while ago and said we shot his waterbuffalo. He wants money. We told him we'd give him money if he gave us information on VC in the area. He told us they hide in the trees and come into the village through a tunnel."

"Every three days," Bertram added. "Prob'ly a couple dozen VC an' half a dozen NVA reg'lars."

"You seem to know a lot. Why didn't you tell us?"

Bertram shifted a bit in his chair, smiled and said, "Why didn't y'all know?"

The CO said nothing.

"Look," Bertram said, "I spen' a lotta time out in the fuckin' field. I know what's goin' on. I hafta know. It's my ass. I mean, shit, if I don't know what I'm facin' I ain't worth a shit."

"I understand that," the CO said softly. "We want your opinion on this course of action. Lieutenant Surrey and I think we can get information from this old guy and we've got him comin' back for the next few days and we hope we'll be able to figure out what's going on."

"Maybe," said Bertram. "But 'member this could be a setup an' he could give y'all information that the enemy wants y'all to have. I mean who's to say this guy's on the up an' up. I wouldn't trust 'im."

"We want to get those VC but we don't want to do it right away. We want to wait for a couple of weeks and then set up an ambush and get 'em either on the way in or the way out. We could also defoliate that woods and hit 'em with airpower."

"Yeah," said Bertram. "I don't think I'd go that fer. I think we can jus' keep an eye on the village for a few nights then hit 'em when it's good for us. We could feed 'em some information, too. Y'know, let him see stuff an' report back if that's what he's s'posed to do."

"How long do you want to stay in?" the CO asked. "You're the only real patrol we've got. I don't want you in too long or out too fast."

"Give us a couple days," Bertram said. "We could use the rest."

"We can send Lark out if push comes to shove," Surrey said. "He did pretty well blowing that tunnel this morning."

"Shit," Bertram said, "Anyone can blow a fuckin' tunnel."

"Lark's here on his second tour. I don't know if that impresses you but it impresses me," the CO said.

"Does he know his shit?" asked Bertram.

"Hard to tell," Surrey said. "He talks a good game and knows what to look for."

Bertram stood up. "I'm gonna get cleaned up and sleep a while. Y'all know where'n to find me." He left the office.

"What do you think?" Surrey asked.

"I'd hate to be standin' between him and the last pork chop," said the CO.

"Let's figure out what to ask for from the old man."

Chapter 14

Majewski stayed awake on guard duty. He rarely had trouble staying awake but this first night after the attack almost everyone else on Green Line stayed awake, too. At least they did for most of the night. Eventually, from some of the bunkers, marijuana smoke drifted skyward.

The following day the old man showed up at the gate again and demanded his money.

"What did you bring us?" asked Surrey through the interpreter.

"He says he told you everything yesterday."

"Tell him the money isn't here yet."

The old man left and returned the following day.

"No money yet, papasan. What do you have for us?"

The old man left and returned the following day.

"The VC came in last night," the interpreter said. "took some rice and asked him why he was comin' here every day. The old man said he showed 'em the dead waterbuffalo and they asked what we were doin'. He said he didn't know anything. He just wanted his money. They left."

Surrey looked at the old man. He could not tell what the man was thinking but he was sure that the old man was getting tired of the runaround he was being given.

That night Bertram took a patrol and checked an area southwest of the village. They found nothing and moved farther west away from the village. The following day the patrol moved north and left the area of the village.

On the Fire Base Majewski kept watch each night. Nothing happened.

When Bertram's patrol came back in Bertram had another meeting with Surrey and the CO. Plans were formulated for an operation in or near the village but only Bertram, Surrey and the CO knew the details and they said nothing to anyone. McGill didn't even know.

The old man did not return to the base for three days. When he did finally show up Surrey and the interpreter met him.

"I've got your money, papasan," Surrey announced. "What do you have for me?"

The old man said something to the interpreter.

"He wants his money."

Surrey took a packet of money from his pocket. It was neatly wrapped with a paper band and it was Vietnamese. He handed it to the old man. The old man jabbered something to the interpreter.

"He wants American money," the interpreter said.

"He ain't gettin' it. Tell him this is what he gets. He didn't give us any information."

The interpreter spoke with the old man and used a lot of gesturing and a lot of firm, gutteral sounds. The old man listened and then looked scornfully at Surrey. He said something to the interpreter.

"He says he will take the money but you sleep with your sister."

Surrey smiled and bowed to the old man.

The old man turned and walked out of camp. Surrey and the interpreter watched him walk across the kill zone.

"Is he one of them?" Surrey asked the interpreter.

"Wouldn't surprise me. He counted us all on the way up. I was watching and could tell."

"Yeah. What do you bet we get hit tonight?"

Surrey was wrong. The VC did not attack that night and did not attack the next night but Bertram took his patrol out at dusk. The patrol left camp and moved North. Nightfall split the patrol. Two men, Sergeant Bertram and Specialist Pitch, moved away from the patrol and disappeared into the tall grass. The rest of the patrol set up camp and built a small fire to make their presence known in the area. Word would surely get back to the VC in the woods that the patrol was miles away and settled in for the night.

Bertram and Pitch moved quietly overland to the village. The village was approximately four miles from the patrol and the two soldiers wanted to enter the village from the far side away from the woods and the stream. The night offered concealment and, when they reached the village, they were confident that they had not been seen.

Bertram and Pitch crawled along the western limits of the village and found the house with the pig sty.

273

Slowly and quietly they moved to the front of the house. The house was made of some sort of plaster that had, in places, crumbled badly. It consisted of one room with a hole in the roof to let out the cooking smoke. There were no windows or doors. Over an opening in the west wall an old brown blanket hung to present a semblance of privacy. The pig pen, they discovered, was separated from the house by a similar blanket.

Pitch positioned himself on the north side of the door, propping his rifle against the wall and bracing himself so he could spring on anyone who attempted to leave the building. When Pitch was in position Bertram carefully moved the curtain slightly and peered inside. He saw a young woman sleeping on the floor. Bertram let the blanket fall back and nodded at Pitch. Slowly Pitch's clawed hand reached for the wall and he dragged his fingernails down the crumbling plaster. The grating was louder than Bertram expected and, for a split second, he was concerned that someone other than the girl would hear. His concern was unfounded. Most of the villagers were asleep and those that weren't were unaware or unconcerned as the girl's house was set apart from the others.

The girl, however, did hear. The noise woke her and she was wary and concerned. Thinking perhaps one of her pigs was making the noise she started for the sty but the sound, she soon realized, was coming from the other door. Slowly she moved toward the door, pushed the blanket to one side and peered out into the blackness. Seeing nothing but still hearing the grating, she pushed the blanket completely aside and stepped out into the night.

She took one step and Bertram's right fist slammed into her cheek with all the force he could muster. Her head snapped to the right, her jaw shattered and blood and teeth flew into the air. The force of Bertram's blow sent her flailing into Pitch's arms and Pitch caught her and smiled.

"Nice punch," Pitch whispered as the girl bled all over his right arm. She had been, until Bertram hit her, a stunningly beautiful girl.

"Get her inside," Bertram said, "and tie her up." Pitch dragged her into the house and let her fall on to one of the bamboo mats on the floor. Bertram picked up Pitch's rifle and brought it inside. Pitch found some wire and tied her hands behind her back while Bertram stuffed a rag in her mouth. When they had finished they kicked dirt on the smoldering embers of the cooking fire and tossed an old mat on the girl.

"You know, Sarge," Pitch whispered, "we ought'a take that there gag outta her mouth. She'll beaucoup strangle on her own blood."

"So what?" Bertram rasped. "Take down that blanket so we can see out into the pig pen."

"I don't feel right 'bout just lettin' her die." Pitch whispered.

"She's a VC. Dyin's what she's good for."

"It jus' ain't right, Sarge."

Bertram thought for a moment. He walked over to the far corner of the room and picked up a bamboo pole that had been propped against the wall. The pole was about four feet long and was strong and smooth. It felt good in his hands.

"She must use this on her pigs," Bertram said as he felt the pole's weight and balance.

Pitch looked at Bertram and shook his head. He knelt down next to the girl and brushed her hair from her face. She was lying on her right side. He could hear girgling sounds as her body began to shake.

"I'll keep her quiet," Pitch whispered mostly to himself. "She won't be no trouble."

Bertram was not paying attention. He was getting the feel of the bamboo by balancing it like a billiard cue and swinging it like a baseball bat.

Pitch reached down and removed the soggy gag from the girl's mouth. Accumulated blood spilled onto the dirt floor. He rolled the girl over onto her stomach and straddled her so her hips were between his feet. Reaching down he slipped the fingers of his left hand under the elastic band of her pants and obtained a good grip. He lifted her by her waistband. She was very light and, with her hips higher than her head, more blood drained. She began to choke and tried to spit but she couldn't and began to convulse. Pitch lifted her higher and shook her as if he were trying to empty a waste basket full of stubborn trash. With his right hand he slapped her on the back and she threw up more blood.

"You'll be okay, honeypot. Jus' breathe through yer nose."

The girl groaned and tried to speak but couldn't. She lapsed into unconsciousness. Pitch let go of her waistband. She fell into her own blood. She would, Pitch knew, be unconscious for quite some time. Perhaps even for eternity.

"She done come to long enough to keep from dyin'." Pitch whispered as he walked over to Bertram.

"So what," Bertram hissed. "Stop fuckin' around an' help me take down this blanket."

Pitch removed the blanket that covered the passage to the pig sty and turned to Bertram.

"How we gonna handle pig boy?"

"I don't know," Bertram answered. "I ain't figured it out yet. We'll have to keep 'im quiet so he don't alert them others."

"You want him alive for information or what?" asked Pitch.

"I ain't decided yet. I'd jus' as soon kill 'im."

"He could have val'able information," Pitch offered.

"I doubt it. He's jus' one a us. I'll probably just grease 'im."

"Suit yerself," Pitch whispered as he covered the girl with the blanket and, referring to the opening to the pig pen, he added, "which side you want?"

"Get your rifle and take that side so y'can cover both them doors. I'll stay on this side and cover them pigs."

Pitch picked up his rifle and walked to the southeast wall. He urinated in the corner, taking care not to splatter his boots. He turned and looked at the girl. Her breathing appeared to have improved. Pitch smiled. He took his assigned position and turned his attention to Bertram.

Bertram seemed very alert. Pitch noticed that all Bertram's senses seemed to be totally active and Bertram seemed to be in a state of controlled agitation. Bertram's hands gripped the bamboo pole, then loosened, then tightened again and again. Every sound was analyzed and every flicker of light and every whisper of wind was felt and analyzed and identified. Bertram's eyes burned into the night and he was coiled and anxious. Within minutes Bertram heard a sound and saw an unusual movement. He crouched and extended the bamboo pole out behind him. His arms moved above his head and he lifted his heels so he was ready to strike quickly.

Pitch could see only Bertram in the dark room. He strained to see out the door and, just as he began to wonder what was out there or what Bertram had seen or heard, he was startled by a diminutive figure that suddenly and silently appeared. Bertram swung the bamboo pole and Pitch flinched in anticipation of the sound of a skull being crushed. Instead the pole smashed into the ceiling and, for an instant, all three men were helpless.

The Vietnamese snapped his head to the right and, with eyes alive with sheer terror, saw Bertram. From where Pitch was standing he could see Bertram's eyes flash with fear and Pitch was astounded. Bertram had destroyed the initial surprise and that stripped him of his most potent weapon. Pitch reacted first. He ran across the room and swung wildly with his rifle butt but, as an M-16 is a short rifle, he missed the Vietnamese completely. His movement did, however, distract the Vietnamese and allowed Bertram time to regain his advantage. Bertram reorientated himself and the pole and, swinging it like a baseball bat, he caught the Vietnamese in the lower abdomen. All the air rushed from the Vietnamese and he crumbled to the dirt. Bertram crouched and brought the pole down on the Vietnamese's back. The sound was thick and solid.

"Son of a bitch!" Bertram bellowed. "you fuckin' shit!"

Pitch, trying to regain his balance, tripped over something and fell to the ground. Bertram brought the pole back up and, still in a crouch, crashed it down again on the Vietnamese. Pitch could hear flesh split and bones snap. As Pitch tried to get to his feet he saw Bertram bring the pole up again. Bertram smashed the pole down again and again and again until Pitch was able to get to this feet. Pitch lunged at Bertram and tried to grab the pole.

"Let go!" Bertram screamed. He was nearly out of breath.

"He's dead!" Pitch yelled as Bertram pushed him away. Pitch stumbled backwards and fell. Bertram raised the pole and again struck the Vietnamese. He slowly and deliberately raised the pole and struck again and then again.

From outside there was movement. Villagers became aware that something terrible was happening. There were shouts in the night and lantern light began to flicker.

Pitch scrambled to his feet and yanked the pole from Bertram.

The pole was covered with blood. It slipped from Pitch's hand and fell to the dirt floor. Bertram's body sagged and he dropped to his knees. Pitch could see beads of sweat and splattered blood on Bertram's face. Bertram, with considerable effort, wiped his brow with his sleeve and sighed. He was exhausted.

"Get up," Pitch ordered, "they're comin'!"

Bertram's eyes now seemed lifeless.

Pitch looked at the two bodies on the floor. The girl was unconscious and the man was dead and covered with blood. Both soldiers and the inside of the building were splattered with blood.

"Get up!" Pitch yelled. "We gotta get outta here!"

Bertram shook his head to regain his senses. He staggered to his feet, glanced furtively around the room, grabbed his rifle and ran into the pig sty. Pitch ran after him and they disappeared into the night.

The pigs, startled and agitated, snorted their discontent.

Chapter 15

Majewski watched the sunrise. He was content to again enjoy that quiet, peaceful time of day. As the sun broke the horizon he saw two figures at the edge of the kill zone. They were waving their hands. Majewski recognized the uniforms as American and motioned the soldiers to approach.

"Pass it along," Majewski yelled to the next bunker. "We've got grunts comin' in. Get the gate ready."

Bertram and Pitch walked slowly to the perimeter. They looked exhausted.

Majewski left his bunker and motioned for the gate to be opened. Bertram and Pitch walked in and sat down on some sandbags.

"What happened to you? Where's the rest of the patrol?" Majewski asked.

"They're still out," Bertram said. "We weren't with 'em."

"They're okay?" Majewski asked.

"I s'pose," Bertram said.

"What happened? You're covered with blood. Are you all right?"

"We're okay. We had somethin' to do," said Bertram.

"Yeah," said Pitch.

Majewski looked at both men and wondered what he should do and say next. The two soldiers before him had obviously been involved in some sort of incident and Majewski did not know what he, as a perimeter guard, should do so he took a pack of cigarettes from his pocket and handed it to Pitch. Pitch took a cigarette and gave one to Bertram. Majewski lit a match and held it up to the cigarettes. Pitch and Bertram inhaled deeply, savored the smoke and exhaled almost in unison.

"You want me to get someone?" Majewski asked.

"CO up yet?" Bertram asked.

"I don't know," answered Majewski. "He doesn't visit us very often."

"We better report in," Bertram said to Pitch. They got to their feet and walked slowly toward the COs office.

Majewski wondered what had happened. He imagined that Pitch and Bertram had set up an ambush but soon realized blood would not splatter on ambushers unless the circumstances were very unique. He decided he would learn soon enough if there was anything to learn so he returned to his bunker and finished his shift.

Sleeping during the day in Vietnam was not very easy. Majewski had mastered it as well as anyone but, after two in the afternoon, fourteen hundred hours Military Time, it was generally too hot to sleep. Sleep was also interrupted frequently by noise from the camp or from helicopters or trucks or work details or just by noises that were different from the ones at night.

Majewski slept well until early afternoon. Then noises and the heat increased and he slept fitfully, waking often, until fairly late in the afternoon. He awoke soaked with sweat. He did not shower as the showers were not turned on and available until after he was posted to his guard duty. He dried off as well as possible with a towel, put on the uniform he had worn the previous day and walked outside. The air was hot and thick. What breeze there was was slight. He judged by the sun's position that it was after three so he stretched, squinted at the sun and walked to the mess tent for coffee.

The men in Bertram's patrol had returned from the field. They had only been out a day and Majewski thought that odd. A patrol of short duration was unusual unless its mission was specific and fairly uncomplicated. The men seemed subdued and that seemed a bit out of place, too. Majewski got his coffee but said nothing to any of Bertram's men. He simply went outside and sat on the sandbags in the shade on the east side of the mess tent.

He had not been there long when Sergeant Lark approached.

"Have ya seen Surrey or Wyandotte?" Lark asked.

"No. I just got up."

"There's a bunch of dinks at the gate. They wanna see the old man," Lark said as he turned and walked toward the main perimeter gate. Majewski sat for a moment but his curiosity got the better of him. He got up and walked slowly toward the perimeter. As he approached he saw the CO and Surrey talking to Lark. Beyond them there were four Vietnamese at the gate, two Vietnamese civilian policemen, the old owner of the dead waterbuffalo and a very small man in black pants and a white sports shirt who looked very alert and bright.

The Vietnamese waited patiently until the Commanding Officer ordered the gate opened and allowed them entry to the base.

Once inside the smallest man stepped forward and presented his identification card with a bow.

The CO didn't bother to look at it. He simply said "Who are you and what do you want?"

The man looked at the American soldiers that had gathered around and said in flawless English "It would be better if we talked in private."

The CO stood silently for a moment. Then he turned to Lark and said "Search him. Search all of 'em."

The man put his arms up and spread his legs. So did the other Vietnamese. The two police officers were disarmed and Lark's search found nothing significant.

"Follow me," the CO said as he led Surrey, Lark and the four Vietnamese to his office. Once inside he sat at his desk and waited for the smallest man to speak. The man stepped forward and stood in front of the Commanding Officer's desk. He bowed and began to speak.

"Good afternoon, Captain. My name is Van and I am an interpreter with the Military Assistance Command on temporary assignment to the Cahn Sats (Vietnamese National Police) in Hue. This elderly gentleman has informed us that soldiers from your camp were operating in and around his village last night."

"Uh, I don't think so," the CO said.

"Two of your soldiers, a sergeant and a specialist fourth class, entered the village and entered the house of a Vietnamese civilian without the owner's consent.

They killed a man and beat a young girl so severly that she may die."

The Commanding Officer sat quietly and said nothing.

"I am authorized on behalf of the government of the Republic of Vietnam, by the village chief and by civilian and military authorities at the Citadel in Hue, to pursue this matter to its lawful conclusion. The paperwork has been filed and will find its way down to you through channels."

The CO said nothing.

"We are here for an explanation. This is a serious matter, Captain. Two Vietnamese citizens are involved and the consequences could be significant."

The CO finally spoke. "I have no idea what you're talking about."

"I see," the man said. He took a notebook and pen from his pocket and wrote something in Vietnamese. "This is serious, Captain. The victims were loyal to the government There is no doubt about that."

The CO sat quietly for quite some time. He leaned forward and said "I still don't know what you're talking about or why you're here."

"We are talking about assault and murder, Captain."

"Why would you think soldiers from this camp would be involved?"

The man gestured toward the old man. "Because this man said so."

"And you believe him?"

"Yes."

"He's probably full of shit."

"He says he provided information to you under duress. He said you would not pay for killing his waterbuffalo unless he gave you information about the village. He said he told you of a house where a VC would come to visit one of the girls. Apparently there was a faulty translation as that particular house is farther south. The house your men defiled belongs to a South Vietnamese officer. The girl was his niece and the young man who was killed was his nephew, a lieutenant in the Army home on leave. He was working with the Popular Forces, the young people that guard the village, and returned to the house to check on the welfare of his sister and was beaten to death by your men."

The CO sat silently.

"The girl was fifteen."

The CO said nothing.

"This man and a number of villagers saw two soldiers run off. We have statements that provide a great deal of information."

"I cannot tell you about operations we engage in," the CO said firmly. "I don't know you from Adam. You could be Viet Cong or North Vietnamese for all I know. But I can assure you that no one on this base was in your village last night."

"That is the position you are taking then?" said Van.

"I still have no idea what you're talking about."

"Then you have provided all the information you intend to provide at this time."

"That's all the information there is," the CO said.

Van pointed at the old man and, in a voice that was firm and determined, said, "This man is old and feeble in many ways, Captain, but he knows what he saw and he does not lie. He lives near that house and heard noises. He looked out and saw both men. He prides himself on his ability to see at night. He knows what he saw. He is suffering a lot and this event has frightened and confused him. He told me he wanted to stop the soldiers but there was no way. He thought they would kill him if he even tried."

The CO said nothing.

"This is a man of honor," Van said. "The girl was like a daughter to him. He has known her all her life and now she is in a hospital with her face destroyed and with her brother dead. He knows the soldiers were from this camp. I know it, too."

The CO again said nothing.

"We will be leaving now, Captain, but we will be back. I expect your cooperation. Do not let it surprise you if pressure is brought to bear."

Van touched the old man's shoulders to indicate they should turn and leave. The Cahn Sats and the old

293

man walked toward the door and Van continued to look at the CO.

"This is not over," Van said softly. "This is far from over."

The CO said nothing for a short period of time. His expression revealed nothing but he eventually said "where did you learn to speak English so good?"

Van leaned over the CO's desk and fixed his eyes on the CO's. Then Van whispered "None of your fucking business."

The CO motioned to the door. Van bowed, turned and walked out of the office. The four Vietnamese stepped into the sunlight and were escorted out of camp.

The CO and Surrey also walked outside. Neither man looked confident or comfortable.

"I have the sinking feeling we're in deep shit, Lieutenant," the CO said.

"So do I," Surrey said as he walked toward the gate and watched the Vietnamese cross the kill zone. They were walking slowly and deliberately, keeping pace with the old man, until the afternoon shadows swallowed them.

Surrey and the Commanding Officer returned to the CO's office. Majewski had long since finished his coffee. He returned to his hooch, laid down on his bed and rested until guardmount. He tried to imagine what had happened to cause a visit from the Vietnamese but he couldn't. He tried to relax. He felt distant and uneasy but managed to doze for an hour.

The night in the bunker passed uneventfully. Someone in one of the bunkers apparently detected movement in the kill zone and fired two clips of M-16 rounds but a search at shift's end revealed nothing. Daylight did bring a helicopter but Majewski was back in his AO and did not see what, if anything, the helicopter brought. It brought officers. Early in the afternoon Majewski was awakened by McGill and told to dress and report to the CO's office.

Majewski soon found himself sitting across the desk from the same Criminal Investigation Division agent that had questioned him after the Biondi-Jackson murders.

The officer read Majewski his rights and then began to speak.

"Specialist Majewski, we meet again."

"Yes, Sir. What's this all about?"

"It's about what happened the night before last."

Majewski sat quietly and waited for the CID man to continue. He didn't so Majewski finally said "what happened the night before last?"

"You don't know?"

"No, Sir."

"Were you on Green Line that night?"

"Sir, I'm always on Green Line."

"It's your sacred calling, then?"

"Yes, Sir."

"What happened in the morning?"

"I went back to my AO and went to sleep."

"I mean before that."

"Sir," Majewski said, betraying slight exasperation. "I really don't know what you're expecting but nothing happened that night. It was quiet."

"What happened at dawn?"

Majewski thought for a moment. "Two of our guys came in from the field, Sir."

The CID man leaned back in his chair and interlaced his fingers.

"Tell me about it, Specialist."

"Two of our guys came in from the field, Sir. I saw them wavin' at us across the kill zone so I alerted the rest of the Green Line so they wouldn't get shot up on the way in. When they got to the gate I had it opened and they came inside."

"Who were they?"

"Two of our guys. Bertram and Pitch, Sir. Bertram's a sergeant and Pitch isn't."

"Where had they been?"

"Beats the shit out of me, Sir. I don't know. Out in the field somewhere, I guess."

"What did they do when they entered camp."

"They sat down on sandbags near the gate and smoked a cigarette."

"Did you talk to them?"

"Yeah. I asked 'em where they'd been."

"What did they say?"

"They said they'd been out in the field, Sir."

"Did you notice anything unusual about them?"

"They were tired but that's not unusual, Sir."

"What about their uniforms?"

Majewski thought for a few seconds.

"There appeared to be blood on 'em if that's what you're after. I asked 'em about it but they didn't say anything. I figured they didn't want to tell me and it was none of my business. After all, it wasn't my blood."

"Whose blood was it?"

"How the hell should I know?" Majewski was becoming more irritated.

"Calm down," the CID man said. "What I mean is did they appear wounded?"

"No, Sir. I asked and they said they were fine."

"No wounds."

"I didn't see any."

"And you don't know how they got blood all over their uniforms?"

"No, Sir."

"What if I told you we have a complaint from the Vietnamese. They say two Americans entered the village and assaulted two Vietnamese civilians. They killed one and perhaps both of 'em."

"I don't know anything about that, Sir."

"Did either Pitch or Bertram mention being in the village?"

"Not to me, Sir. We didn't talk long. If you think they're involved why aren't you talking to them?"

"That's just it," the CID man said. "We can't find them."

Majewski sat quietly for a few seconds not knowing what to say or what would be said next. The CID man pushed a pack of cigarettes across the desk. Majewski took one and lit it. The smoke filled his lungs and seemed to heighten his senses.

"Where did they go after you talked to them?"

"I don't know, Sir. They headed this way. I don't know if they came here or went back to their AOs. I returned to my post and finished my shift."

"Did they mention the Commanding Officer at all?"

Majewski thought for a moment. He knew that Pitch and Bertram had mentioned the CO.

"I think they did," Majewski said, "but I don't remember the context."

"Then you don't know where they went when they left you."

"Sir, when I'm on Green Line my concerns are with what's out beyond the perimeter. Not what goes on inside."

"Most commendable." the CID man said. "So you don't know if they talked to the CO or to anyone else."

"I don't know, Sir. I went back to my post and finished my shift."

"Do you know if Bertram and Pitch left the base during the day?"

"Which day?"

"Yesterday."

"No. I don't know."

"What did you do yesterday?"

"Slept, Sir."

"Did you hear any helicopters come in?"

"Not that I recall, Sir. They come and go. It's no big deal. They're always around. If I am asleep and one wakes me up I go back to sleep."

"Did that happen yesterday?"

"Not that I recall."

"How about trucks or Jeeps? Did you hear anything like that?"

"Not that I recall, Sir."

"Could Bertram and Pitch get out of camp without being seen?"

"By me they could've, Sir. I was sleeping. GIs come and go."

The CID man lit a cigarette and Majewski extinguished his in the CO's ashtray.

"So you saw them come in to camp," the CID man said as he exhaled, "and you saw them come this way but you didn't see where they went and you didn't see them with or talking to anyone else. You finished your shift and went to sleep, is that right?"

"Yes, Sir."

"And you don't know if they're still on the base or if they've left."

"That's right, Sir, I don't know."

"Could they have got off base last night when you were on guard duty?"

"If they went through my sector I would've seen 'em, Sir."

"You're sure," said the CID man.

"Absolutely."

"Could they have gotten out through any other sector?"

"Probably. But they didn't go out through mine."

"Okay. Do you have anything to add?"

"No, Sir. I don't know what's happenin' and I don't care. I wish I was better at followin' the advice my mother gave me years ago."

"What advice is that, Specialist?"

"She took me aside one day," Majewski said in earnest, "and told me to beware of people that are into weird shit."

The CID man smiled. "That's good advice. Your mother is quite insightful."

"I'm thinking of having it sewn into a sampler I can hang above my bed next to my short-timer's calendar."

"Good idea," the CID man said. "That'll be all."

Majewski returned to his AO and tried to get back to sleep. He had no idea what had happened but he knew that he was not involved. He did wonder what had become of Pitch and Bertram but didn't spend much time speculating as he figured he would eventually find out.

That night Green Line was alive with rumor and speculation. Each man on Green Line had been interviewed by the CID man. There was no doubt that Bertram and Pitch had been in the village and had attacked the two Vietnamese. There was no doubt, too, that Bertram and Pitch were no longer on the base. Rumor had it that even their footlockers and personal possessions were missing. No one knew who had cleaned out the AOs or when it had been done but done but new footlockers were in place and the hooch was waiting for new tenants. Speculation assumed that someone in Supply would know what had happened but Supply didn't know. Supply had been asked by the potheads and Supply had no answers. Did Bertram and Pitch slip out of camp at night? It was certainly possible. Did they leave by helicopter or truck? That was also possible. No one knew anything for sure but everyone enjoyed speculation. Speculation was less boring than duty.

The night passed quickly. The CID man was still on the base and he had talked with everyone on Green Line and everyone that had initially gone out in the field with Bertram and Pitch. He did not talk to the officers. A Colonel from Battalion flew in and talked briefly with the CO and Surrey. McGill was sent out of earshot and no one knew what the Colonel learned except the CO and Surrey and they were not volunteering information.

After the meeting in the CO's office the Colonel made a brief inspection tour of the perimeter. He wrote some observation notes in a small notebook and seemed particularly interested in an area in the northwest sector. Surrey and the CO stood nearby. The Colonel occasionally pointed or gestured toward the kill zone and to the nearby bunkers and the CO responded with his own series of gestures. Surrey said nothing. He seemed strangely detached from everything and everyone.

The Colonel's visit was brief. He returned to his helicopter, took a salute from the CO and Surrey and flew off in an easterly direction. The CO and Surrey returned to the CO's office and the camp was quiet until sunset when rumors again flew and speculation abounded.

At two thirty-seven the northwest sector took and returned rifle fire. No one was hurt and a lot of rounds were fired by the bunker rats into the kill zone. Sunlight brought a thorough search of the area but nothing significant was found.

When the patrol returned to the base the CO sent them out again and the second search revealed a bloodstained shirt at the woods edge of the kill zone. It was an American uniform shirt or, as the Army preferred, blouse. The nametag had been ripped off as had the sergeant's stripes. It was obviously the shirt Bertram had worn in the village.

The CO held the shirt up when it was presented to him by the man that found it. He turned it this way and that and made sure those around him saw that he was inspecting it thoroughly.

"We'll send this to Battalion," the CO said as he handed the bloody shirt to Sergeant Elmore. "Maybe they can make something out of it."

Elmore took the shirt to the CID man and, upon taking it, the CID man laughed.

The CO walked to his office and put a call through to Battalion. An hour later a helicopter landed on the PSP and the same Colonel stepped back onto the base. Men close enough to the helicopter pad saw the CO approach the Colonel. The Colonel, yelling loud enough to be heard over the sounds of the helicopter, said "I understand you've found something, Captain."

The CO saluted and said "Yes, Sir. Right this way."

The Colonel and the CO walked toward the CO's office. Surrey and the CID man followed. Once inside the office the CID man handed the blouse to the

Colonel. The Colonel put the blouse on the CO's desk without paying it much attention.

"Where was this found?" he asked.

"At the far end of the kill zone, Sir," the CO said, "out to the northwest."

"I see. I assume it belongs to that sergeant."

"We haven't determined that yet..." the CO began but he was interrupted by laughter from the CID man.

"You both are so full of shit!" the CID man said as he turned and left the office.

The CO and the Colonel stayed in the office. Surrey strolled outside.

The CID man was sitting on some sandbags near the helicopter pad lighting a cigarette. Surrey approached and lit a cigarette of his own.

"You mind if I sit down?" Surrey asked.

"Help yourself," the CID man said. "Are you part of this bullshit?"

Surrey sat quietly for half a minute. He savored his cigarette and said "Not wholeheartedly."

S. R. Larson

"Good. I would like to think you could come up with something better than 'the dog ate my homework.'"

Surrey sat quietly and watched the cigarette smoke rise.

"I know Van," the CID man said. "He's a tough little bastard. He'll tear this story to shreds and smile while he does it. What is it we're supposed to believe? Two renegade soldiers entered the village and beat the shit out of a couple of suspected Viet Cong then came back here and snuck out again to be swallowed up by the jungle where they'll live off the land and fight for truth, justice and the American way. Get serious."

Surrey shrugged.

"Are they back in the States yet?" the CID man asked.

Surrey said nothing.

"How did you get 'em off the base?"

Surrey inhaled deeply but the only thing to come out of his mouth was smoke.

"I think the Colonel arranged for them to be hustled off the base in a chopper or supply truck. I think they're back in the States drinkin' beer and makin' babies."

Surrey finally spoke. "I really don't know what went on. We had information that there was VC activity in the village. We got some information from the old man but didn't trust him. He could easily have been Viet Cong. We discussed some operations but nothing like what happened. That I can assure you. If it was Bertram and Pitch in the village I don't know about it. I know they came back here but if they left the base, the left it without my help or knowledge."

"Sleight-of-hand," the CID man said.

"Listen," Surrey said softly. "I'm short. No one is supposed to know this but I'm going back to the States in about a week and a half. I don't want to fuck that up by getting involved in something like this. I mean, I just don't need the aggravation."

The CID man tossed his cigarette away.

"Lieutenant," the CID man said, "I checked you out before I came up here. You're on the Battalion shit list. They consider you a fuck up. I know they pulled you out of the field and barred you from re-enlistment so cover your ass. They may be trying to find a way to hang all of this on you."

"I thought of that," Surrey said.

"I don't know what really happened. I'm just doin' my job with what I have available. What you have to worry about is Mr. Van. He'll do his job with what he has available, too, and he's a tough little son of a bitch."

Surrey flipped his cigarette butt into the air. It landed on the sand and continued to smoke.

"Van is brilliant," the CID man said, "but he won't have to be very smart to see through this bogus story. I would strongly suggest that you and the CO and that chunk of birdshit in the office get your shit together. Try real hard to come up with a better story than you have now."

Surrey lit another cigarette. He turned his eyes skyward and spent the next minute watching the passing clouds. The CID man looked up, too.

"You better get your shit together," the CID man said. "Or you'll be standing tits deep in shit."

310

Surrey and the CID man heard the CO's office door open. They saw the Colonel make a circling motion with his right arm. The helicopter blades slowly began to move and dust blew on Surrey and the CID man. The Colonel walked slowly toward the helicopter. He was carrying the bloody shirt and the CO was following. Dust and sand blew harder as the helicopter increased its power. Surrey and the CID man stood up and watched the Colonel get into the helicopter.

The CO ducked his head, stepped back, held on to his cap and watched the helicopter slowly rise from the pad.

The helicopter climbed slowly into the air and moved in a southeasternly direction. It followed the narrow dirt road that led to and away from the camp.

Surrey and the CO walked together back to the CO's office. The CID man walked toward the latrine and, over the woods at the edge of the kill zone, the helicopter lurched as a barrage of small arms fire slammed into it. It climbed as smoke began to roll from its engine. It first cleared and then disappeared behind the trees. A flash of fire and the sound of an explosion followed and a column of grayblack smoke rose over the trees.

Shouts rose from the towers and bunker line. Faint sounds of rifle fire and more explosions were heard from the area beyond the trees. Surrey and Captain Wyandotte ran to the perimeter and, for a few seconds, watched smoke billow into the air.

"Get some men," the CO shouted to Surrey. "Any men!"

Surrey ran to the nearby hooches and commandeered every man not on duty. Majewski had heard the helicopter leave and had heard the commotion. He dressed and was buttoning his shirt when Surrey appeared.

"I'm going to need you for this one, 'Ski," Surrey said. "Get your rifle and form up at the gate."

Majewski finished buttoning his shirt. He wondered what was happening and why he had been singled out for a mission when he was perfectly content being a Green Line bunker rat. A feeling of dread slammed into him and he felt weak and lightheaded. He sat down on the bed and, ever so slightly, began to shake. His throat became dry and his chest began to tighten and he found it difficult to breathe. He wondered what was happening to him. It seemed as though the walls were closing in so he forced himself to this feet, grabbed his rifle, a bandolier and his flak jacket and staggered out into the sunlight.

Soldiers were running for the perimeter and those that were already there were shouting and pointing. Majewski saw smoke but didn't know where it was coming from. He knew the area well enough to know that the smoke was fairly close to the road but the thought of a helicopter crash never occurred to him.

When Majewski reached the perimeter he quickly learned the origin of the smoke. Surrey arrived, formed up the men and, at a trot, they left the Fire Base.

Majewski hated running. Running by itself was bad enough but running in Vietnam with a rifle and bandolier and a flak jacket was sheer torture. Most of the other soldiers felt the same way and the column sagged and separated. The column slowed, reformed and walked in an orderly fashion along the road.

Two helicopter gunships appeared and circled the smoke. They did not land but did strafe the woods with machinegun fire and two rockets.

The footsoldiers approached the wooded section at the edge of the kill zone and, staying on the road, they moved quickly toward the rice paddies. There they saw the Colonel's helicopter aflame in the rice paddy about fifty yards from the road. Surrey leaped from the road into the rice paddy. The rest of the soldiers followed in due order, some jumping, others sliding and others, like Majewski, slipping into the paddy with cautious trepidation. The water was warm and it stank. It was less than knee deep but the mud gave more than Majewski expected.

By the time Majewski had sloshed his way to the helicopter Surrey and most of the other soldiers were already there. Inside the helicopter two people had been burned to death, their bodies charred and folded into distorted, peculiar, unnatural positions.

"Check him out, 'Ski!' Surrey yelled as he pointed to a body near the helicopter.

Majewski knelt down next to the body. The dead man was lying face down with his arms pulled curiously next to the body. Majewski had expected the arms to be outstretched as if to break a fall. The water around the body was pink.

Majewski turned the body over and saw the eyes, wide open in terror, of a young man. The eyes were powerful and seemed to fix directly on Majewski's face. Majewski flinched at the thought that the dead man might be focusing on him and he tried to get to his feet. He couldn't. He seemed fastened to that particular spot in the rice paddy so he returned his attention to the dead man. The dead man's face was wet and muddy from the rice paddy and his hands were clutching at his throat. Majewski slowly moved his left hand to the dead man's hands and cautiously pulled them away. The dead man's throat had been cut from just under the right ear to just beyond the midpoint of the neck.

"Lieutenant!" Majewski shouted. "You better see this!"

Surrey splashed his way over to Majewski and looked down at the dead man.

"Jezus," he muttered.

"This didn't happen in the crash," Majewski said.

"I know. Someone came out of the woods and slit his throat."

Majewski nodded and folded the dead man's hands back to their death position. He looked up at Surrey. Surrey was watching the tree line to the west of their position and Majewski realized he was kneeling in a rice paddy. He attempted to get up but Surrey pushed him violently and screamed "Hit it!" just as rifle fire erupted from the tree line.

Surrey dove over Majewski and the dead man and landed in the muddy water to Majewski's right. Bullets screamed overhead. Some slammed into the burning helicopter while others found more fleshy targets. Additional bursts of rifle fire came from the woods to Majewski's right. The Americans were in a crossfire and spurts of water sprang into the air as bullets pounded the rice paddy.

Majewski scrambled over the dead man and yanked the body so it angled slightly to his left. He got as low as he could in the water and mud and used the dead body for cover and concealment.

Majewski had let his rifle go at some point and had no idea where it was. He didn't care where it was. He was interested only in survival.

Overhead the helicopter gunships opened fire. Tracer rounds slammed into the tree line and water splashed as bullets crashed and casings fell into the rice paddy.

Three mortar rounds impacted near the burning helicopter. Shards of shrapnel splayed violently through the air and water and mud splattered Majewski, the dead man and Surrey.

Surrey crawled from his position on Majewski's right to the burning helicopter. He used it for cover and began firing his M-16 at the tree line. Overhead the gunships continued to fire and soldiers farther to Surrey's left opened fire.

Majewski covered his head and pulled his knees up to his chest. His M-16 laid in the water on the far side of the corpse.

Someone beyond the helicoper fired rounds from an M-79 grenade launcher into the tree line and Surrey turned his fire to the trees on the right. Mortar rounds again hit near the burning helicopter and there were shouts and screams from the tree line and from the rice paddy.

One of the gunships concentrated its fire from above the rice paddy while the other gunship moved around and positioned itself over the trees so its fire could be directed downward from behind the enemy position. Hundreds of machinegun bullets pounded the tree line and M-16 fire poured in from the rice paddy.

The AK-47 fire lessened. Shouts directing fire could be heard from an area beyond the burning helicopter and, within a few seconds, a barrage of M-16 fire silenced the remaining AK-47 fire. The attack was over.

Chapter 16

Majewski used the dead man to help push himself up after the attack ended. He checked himself for pain and wounds. He found nothing notable and realized he did not have his M-16. He searched for it by probing with his right foot and, when it was found, Majewski picked it up. It was covered with mud and the assorted slime that covers the bottom of rice paddies. Majewski rinsed it off in the water at his feet.

Surrey was standing near the helicopter shouting orders and pointing at the tree line. Beyond him two soldiers were dragging a wounded man toward him and others were kneeling over the fallen and wounded. The helicopters above were still circling and would fire periodically into the woods.

Surrey turned and looked at Majewski. Surrey's eyes flashed with intensity and he began to shout and gesture at Majewski.

"Does that work?" Surrey yelled.

"What?" Majewski yelled back.

"Your rifle! Does it work?"

Majewski shook his rifle and noticed, for the first time, that there was a clip in it. He did not recall inserting a clip so he thought for a moment that he may have picked up the dead man's rifle but soon he recognized it as his own.

"I don't know! It looks…"

"C'mon," shouted Surrey.

Majewski dreaded the prospect of going into the woods but knew what Surrey had in mind. He sloshed through the muddy water and stood, with seven other men, near Surrey.

"Spread out," Surrey ordered, "and head for the woods!"

The men stood silently for a few seconds.

"C'mon, follow me!" shouted Surrey. "Get a move on!"

The soldiers followed. They spread themselves out and moved cautiously toward the tree line.

There was no rifle fire from the trees and, overhead, the gunships provided cover. Majewski, Surrey and the others splashed their way to the edge of the rice paddy and climbed up on the higher ground in front of the trees.

There were sounds from the woods, groaning sounds from someone somewhere and odd, cracking, splintering sounds that seemed to come from the trees themselves. The woods was terrifying, strange and frightfully unfamiliar. Majewski stepped cautiously and felt his chest tighten. He became lightheaded and dizzy and his hands began to shake. He dropped to his knees and felt as if everything was closing in around him. He shook his head and looked up as if trying to find an escape. Shafts of sunlight suspended smoke in an eerie, macabre chamber of forms and bewildering shadows. Majewski spread out his hands and felt as if he was hovering just above the ground. He was wet and very afraid and certain he was going to die.

There was gunfire to his left and bullets whizzed overhead and slammed into trees. He flattened out instinctively. Shouts could be heard and more shots were fired.

Majewski looked to his left but was so low that he could see nothing except matted grass and his left hand, which was twitching.

From his right there was an explosion and he felt the ground beneath him vibrate. Dirt and stones and pieces of metal pelted him. He heard someone shout and turned to see someone run past his position. For a few seconds Majewski laid motionless in the grass, then he sprang to his feet and ran after the other soldier. He was, for a second, surprised by the fact that he was functioning and capable of such swift and deliberate movement. He seemed to glide effortlessly over the ground as if his feet were barely touching and he felt the most bizarre sense of freedom for a few seconds before the man in front of him disappeared. The ground had opened and the other soldier vanished.

Majewski veered to the right and flailed past the hole that had swallowed the soldier. He stumbled and fell. Hitting the solid ground pushed all the air from his body and he gasped and clawed at the dirt and grass.

The other soldier had fallen through the concealed cover of a booby trap into a pit and was impaled on sharpened bamboo stakes. Majewski could neither see nor hear the other soldier but he seemed to know that the soldier was dead. Majewski was wrong. The soldier wasn't dead but had a bamboo stake through his left foot and another through his right thigh. Blood was oozing out of each wound and the soldier was terrified.

Majewski still could not catch his breath. His chest ached and each gasp brought sharp stabs of pain. He was certain he had been seriously wounded and sure the wounds were going to be fatal. He was wrong again. Eventually his breathing regulated and air again found its way into his lungs. He was not wounded but he was frightened.

Others had seen the soldier fall into the pit. Help was immediate. Another soldier was lowered carefully into the pit and the stakes were hacked off with the edge of an entrenching tool. Each hacking blow caused the wounded soldier to scream in pain.

When the stakes were severed the soldiers were pulled out of the pit and tourniquets were applied to the legs of the wounded man. He was carried back to the rice paddy.

Majewski had been unable to help. Someone had helped him to his feet but he still was not breathing correctly. His cheeks were wet from tears and his entire body was trembling. He felt as if he was going to implode and, seconds later, he felt as if he was going to explode. He dropped to his knees and let his head fall forward. He was dizzy and gasped again for breath but there did not seem to be any air for him. He coughed and tried to clear his throat. Someone slapped him on his back and told him to inhale deeply. Majewski collapsed and laid helplessly in the tall grass. He was certain that he was going to die.

Lieutenant Surrey stood near his men and divided his attention between the sights and sounds of the woods and the wounded soldier.

Two soldiers were assigned to carry the wounded man back to the burning helicopter and the rest were ordered to spread out and be careful. "Get Majewski up," Surrey yelled. "He ain't hurt."

Majewski was pulled to his feet. He was handed his rifle and pushed toward the other men. His chest heaved but his breathing was now better and he was able to cope with physical movement.

Surrey heard groaning from near the booby trap. He found a spiderhole and, inside, a Vietnamese soldier that had been shot in the cheek. Surrey reached down and, with one hand, pulled the soldier out by the hair and left him sprawled on the ground.

The Vietnamese groaned and was barely concsious. Surrey stood over him. The Vietnamese was wearing a greenish gray uniform. Surrey searched the shirt pockets and found nothing. He rolled the soldier over and checked the pants pockets. He found some Vietnamese money and an identification card. He slipped the card and money back into the soldier's pocket. Then he pointed the barrel of his M-16 at the base of the soldier's skull and fired one round. The soldier's body twitched and died.

Majewski, like some of the other soldiers, had walked up close to Surrey. Surrey turned to Majewski and said "Sometimes you have to stop bein' a pussy."

Majewski said nothing.

"Fan out," Surrey ordered and the soldiers moved farther into the woods.

Majewski was numb but his breathing had improved. He was able to keep up with the others as they moved cautiously between the trees. Three more Vietnamese soldiers were found. Two were dead and the other had been severely wounded by rounds from the gunships. Surrey again leveled his M-16 and fired. The wounded soldier died instantly.

No weapons were found near the dead Vietnamese. Comrades had obviously taken the rifles and ammunition before leaving the area. Surrey gathered the men together, made a quick count and said "turn around and get the hell out of here! We've done enough."

The soldiers wasted no time getting back to the rice paddy. A Medevac helicopter landed near the burning helicopter and the dead and wounded were quickly placed aboard. He helicopter rose, spraying water and mud over the soldiers below.

Majewski was exhausted. His chest still hurt and he stood in the water and trembled uncontrollably.

Surrey called the remaining soldiers together and said "let's get back to camp. Gather up all your shit an' get the hell outta here."

Majewski remembered little of the trip back to the Fire Base. He was wet, muddy and tired physically. Mentally he was completely confused and exhausted. He had been perfectly content with an average day in camp until the helicopter was shot down. Then he had been hurled into a situation that had terrified him and, thinking back, he began to be mentally bothered by the statement Surrey had made.

"Sometimes you have to stop bein' a pussy."

The Fire Base was a welcomed sight. Majewski entered with the other soldiers and went directly to his AO where he stripped off his clothes. He checked himself over for wounds but found only a leech fastened to his calf. He took a cigarette, lit it and burned off the leech. He picked up a towel, wrapped it around his waist and walked to the shower. Other soldiers were there before him and someone, probably McGill, had turned on the master valve. The water was strangely cold to Majewski. He showered and returned to his hooch where he put on cleaner clothes. He was exhausted and wanted to sleep but knew there were things that had to be done first. He sat on his bed and began cleaning his rifle. It was filthy and it hadn't been fired. Mud and torn blades of grass clogged the mechanism and Majewski doubted the piece would even function.

He took a rag from his footlocker and began rubbing it across the stock. His mind drifted back over the day. For the second time Majewski had fallen on a dead man. He had used a dead man for cover and concealment. He had seen the gash in the dead man's throat and it had stunned him but not enough to keep from using the corpse for protection.

Majewski began to tremble with the realization that, for the second time in a few days, someone had run past or jumped over him in the heat and confusion of an attack. One of the sappers had cleared his prone body with ease when the base was attacked and, before crashing into the pit, an American soldier had effortlessly hurdled him.

The afternoon had been frightful, macabre, gruesome, strange and unfamiliar. He had been very afraid and ineffective and, as he sat on his bed with his rifle and towel, a tear fell from his left eye and landed on the black rifle stock. Slowly the tear trickled around the stock and fell onto Majewski's leg. He began to shake violently and the tears flowed. He was crying and he couldn't breathe. He put the rifle on the footlocker and laid back on his bed. His head seemed to be swimming and he put his right forearm over his eyes to mask his tears. He did not want anyone who might happen to enter his hooch to see him cry.

Chapter 17

The night passed with prolonged dread for Majewski. He spent his bunker time keeping a tenuous rein on his emotions. He leaned his rifle up against the sandbags and endured the sad hours of mental and physical solitude. Bitter memories fought with flights of fancy and each creeping shadow brought with it new fears and anxieties. Majewski stayed awake and remained exhausted.

Daylight brought another visit from Mr. Van. He arrived at the Main Gate in a Renault and honked for admittance. Lieutenant Surrey was summoned and the gate was eventually opened. Mr. Van parked his car and walked with Surrey to the CO's office. McGill was sent from the building. The CO sat at his desk. Mr. Van stood in front of the CO's desk and Surrey sat on a footlocker.

"I want information about the incident in the village," Van said.

The Commanding Officer said nothing.

"I want information and I want it now. I am authorized to take whatever means necessary…"

"Fuck you," said Surrey. Van turned to his left and looked at Surrey.

"You ain't gettin' jack shit!" Surrey yelled. "Your little Viet Cong buddies shot down a helicopter and killed three men yesterday. I got four wounded men so you don't get a fuckin' thing!"

"I saw the helicopter as I drove up, Lieutenant," Van said. "I don't know what happened yesterday. I am interested in what happened in the village."

"I'll tell you what fuckin' happened," Surrey shouted. "That dipshit village protected thirty or forty Congs that shot down a helicopter and shot up the patrol sent out to rescue the Americans they murdered! That's what fuckin' happened, Charlie!"

"I don't know who shot down the helicopter," Van said, "but it wasn't anyone from the village."

"I didn't say it was someone from the village, you stupid shit! I said the village provided food and information for an NVA unit or for a band of Viet Cong. That's what I said!"

"How do you suspect the village of involvement?" Van asked.

"What?" Surrey answered.

"How do you know the village was involved?"

"Oh, I suppose it's sheer coincidence that a helicopter got shot down. I suppose you'll tell me next that it was the Americans who shot it down."

"I don't know who shot it down. I don't know anything about it. That's not what I'm here for."

"I know there are at least four dead dinks in that woods. I extinguished two of 'em myself and they had to come from somewhere."

"I don't know where they came from. I am only interested in what happened in the village..." Van was interrupted.

"Get out of my office!" The CO shouted. "Get out and stay out!"

Van turned to the CO.

"You have not seen the last of me. This situation is serious and I will be back. Battalion is involved and I will have answers. You deny your soldiers were in the village and then accuse the village of shooting down your copter. You can't have things your way all the time. Why would anyone believe you at all?"

"There's the door," the CO yelled. "Feel free to let it hit you in the ass on the way out."

Van bowed, turned and left the office. He walked to his car and started it. The gate was opened and Mr. Van drove off the base and down the kill zone road.

Surrey and Wyandotte watched until Van's car could no longer be seen. Both men seemed agitated as they returned to the office. Midmorning brought a return visit to the woods by the helicopter gunships. Enough incendiary rounds were fired to set the woods ablaze and the gunships moved to the woods nearer the village where that forest, too, was ignited.

The afternoon demanded another patrol to the area of the rice paddy. Shots had been fired from the woods at the gunships and Surrey was again assigned the task of clearing the woods.

It took time for the fire to burn itself out. The woods smoldered and Surrey's men, Majewski among them, proceeded cautiously.

Majewski was near exhaustion from the previous day and the subsequent night. He did not sleep much in the morning as the gunships provided quite a show and a lot of noise. He had watched for a while from the perimeter as the woods was pulverized and this day's patrol seemed far less menacing than the previous day's had proved to be.

The men moved cautiously along the dikes and near the road at the edge of the rice paddy. The shell of the burned helicopter slumped in the muddy water.

The burned bodies of the Colonel and the pilot had long since been removed and that task certainly must have been unpleasant.

Surrey seemed tired and distant. His enthusiasm for such missions had waned considerably in the last day and he seemed annoyed at having been given such an assignment. He had, after all, been barred from leading men into combat and was scheduled to go back to the States in a few days.

"I want you men to be careful," Surrey said as the patrol moved along the edge of the rice paddy. "We're going to go along the dikes and into the woods but we aren't going in very far. We'll ghost for a while."

Majewski liked the plan. He was not interested in exploring the woods. He walked behind Sergeant Elmore and, as they turned to walk from the road to one of the dikes, Majewski noticed a cloud of dust off in the distance. He called to Elmore and Elmore saw the roostertail of dust, too. Something was moving rapidly along the road and, as the object neared, both Majewski and Elmore recognized it as Van's Renault.

"Here comes that dink," Elmore said. "Headin' for the camp."

As Majewski watched the car approach he saw a flash of light and the car disintegrated in an impressive explosion. Glass and metal blasted skyward and rained down on the road and on some of the men.

Majewski instinctively dropped to the ground and covered the back of his head and neck with his arms. Elmore jumped into the rice paddy. Surrey dropped, rolled to the edge of the road and scrambled halfway down the embankment. Debris landed where he had been standing.

Van and his car were gone. The blast caused a smoldering crater in the road and scattered the men. Men along the dikes stood and watched the results of the explosion with detachment. Men nearer and on the road itself were feeling the effects. Ringing in the ears and shortness of breath caused the proximity soldiers to check themselves for wounds and damage. Surrey scurried back up the embankment and approached the car. Elmore sloshed and splashed in the rice paddy. Majewski saw him and was reminded of Elmore's adventure in Lake Piss Tube. Slopping through variations of watery substances must have been Elmore's Vietnam fate.

The blast and fire had incinerated Van.

Surrey stood fairly near the car and watched it burn.

Majewski got up and helped Elmore out of the muddy rice paddy.

Together they walked to the mangled remains of the car and stood next to Surrey.

Surrey stood silently for a minute and watched rings of ripples expand across the water.

"I think this will about conclude our mission," Surrey eventually said. "We'll fire some ammo into the woods and get back to base."

The men were agreeable. Soldiers on the dikes were called back to the road and hundreds of rounds were fired at the tree line.

Surrey continued to stand near the car. He took a small notebook and pen from his pocket and checked his watch. He wrote something in the notebook and replaced it. Elmore and Majewski were still close by and Surrey turned and looked at them.

"He must've hit an anti-tank mine. There ain't nothin' left."

Elmore agreed and Majewski offered no comment at all.

"It could've been here for days or it could've been planted any time since yesterday," Surrey stated and then he softly muttered "this situation is gettin' outta hand."

Elmore turned and fired his M-16 into the woods. Majewski considered doing the same but instead handed his rifle to Elmore. If last night's cleaning had been inadequate Majewski didn't want to be the one to find out.

Elmore took Majewski's rifle, pointed it at the woods and pulled the trigger. The M-16 fired flawlessly. He handed the rifle back to Majewski without comment.

"Let's form up and get the hell outta here," Surrey said. "I'm ready for a nap."

Elmore gathered the men and they all returned to the Fire Base.

The Commanding Officer was waiting at the gate.

"What happened out there?" Captain Wyandotte asked.

"Mr. Van got blown up," Surrey said. "Must've hit a mine of some sort.

The CO could not hide a skeptical look. He and Surrey walked to the office.

Majewski walked slowly to his hooch. He would clean his rifle and sleep for a few hours before guard duty. His legs felt heavy and his arms were tingling. He did not care about Van. Seeing the car blow up had been interesting. He had never seen anything like that at all and the fact someone had died did not particularly bother Majewski. After all he was not dead. Someone else was. Sleep came easily. Majewski slept for four hours before McGill woke him for guardmount. Coffee accompanied Majewski to his bunker and the night passed slowly without incident.

Majewski allowed his mind to roam but, when it settled on the events of the last two days, he pushed memories from his peaceful past into the immediate. He remembered automobiles he had driven or owned. He remembered women he had been involved with and friends from his past. He remembered warm, humid midwestern summers and cold, crisp winter nights. He remembered Christmasses of his youth and school days and the occasional pleasant triumphs and the frequent stinging humiliations of childhood. He remembered, as he looked out over the kill zone, life as it had been.

Morning brought the hope of sleep again. Majewski left his bunker when relieved and went directly his bed. He slept solidly for six hours until McGill woke him with "the CID guy wants to talk to you."

Majewski dressed slowly and ran a comb through his hair. He found a cap and made sure all his buttons were buttoned. He laced up his muddy boots and walked to the hooch being used by the CID man.

"Specialist Majewski," the CID man grinned. "We meet again."

Majewski took off his cap and sat down.

"I want to talk to you about yesterday."

"What about yesterday?" Majewski asked.

"Let's talk about Mr. Van and his accident."

"He was driving down the road," Majewski said, "and his car blew up."

"You saw it?"

"Ya."

"Tell me about it."

"There isn't much to tell," Majewski said as he stirred in his chair. "We were walkin' along the road and had just stepped onto a dike and I saw a cloud of dust and saw a car approach so I alerted Sergeant Elmore and he was watching it and it blew up."

"Do you know what caused it to blow up?"

"No. Lieutenant Surrey and Sergeant Elmore suspected that it hit an anti-tank mine."

"Do you think that's what happened?"

"How the hell should I know? I just saw it blow up. I don't know what it hit."

"Did it hit something or did something hit it?"

"What do you mean?"

"Did you see anything hit it?"

"Like what?"

"Like a mortar round or rocket or M-79 grenade."

"No. The car was comin' up the road toward us and blew up. That's all I saw."

"Do you know anything about the man that was driving the car?"

"No."

"He was investigating the incident in the village. For the last few days he had been putting a lot of pressure on Battalion and on the Commanding Officer of this company. He was accused by your Lieutenant Surrey of being a Viet Cong sympathizer and of having something to do with that helicopter being shot down."

"What's that got to do with me?"

"We're just interviewing everyone who was out there."

"Well I was there but I don't know anything."

The CID man leaned back in his chair and interlaced his fingers behind his head.

"Did you see Lieutenant Surrey when the car blew up?"

"He was standing between me and the car."

"Was he holding anything?"

"Anything like what?"

"A detonator."

"No, He was holdin' his rifle. Nothin' else."

"Are you sure?"

"Positive. He was within a few feet of me and all he had was his rifle."

"You didn't see anything else."

"There wasn't anything else."

"Okay. What did he do when the car exploded?"

"I don't know. I hit the ground and I guess he did, too. Sergeant Elmore jumped into the rice paddy. I heard the splash."

"So the car exploded and you hit the deck."

"Yes. What was I s'posed to do? Catch it when it came back down?"

"I suppose your survival instinct took over."

"Yes. I suppose so."

"So what did Surrey do then?"

"When?"

"After the explosion. When it was safe."

"He went over close to the car and checked things out."

"Did he say anything?"

"When?"

"When he was checking out the car?"

"There wasn't much to check out. I was still on the ground when he went over to the car. I helped Elmore outta the rice paddy and he and I went over to check things out, too."

"You went over to where Surrey was?"

"Yes."

"What did he say?"

Majewski sat silently for a few seconds. He was trying to remember.

"I don't know that he said anything," Majewski finally said. "I don't remember him sayin' anything. He probably speculated about what happened to the car."

"You don't know what he said."

"Didn't I just say I don't remember?"

"Yes."

"Then I don't remember."

"Then who said it must've hit a mine?"

"I don't know. I suppose it was Lieutenant Surrey but it could've been Elmore."

"But you don't remember."

"No. All I know is that it wasn't me. I heard someone say somethin' about a mine but I don't remember who it was."

"It could've been Surrey, though."

"What's with you, man!" Majewski flared. "I just told you I don't remember. I've said that five or six times! How many fuckin' times do I have to say it before you believe it?"

"Now don't get huffy," the CID man said as he rocked forward on his chair. "I'm just trying to find out what happened."

"I told you what the fuck happened! I told you what I saw. If you don't believe me, ask someone else."

"I have asked someone else. In fact I've asked just about everyone who was out there."

"Then why do you keep asking me the same thing over and over again? Jesus, I told you what I saw! The fuckin' car blew up! Surrey had nothin' in his hands except his M-16. Elmore and I stood next to him and if he said anything, I don't remember what it was. Why is that so friggin' hard for you to grasp?"

"Specialist Majewski," the CID man said. "This situation is very complicated. Isn't it suspicious to you that the two GIs that entered the village and killed the Vietnamese disappeared. The only trace of 'em was a shirt that was obviously planted. A Vietnamese investigator grabs the story and hangs on like a terrier and gets Battalion involved. Battalion sends out a Colonel to investigate and his helicopter blows up.

Who shot it down? The Viet Cong or the missing GIs? Then the investigator himself blows up. Doesn't all that seem strange to you?"

Majewski sat quietly for a few seconds. Then he leaned forward and began to speak slowly and deliberately.

"I don't give a rat's ass what happened in that fuckin' village. I don't know what happened to Bertram and Pitch. I don't care what happened. I don't know where they are. I don't care where they are. I had nothin' to do with the village.

"I was out there when the helicopter was burnin'. I found the crewman with his throat cut. That bothered me a lot at the time but now it don't mean nothin'. I nearly got my ass killed in that fuckin' woods tryin' to find whoever killed the helicopter and I don't give a shit who it was. I don't want to get killed over a dead fuckin' helicopter! I don't give a shit about the guy that blew up yesterday. His car hit a fuckin' mine. That's not my fuckin' fault. I was just close by. That's all there is to it."

"So you don't care about this situation at all?"

"No. I couldn't care less. Here it is the first of December and my tour is up at the end of January. That's two months from now and I want to get the hell out of here alive. That's what I'm interested in! Nothin' else."

"Things are complicated."

"Yes, but I ain't the one that complicated 'em! I'm just here! That's all! Not gettin' killed is what's important to me. I don't give a shit about anythin' else."

"Okay. I can understand that," the CID man said. "We've talked often in the last few months. You've been on the fringe of a lot of incidents over here and that's sort of suspicious but perhaps I am reading more into these situations than there is. I just have a job to do when crimes have been committed. One thing leads to another. I check out an incident and that leads to something else and that leads to something else and that leads to something else. I have to pick and choose and decide what's important. That's my job. I need information and I'll get it any way I can. If that means upsettin' a few people around here then that's what's going to happen. If you don't like it, tough shit."

"Okay. Instead of sittin' in here on your dead ass why don't you go out into the field and gather your information first hand. Have you been to the village? Have you been to the rice paddy or to the woods? Have you done anything except sit here and insult those of us who have been doin' our jobs the best we can? Do you know anything on your own?"

The CID man sat silently. After a few seconds he pointed to the door.

"Get the fuck outta here," the CID man said. "I'm through with you."

Majewski got up slowly and walked out of the room. He was pleased he had spoken his mind. Stepping outside into the sunshine lifted his spirits and he actually looked forward to a night in the bunker. He went back to his hooch, kicked off his boots and laid down on his bed. He knew the CID man was only doing his job but Majewski had had enough of trying to follow what had been happening. He was exhausted by everything. He was tired and hungry and, while his spirits were up for the time being, he was still concerned about the fear and anxiety he had been experiencing.

"Two months to go," he said to himself as he settled on to his bed. "Sixty days and gone."

Majewski awakened in time to eat before guardmount. He carried coffee and his rifle to the bunker and settled in for what he hoped would be a quiet, uneventful night.

The first two hours passed quietly. He was alone in the bunker and, to his left and right, other bunkers were manned by at least two soldiers. A Starlight Scope was passed from one bunker to the next so each bunker had it for part of the night. It was a comforting device.

Majewski used the Starlight for an hour. He detected movement at the edge of the kill zone but it was indistinct and too far away to be an immediate concern. When he turned the Starlight Scope over to the next bunker, he told the shitbirds he had seen movement at the edge of the kill zone.

"We'll keep our eyes peeled," a smoker in the next bunker said.

Majewski settled back into his observation routine. He moved his eyes slowly from left to right and from near the perimeter to as far out into the kill zone as he could see. Flares occasionally dangled in the sky and things were quiet for another half an hour until the next bunker opened up with small arms fire.

"There's somethin' out there, man!" a soldier yelled. "I kin see somethin'!"

Majewski followed the tracers into the kill zone. He could see nothing but the bunker with the Starlight Scope was the bunker that was firing. Majewski waited for the firing to stop and for the officer or NCO in charge of Green Line to come and check on all the fuss. Lieutenant Surrey spent a fair amount of time in the firing bunker and then walked over to Majewski's.

"Hey, 'Ski, you okay in there?"

"Yeah," Majewski said, "c'mon in."

Surrey entered the bunker and took off his steel pot.

"What were they shootin' at?" Majewski asked.

"They saw someone in the kill zone and called it in. I told them to fire things up. They did hit whatever it was they were shooting at. We'll go out in the morning and see what it was."

"I thought I saw somethin' way down range so I told 'em about it."

"Well, they shot it."

"Let's hope that's all there is tonight. My nerves are fairly shot the way it is."

"These last few days," said Surrey, "have been a bitch for us all. Did that Criminal Investigation guy talk to you?"

"Yep. He and I got into it. He kept hasslin' me about things I couldn't remember."

"He raked me over the coals pretty good, too," Surrey said. "Seems to think I masterminded this whole thing with Bertram in the village."

"Yuh," Majewski said. "He kept askin' me what they said when they got back to the base. I didn't remember. I don't think they said anything about where they'd been."

"So don't worry about it," Surrey said. "If you don't know, you don't know."

"I've jus' got to the point where I don't care at all anymore. I just want to do my job and go home."

"That's what I'm doin'," Surrey said with a smile. "I leave for the States in the morning. I'll be home in a couple of days."

Majewski was stunned. He could manage only a "no shit!"

"No shit. I'm on my way. I was banned from re-enlistment for that hassle with Loomer so I'll be out of the Army in just a few days."

"That's great!" Majewski said with genuine good will. "That's really great."

"Yeah, so if I don't get shot tonight I'll be just fine."

"Then you'd better get the hell off Green Line. Who knows what hornets' nest the guys next door stirred up."

"Ski," Surrey said seriously as he shook Majewski's hand, "you take care and keep your shit together. I want you back in the States in one piece."

"That's what I want, too, Lieutenant."

"So keep low and don't be takin' any chances. I know what your bag is. I tried to keep my men as safe as possible and sometimes I failed but I always tried."

"I know you did."

"Noland's death really bothered me," Surrey said. "He and I used to talk a lot. You probably don't know that but, yes, we talked a lot. Did you know he wanted to be a teacher?"

"No. We didn't talk much about what we wanted to do. We talked a lot about what we were expected to do."

"I s'pose," Surrey said softly. "He was a pretty bright guy."

"There are a lot of bright guys over here. A lot of dumb fucks, too, but there are a lot of guys who could really make a difference."

"Well, I ain't gonna be one of 'em for much longer," Surrey grinned again. "I'm so short I'd have to stand on my tiptoes to scratch a snake's belly!"

"Scratch away," Majewski said. "I'll see if I can find Grasp."

"Thanks, 'Ski. You take care and I hope I never see your sorry ass again."

"Good luck, Sir," Majewski said as he delivered a proper salute.

Surrey seemed a bit surprised but returned the salute and left the bunker.

Majewski's attention returned to the kill zone. Flares illuminated the sky and part of the countryside. Majewski did not see anyone lying dead in the zone but he would know soon enough if anyone was, indeed, there.

The rest of the night passed uneventfully. Surrey's last day at the Fire Base dawned with pink clouds. A patrol was sent out and found a dead dog in the kill zone. It had been shot numerous times by the bunker rats and someone buried it with an entrenching tool. Movement, after all, had been movement.

Majewski returned to his AO and stored his M-16. He went to the mess tent and had some breakfast and coffee. He was tired and the thought of Surrey's departure was, in a way, upsetting. Surrey had taken care of him. Majewski had a great deal of respect for

Lieutenant Surrey and Surrey's departure would cause adjustments.

When he finished eating he walked toward his AO. McGill met him and handed him a letter.

"This came in yesterday on the water truck," McGill said. "I didn't get it sorted before guardmount so I thought I'd deliver it now."

"Thanks," Majewski said as he took the letter. "I appreciate it."

He walked to his hooch, kicked off his boots, flopped down on his bed and opened the envelope. It contained a Christmas card. The card showed a house in the middle of a field of snow. From the chimney gray smoke rose into a starry night. Inside the card read "Merry Christmas and Happy New Year! May the Spirit of the Season Sustain You in the Coming Year." The card was signed by his aunt.

There was a piece of paper inside the envelope. It was a handwritten letter that read:

Dear Anton,

We wanted to get this card to you early because we don't know how long it takes to get mail to Viet Nam. We want to wish you a Merry Christmas. We hope you will come home soon and that you are safe.

Aunt Cecilia prays for you every night and you are in our prayers, too. We don't know what you are going through. We just hope you are O.K.

Have a Merry Christmas. We love you very much.

Aunt Janet and Uncle Loui

Majewski read and reread the letter. Tears formed in his eyes and he became very, very depressed. He sat up on his bed, opened his footlocker and found some paper and a pen. He closed the footlocker and put the paper on the lid. He took the pen and began to write "Dear…" but the paper remained blank. The pen put a ridged line in the paper but there was no ink. The ballpoint was dry.

Majewski moved the pen off the paper and looked at its tip. Then he began to tremble slightly. Tears dropped from his eyes and landed on his pants legs. He thought of Noland. Noland had said, on the morning of the last day of his life, that he had written a letter home the previous night. Majewski had not written anyone since he wrote to Janet and Lou shortly after Noland's death and he decided not to write anyone now. He put the paper and the pen back into the footlocker and laid down on the bed. He was tired and depressed.

Chapter 18

He watched clouds pass across the face of the moon and became familiar with the subtle changes of color, the grays, blues and touches of pink, moonlight created. He became intrigued by the path of the moon and was fascinated by the fact that just about a year and a half earlier man had walked on its surface. For how many centuries had man marvelled at the night sky? How much speculation had there been over the years on the nature of the moon? How many men actually knew anything about the moon? How many men, like himself, knew nothing for sure but simply enjoyed viewing?

To fill those lonely hours in the bunker Majewski began to alternate between watching the kill zone and watching the stars. He became fascinated by the awesome vastness of the universe and by his own insignificance.

The night sky made Majewski feel very insignificant. His life meant nothing in the vastness of space and time. Above him the universe moved in its own spendor as it had done for millions of years before him and as it would do for millions of years after him. An endless universe constantly expanding and unconcerned about life on this inconsequential, paltry planet coursed above him through millions of miles of empty space and through the most pure time. Majewski realized he could find a purpose for God in the universe. God could bring the vast majesty of the universe to mankind. He could make the universe understandable and God could give comfort to insignificant man.

God was available so sense could be made of things on earth but God brought along questions, too. Why, God, with so much space and time in the universe, did a bullet hit the exact spot at the exact time that Noland's head happened to be occupying that particular space in time? Would change in a unit of time or a measurement of space have caused that particular small piece of speeding metal to miss Noland entirely? If the bullet had been fired a fraction of a second earlier or later would it have combined with other forces of space and time to cause a change in its path? Could Noland have avoided the impact by walking faster or slower? Why, with all the space and time in the universe, had forces combined to send bits of Noland's skull cascading through limited space for a limited time until they fell into the tall grass? Could the bullet have missed if something somewhere in universal time and space had been different?

He didn't know and God didn't answer in any evident way but Majewski began to accept that he was helpless in the universe and insignificant in time and that, oddly, gave him comfort. He did not have to understand. He did not have to really believe. All he had to do was accept the fact that there was an endless universe and powers beyond any ability to reason or control. He was powerless in the flow of time.

The universe was beyond his influence or understanding but he had power over the immediate as, inside that bunker, he could reach down and touch dirt and sand and he could control that specific and tangible part of the universe.

Majewski knew that, at any given time, there could be hundreds of thousands of people looking at that same sky and yet there was no one else in the world seeing and interpreting that sky from the same place at the same instant in the same terms as he and that made the stars and the moon and the entire universe his and his alone.

Each sunset, each night and each sunrise would become specifically his for the enjoyment nature and space provided. He was an observer unable to influence anything other than his most immediate space and he became comfortable with that and, except for the occasional seering rage at forces beyond his earthbound control, he accepted his role in space and time. He was a soldier. Life had become that simple and that complicated. No control beyond the most immediate limits of time and space or beyond the range of his weapons.

Looking at the stars provided an escape from the horizon. There were field of vision limitations when Majewski's attention was on the kill zone. He could only see so far and so well with an unaided eye. He needed flares or a Starlight Scope to really see in that limited area and yet he could look at the sky and see for millions of miles.

The kill zone was different and more active. It provided light and movement and was its own dangerous little universe. It provided excitement and boredom and a way to spend the night.

Bunkers and towers were arranged to provide overlapping fields of vision on Green Line. Being in a tower increased one's range of vision and most activity was spotted by soldiers manning the towers.

Bunkers were there to concentrate fire at ground level and to direct fire into specific areas from different directions. Bunkers provided better protection for those inside because they could be easily thickened and reinforced with sandbags.

Towers were vulnerable. The Californian had found that out shortly before he died. The Californian's tower had been rebuilt, renamed "Folsom" and remanned with a full complement of potheads. There were two bunkers between Majewski's bunker and the new tower. There was one bunker between his bunker and the next tower to his left. He felt secure in his bunker because he felt it was of no strategic consequence. He could watch the kill zone and watch the sky. There was worse duty.

The day following Surrey's departure brought his replacement's arrival. The new Lieutenant approached the camp in a Jeep but, when the Jeep neared the gate, it slowed to a stop. The Lieutenant stepped from the Jeep, shouldered his M-16, sauntered to the gate and was admitted. He walked confidently onto the base and proceeded directly to the Commanding Officer's office. The soldier that had opened the gate looked at the Lieutenant's driver. The Lieutenant's driver shrugged. The gate guard motioned the Jeep through the gate.

"I can't leave this gate open. It lets out all the heat!" the gate guard shouted.

McGill was sitting at his desk when the new Lieutenant entered. He remained seated.

"On your feet, soldier," the new Lieutenant said, "I'm Lieutenant Melloy and I'm here to see the Commanding Officer."

McGill moved exceptionally slowly. "I'll see if he's in, Sir."

The CO, as McGill well knew, was in his office. He nodded to McGill and the new Lieutenant entered.

"Lieutenant Melloy reporting for duty, Sir," Melloy said with a salute.

The CO returned the salute. "Sit down, Lieutenant. I'm Captain Wyandotte."

"Captain, I'm here for a couple of reasons. I'm replacing the Lieutenant who left for the States and I am here to be in charge of the artillery pieces that are going to be brought in."

The CO sat silently. He squirmed a bit in his chair and said "Battalion has been hinting for a couple of weeks that something big was going to happen. Are you it?"

"I may be," Melloy said.

"Putting back the artillery, huh. What are you bringin' in?"

"Two 105mm howitzers, two five men crews and an NCO. Battalion will supply the support and the details."

"We've got three or four conexes full of one oh five ammo from the last time we had artillery here unless, of course, the rats ate it. I haven't checked recently."

"We'll take care of everything, Sir."

"What are you going to be shooting at, Lieutenant?"

"I have information that VC and NVA units are operating in this area. They shot down a helicopter a few days ago as you well know. Battalion is, how shall I say it? Not amused. They want something up here that will toss some shit down on top of whoever's out there."

"And you can do that?"

"Yes. We know where they are but we don't want to defoliate because this is good ricegrowin' land and we'll keep the good will of the dinks if we don't fry their fields. If we lob some shells into the woods occasionally they shouldn't get too pissed."

"If you bring artillery in here that village will know about it before it even gets here. You can't take a piss up here without them knowin' it."

"So what if they know?"

"Yeah," the CO said softly. "So what."

"We'll be truckin' the pieces in tomorrow. It won't take long to get set up. We could hit 'em tomorrow night."

"If you bring that stuff in tomorrow do you really think there'll be anyone in the village tomorrow night? I'll tell you one thing. Whatever unit is in the woods won't be there tomorrow night."

"We thought of that," Melloy smiled. "We're hoping to control where that unit goes. We're not the only artillery in this area, you know."

"Oh, I see," said the CO. "you make a big show of bringin' in the hot stuff and the dinks think they're the target so they move to another place they think'll be safe only to find out they've been targeted by a whole different artillery setup and, by the time they realize it, they're splattered all over the countryside."

"Something like that," Melloy said, "except we aren't really a decoy. There are plenty of targets in this area. They've just been neglected a bit but the Vietnamese are taking over the war now and we're pullin' back and you can bet your sweet ass that when the North decides to kick some ass, they'll start kickin' up here in I Corps. We're too close to the DMZ to be taking all this lightly."

"No one around here is taking anything lightly," the CO said. "We're doing our job."

"I know you are and Battalion knows," Melloy said. "It's just that we want to keep the slopes off balance and the easiest way to do that is to fuck with 'em."

"Bringing artillery in to the base makes us a target again," Captain Wyandotte said. "We weren't capable to bein' much of a threat to anyone as long as we remained just a bunch of grunts. Now we're important. I'm going to have to give a lot of consideration to pulling our patrols in and keeping 'em in."

"That would make sense but only if they aren't your first line of defense."

"They're out there checkin' things out. Seeing what's happenin'. They're lookouts more than anything else. If they do engage the enemy it's more by accident than design."

"Bringing in the artillery will be a good thing," Melloy stated confidentally. "It'll take some of the pressure off your grunts."

"We'll see," said the CO, "but I still think it'll create more problems than it'll solve."

"We're just cogs in the big green machine, Captain. We do what they tell us."

"Let's hope they know what they're doin'," the CO said.

"I think Battalion's right on track with this. I'm only a Lieutenant. I don't know shit. I get called in and told what to do and I do it. I knew this was coming, though. I could feel it."

The CO didn't say anything and he didn't seem particularly interested in what the Lieutenant had to say.

"Something had to happen. There were too many officers standin' around with nothin' to do. The ARVNs are supposed to be taking over this war. I'm kind of surprised they didn't assign any of those little pricks to this project. Battalion's trying to get them more integrated with our units so I'm kind of surprised they didn't saddle me with any of 'em."

"Maybe Battalion didn't know which way the guns would be pointing."

"That could be. Who knows what they're thinkin'!"

"I certainly don't," the CO said. "That village doesn't like us much. You may end up sightin' 'em in."

"I already have," Melloy said as he tapped his shirt pocket with his right index finger. "My book's right here."

"All the info, huh?"

"All the fuckin' numbers," Melloy said.

"Keep 'em handy," the CO said. "I'd be willing to bet you'll need 'em."

"My toys and my NCO and my men'll be here tomorrow. Can this base accommodate us?"

"McGill out there will find places for you and your men. Some of your guys will end up in tents but there are a couple of hooch AOs open. We've had casualties and deaths."

"Thank you, Sir," Melloy said as he saluted. "I'm looking forward to this."

Melloy left the room. The CO stood up, lit a cigarette, shook his head and said "The shit will hit the fan. The shit will definitely hit the fuckin' fan."

It didn't take long for word of the impending artillery to get out. Green Line was alive with speculation as to what would or would not happen and Majewski, alone in his bunker, watched the stars.

The next day trucks towed the howitzers to the Fire Base. Soldiers assigned to the pieces as crew rode in the back of the trucks and Melloy met his men at the Main Gate. He took charge of positioning the artillery and his men worked quickly and knowledgeably. The howitzers were soon in place.

The men were assigned to available hooch AOs and some ended up assigned to tents. Lawnchairs were among the gear the artillerymen brought to the Fire Base. Lawnchairs and beer. They had a number of portable tape players and soon settled in to an afternoon of beer and music.

They were joined in short order by various established members of the Fire Base complement and the good times did roll. The afternoon took a toll on the Green Line crews as a number of shitbirds assigned to duty in the bunkers missed or showed up drunk for guardmount.

Majewski was not amused by the situation. Sergeant Elmore was not amused, either, but Elmore was in a position to do something to alter the state of affairs. He sent sober men out to round up the missing and, when all the soldiers were accounted for, Elmore treated them to a brisk session of calisthenics. Elmore was capable, loud and demanding when it came to conducting punishment calisthenics and there was a lot of groaning and complaining and vomiting. Suffering embraced the drunks and it did not take long for them, even the most inebriated, to realized they had not done a bright or prudent thing when they chose drunkeness over duty.

Majewski sat on nearby sandbags and watched the calisthenics with total amusement. Seeing drunks do structured pushups under the watchful disdain of Sergeant Elmore was complete joy to those who weren't drunk. When a drunk would be in total distress, Elmore would lean over him and shout insults and instructions. The more miserable the drunk, the more insulting the sergeant. Agony abounded and punishment continued until the drunks were sober enough to man their assigned positions.

The artillerymen partied on into the night and paid no attention to the Green Line drunks.

Majewski spent a quiet night in his bunker. Elmore stopped by around midnight and said "I don't like you much, 'Ski, but I can depend on you. You don't get drunk and you don't sleep."

Majewski said nothing and Elmore left without further comment.

Except for the occasional mad minute when the semi-drunks and potheads fired their weapons into the kill zone, the night passed without incident. The morning sun assaulted bloodshot eyes and Majewski welcomed the daylight by striding confidentally away from his bunker when he was relieved. Other soldiers stumbled and staggered into their morning hangovers and the artillerymen slept late and, to a man, missed the morning mess.

Majewski slept until mid afternoon. The previous afternoon's revelers slept even later. The artillerymen rose around noon and prepared for action by drinking large amounts of coffee and the occasional beer. Hair of the dog.

Elmore defended his calisthenics to the CO by stating "I don't give a shit if them assholes have to stand knee deep in their own puke, there ain't gonna be no fuckin' drunks on my Green Line." The CO subsequently informed Lieutenant Melloy that there would be no more drinking by his men. Melloy informed his NCO and the NCO informed the artillery crews but the NCO's admonition would have been more effective had he not been holding a can of beer when it was delivered.

Late in the afternoon the artillery crews assembled at their howitzers. Lieutenant Melloy directed the allotment of ammunition and targeting. At 1615 hours the howitzers were fired and high explosive rounds were sent crashing into the woods near the village. Trees shattered and splintered. Villagers ran in confusion looking for places of cover and safety. Thirty rounds from each howitzer smashed the forest but the artillerymen were unaware of the effects of their work. They did not know if any Viet Cong or NVA soldiers were even in the woods. It didn't really matter. The point was that the woods could easily be pulverized and that meant it could no longer be effectively used by anyone. The villagers realized quickly that their village was also extremely vulnerable and the reality was disconcerting. No place was safe.

The Fire Base was a Fire Base again. Outgoing rounds whistled across the kill zone on their lethal trip to the woods. Soldiers with lingering hangovers suffered and Majewski was uneasy. Artillery sounds didn't bother Majewski but he was concerned about the effects on the enemy. If the artillery killed the Viet Cong and NVA soldiers it was good. If it annoyed them and caused them to reconsider the Fire Base's place on their target list then the artillery was something to worry about.

Majewski doubted the Vietnamese had anything in the area comparable to the howitzers but felt certain that, if they did, the Fire Base would quickly find out.

Howitzers didn't have to miss a target by much to miss but they were certainly capable of disrupting a given area at any given time. Artillery was power. Majewski wondered why the Vietnamese hadn't used artillery against the base if they did, indeed, have it. Perhaps the base wasn't important enough and, if they did have artillery, why tip their hand by firing it at a relatively insignificant installation like the Fire Base? Save the surprise for a more important target. But two howitzers made the Fire Base a more important target. Two crews of drunks who knew how to fire artillery became more important than drunks and potheads who fired rifles into their immediate kill zones during the occasional mad minute. Artillery changed the situation.

Majewski arrived for guardmount in time to note that the soldiers that had been drunk the day before were now sober. Being sober did not mean they were necessarily alert and it certainly did not mean they were enthusiastic. They were simply there.

Elmore lined everyone up and made a big show of walking down the line glaring at each and every Green Liner. Even the most stupid shitbird knew better than to show up drunk. Elmore decided glares alone were not intimidating enough. He sent every soldier not in proper uniform back to his respective AO for a proper uniform. Eventually olive drab T-shirts were covered by proper shirts. Shirts without sleeves were changed to shirts with sleeves. Pants were properly bloused. Buttons were buttoned. Boots, if not properly polished, were polished or at least the biggest, most offensive chunks of whatever were removed. Flak jackets and steel helmets were required. Rifles were clean or they were cleaned. Majewski himself was sent to shave and he was not alone. At least a dozen Green Liners dry shaved and, finally, when Elmore was satisfied, all were posted properly and the night in the bunker officially began.

Majewski paid very close attention to the edges of the kill zone. He was surprised by how much he could actually see and he remained alert for any and all movement.

Sergeant Elmore visited each tower and bunker and arrived at Majewski's bunker at midnight.

"What did you think of the artillery fire this afternoon, 'Ski?"

"I don't know."

"Think it did any good?"

"Depends on what they were shootin' at and if they hit it."

"They was shootin' at the woods outside the village."

"Can they hit it from here?"

"Sure. It's only four or four and a half miles away."

Majewski was silent.

"They could hit it at twice the range," Elmore said confidentally.

"Really? I don't know anything at all about artillery."

"Yeah, those one oh fives're terrific."

Majewski was silent again.

"Just keep your eyes peeled," Elmore said. "I wouldn't be s'prised if the fuckers hit us tonight jus'a pay us back for hittin' their woods."

"That thought has certainly occurred to me," Majewski said without trying to sound sarcastic.

"Yeah, keep a sharp lookout. They'll probably hit us on the other side of the camp nearer the artillery but who can say for sure, right?"

"Right. If they come in from over there, I'll see 'em."

"Good," said Elmore. "I know I can trust you."

"I won't let you down, Sarge," Majewski said. "I'll keep an eye on things."

Elmore nodded and left the bunker. Majewski shook his head and returned his gaze to the edge of the kill zone. The stars were not his concern. He was determined not to be caught by surprise should the Vietnamese wish to express their anger over the artillery. They didn't. The night passed quietly.

For the next week Melloy and his artillerymen fired into the countryside. Targets were altered and firing times changed depending on intelligence reports supplied by helicopters and spotter planes. Each fire mission was evaluated and Melloy would choose and chart each upcoming target. The woods outside the village remained an active target. Melloy was convinced supplies were stored there. The forest near the burned helicopter was also hit. Smashed and splintered trees were ignited by an ammunition cache that had been ignited by an artillery barrage and a section of the woods burned for two days.

The Vietnamese were annoyed but there was little they were apparently willing to do. Mr. Van was no longer available to the villagers so the old man with the dead waterbuffalo approached the base waving a white flag. He was admitted and Captain Wyandotte talked to him through the interpreter.

"What does papasan want?" the CO asked.

The old man chattered and the interpreter spoke.

"He says he wants us to stop shelling near the village."

"Why?"

"Because he doesn't like it."

"Tell him to roll in shit."

"I can't tell him that," the interpreter said.

"Okay, tell him we're killin' the VC he said weren't there."

The interpreter had trouble with that phrase. It took a long time to convey the Commanding Officer's meaning.

"He says he's not a VC," the interpreter said when the old man responded, "and there ain't none in the woods."

The CO smiled and said, "Tell him to turn around and walk off this base or I will take out my pistol and put a bullet right between his lyin' fuckin' eyes."

The interpreter did as well as he could with that phrase. The old man stood silently for a moment. The contempt he felt for the CO and the Americans on the base was very evident. He turned very slowly and walked with a deliberate and dignified gait to the Main Gate. He stepped off the base, walked past the concertina wire and crossed the kill zone on the approach road. He did not look back. He did not look to either side of the road. His movements were natural and unsuspicious. The terrain was obviously very familiar and now he knew where the artillery was as it had not been difficult to spot.

Melloy and Wyandotte watched the old man walk away.

"Who's that?" Melloy asked.

"Just an old Viet Cong," the CO said.

"Are you just going to let him walk away?"

"Let's see what happens."

"Do you think something will?"

"Yep. Sometime soon. I was watchin' his eyes. He checked out the position of every piece. Expect company."

Chapter 19

No one knew for certain how the artillery was affecting the Viet Cong or the NVA soldiers. It had obviously annoyed the villagers but the nights remained calm on Green Line and there was no indication that the Viet Cong were even still in the area.

Majewski was suspicious of the peaceful nights. He would have liked to believe that the artillery had ended ground attacks by the neighborhood Viet Cong but he was reluctant to embrace that idea in full. He was respectfully suspicious enough of the Vietnamese to realize they were capable of carrying a grudge and of transferring that grudge to vengeance. Majewski didn't want the Vietnamese to attack and yet he kept wondering why they didn't attack.

Early on the afternoon of the tenth of December McGill awakened Majewski with the announcement that Majewski was wanted in the CO's office.

"Why?" asked the groggy Majewski.

"I can't tell you. Just get dressed and get over there pronto."

"Shit," mumbled Majewski. "Now what?"

Majewski dressed and walked to the CO's office. There were six other men waiting to see the CO. Two more soldiers showed up after Majewski's arrival and, when McGill was satisfied with that all called were present, the CO entered.

"Men," Captain Wyandotte said, "All of you have at least ten months in country. That means you're eligible for a reduction in your time of service here in Vietnam. If you choose to accept this drop you will leave the country in, oh, a week and a half. You can choose to turn down this drop and serve out your required time or you can extend your tour of duty. It is all up to you. If you wish to follow any of those three options tell Specialist McGill and he'll take care of you."

A festive cheer rose from the assembled men. The CO left the building.

The possibility of going home in a few days both delighted and frightened Majewski. The prospect unnerved him in that it made him even more fretful and restless. In a few days he would be off the Fire Base and back in the States. That was a wonderful expectation but it was still something that off in the future. The immediate situations and conditions made serious demands on Majewski's attention. The United States was a long way off physically and Majewski knew he had to keep it a long way off mentally. He still had responsibilities, concerns and fears that centered around the kill zone. He was not back in the States yet. He was still in Vietnam.

While Majewski concentrated his efforts on maintaining his perspective other soldiers that had received drops were not reluctant to celebrate. Word spread quickly around the camp that drops had come down. Joy was unrestrained. One particularly happy and nimble soldier executed a remarkable series of backflips from the CO's office to his hooch while another dropped to his knees and openly thanked his Lord and Maker for allowing him to survive his Vietnam ordeal. Another danced, bobbing and weaving, all the way to the perimeter wire where he turned, dropped his pants, bent over and displayed his buttocks to the kill zone.

Soldiers that weren't leaving reacted in varying ways. Some were happy for those that were leaving, others were resentful, others accepted the situation and still others wanted AO's or personal possessions that could be left behind.

"Can I have your fan?" was one of the first questions asked by those staying.

"Short! Short! Short! Short! I'm one short son of a bitch! I'm so short I'd have to stand on my tiptoes to kiss a gnat's ass!"

There were a lot of sexual rantings, too.

"I'm goin, home an' get me some round eye!"

"I'm gonna kiss the baby on the forehead, grab its mamma and make another one."

"Time to do the hot an' nasty!"

"Home stuff!"

Majewski went to his hooch and laid down on his bed. He did not want to think ahead. He wanted to keep his mind in the present and reflect a bit on the past.

Noland was dead. Norris had left months ago. Surrey was back in the States looking for a new line of work. Virtually all the soldiers he had been in the field with were gone. Soldiers had come into his acquaintance, stayed for varying periods of time, and drifted off. Some visits had been short, like that of California and the guy that had fallen into the pit. Others had been enduring temporal episodes of varying significances, like Sergeant Elmore, McGill and the CO. Other people, known for but a split second, had engraved impressions on Majewski's memory. The sapper that had jumped over him and the Vietnamese soldiers near the tree that had been shot on his first patrol and the soldiers that had been killed when the ammunition conex blew up all entered his life for short, intense periods of time then disappeared only to reappear periodically and, at times, intrusively, in Majewski's mind.

Majewski thought back over the year. He thought of all the deaths and the woundings and the agony he had observed. He thought of the soldier lying with his throat cut in the rice paddy and of the CID agent that seemed to suspect him of everything in Vietnam that couldn't be easily solved. He thought about the total absurdity of sharing a bunker with a Burmese python and he thought of Sergeant Elmore chin deep in a lake of rancid urine and, while some of the memories were pleasant and amusing, others were dark and sinister and unnerving.

Majewski could feel his chest tighten under the influence of certain remembered instances. Some memories made him want to leap off his bed and run as fast as he could to nowhere. Others soothed and relaxed him. Those were the memories he wanted but they were the ones that were so difficult to recall when the dark ones were so powerful.

Majewski began to sweat. He realized his hands were trembling and he felt lightheaded. Home was a concept that was still impractical. The kill zone would be his concern for the next few days. It was all he would allow himself to think about.

That night on Green Line Elmore came around again.

"I hear you're gettin' one of them drops," Elmore said as he entered Majewski's bunker.

"Yeah," Majewski answered. "I guess so."

"Got any plans?"

"Yeah, making it out of here alive. That's my plan."

"Things is pretty quiet. Not much happenin' around here no more. I think the friggin' artillery done put an end to any gook activity in this sector."

"I hope you're right. I don't need a lot of bullshit before I go."

"They've been sendin' out 'copters an' spotter planes to see what's happenin' in this area an' things have been looking pretty good. Battalion has to 'Vietnamize' this war, you know. Turn over what we've been doin' to the South Dinks. We've shown 'em what to do an' how to do it so now it's up to them guys."

Majewski shook his head.

"I personally don't trust them ARVNs," Elmore offered. "They're slick. I imagine most of 'em's VCs anyway. They'd justa soon kill us as look at us."

Majewski said nothing. He was looking out over the kill zone and thought he saw movement.

"I'll be headin' out pretty soon, too," Elmore said. "Them drops'll keep comin'."

Majewski continued to study the kill zone. He was sure there had been movement.

"Do ya see somethin'?" Elmore asked when he noticed that Majewski didn't seem to be paying attention to what he had been saying.

"I thought I saw somethin' out there but I'm not sure."

"Where?"

"Just to the right of that big tree."

Elmore took a pair of field glasses from his web belt and handed them to Majewski. Majewski studied the tree line but shook his head and said "I don't see anythin' now."

"Shadows," Elmore said. "We shoot a lotta shadows."

Majewski handed the binoculars back to Elmore. Elmore replaced them on his belt.

"I'll go over to the tower and tell 'em to keep an eye on that section of the KZ," Elmore said as he left the bunker.

Majewski shook his head. He was certain he had seen movement. What would cause a pecular shadow if it was not some sort of movement? The wind was not a factor. It was virtually nonexistent. Animals in the kill zone were somewhat frequent. A dog had been shot a few nights earlier and that was a bit odd but not outside of the realm of happenstance.

Majewski was willing to admit he could have been mistaken and whatever he had seen was due more probably to nervousness about his imminent departure than to any real threat. He nonetheless kept alert, peering out of the viewing hole and even, on three occasions, leaving the bunker to crawl on top so his perspective would change.

He became reluctantly convinced that something was happening at the edge of the kill zone. He could not tell what but there seemed to be activity to the right of the big tree. He alerted the tower and they concentrated their vision but saw nothing suspicious.

He called Elmore on the field phone and, in due time, Elmore appeared with a Starlight Scope.

"I know there's something out there, Sarge," Majewski said as he peered through the Starlight Scope. The images at the end of the kill zone were not cold. Heat from bodies showed up and there was, indeed, movement.

"There! I was right. The fuckers are out there!" Majewski was duly alarmed.

"Lemme see," Elmore said and took the Scope. He stared for a few seconds and then said "Damn, man, we're gonna catch some fuckin' shit!"

Majewski handed Elmore the field phone.

"Pop some fuckin' flares," Elmore ordered, "and alert the tower and the next two bunkers."

Majewski ran out of the bunker and popped two flares. The sky over the kill zone in the general direction of the movement shimmered in white light.

"We got somethin' out beyond the kill zone," Elmore yelled into the field phone. "Get them artillery drunks up and throw some shit out there. They're beyond our fuckin' grenade launchers!"

Majewski tried to accurately pinpoint the activity but the countryside seemed to change under the flickering light from the flares. Things looked very different.

"Get yer ass back in here," Elmore yelled, "and put on your steel fuckin' pot. Jeezus."

Majewski scrambled back into the bunker and Elmore scrambled out.

"I'm gonna 'lert the rest of the line," Elmore yelled. "Keep an eye on things out there."

Majewski was alone. He was directly across from some sort of enemy activity but he did not know what to expect. He found his steel pot and put it on. Dirt fell onto his head from the inside of the helmet so he took it off and brushed his hair with the palm of his hand. He fastened his flak jacket and inserted a clip into his M-16. Outside long shadows crept across the kill zone as the flares drifted closer to the ground. It would take time for Majewski's eyes to readjust to the dark. He lowered his head and closed his eyes.

"Please, God, don't let it happen," was all he said under his breath. He could feel his hands tremble and his chest tighten. The hair on the back of his neck stood up and his legs began to cramp. He tried to stand up but didn't have enough room so he laid down on the ground to stretch out his legs.

He could hear shouting along the perimeter and gunfire erupted. It was American M-16 fire.

Majewski pulled himself up enough to look through the viewing slit. The first thing he saw was a flash of light from the woods. He knew enough to duck and, a split second later, he heard the report of an artillery piece and the whistle of an incoming round. A horrendous explosion shattered the night and seemed to push all the air off the earth. Sand and dirt stung Majewski's cheek and the sandbag back wall of the bunker disintegrated.

Majewski was flat on the bunker floor when the next round slammed into the camp. It was farther behind him and the third round farther off yet so Majewski clawed his way to his knees and looked out across the kill zone. Smoke was rising from the tree line. M-16 tracer rounds were arcing near the smoke and Majewski knew what had happened. The

Vietnamese somehow had moved an artillery piece into the woods or uncovered one that had been hidden there and the Fire Base was now a target. But why just an artillery attack? An artillery piece was a valuable weapon to the Vietnamese. Why use it without infantry?

Majewski immediately turned his attention to the area of the Kill Zone nearer the base. He didn't see anyone but did hear AK-47 fire from quite a distance behind him. That was it. Artillery fire from the south and an infantry attack from the north. Majewski turned and looked behind him. The back wall of the bunker was no longer in place. Sandbags were strewn over the floor. Surely some must have landed on him, he thought, but he knew he was complete and nothing hurt. He wasn't bleeding and his crotch was intact so all was well for that particular instant.

He could not see across the compound but M-16 fire from the northern section of the perimeter had become more intense. Mortars and M79 grenades exploded frequently and there was a lot of shouting. Majewski couldn't help. He was assigned to that southern bunker and, as the fourth artillery round whistled overhead, he hurled himself to the sand floor and covered his head.

The round exploded beyond the CO's office quite near the one-oh-fives. Majewski didn't know it but the artillerymen were springing into action. They turned one of the artillery pieces around so it faced north and fired a round through the perimeter concertina wire at a very flat trajectory. The north and flanking sides of the perimeter Green Line opened up with rifle and machinegun fire.

The artillerymen reloaded and fired again through the north wire while another crew readied the other howitzer for fire to the south.

The Vietnamese fired one more round into the base. It slammed into a hooch and collapsed a bunker.

A round from the southern howitzer shattered trees in the woods beyond the kill zone. That round was not close to the Vietnamese artillery but the firing continued in an effort to range in the enemy. The Vietnamese artillery stopped firing. Their crew was probably pushing it or dragging it through the woods to be used again.

While some soldiers fired from the bunker line others ran to the collapsed bunker to try to free anyone trapped inside.

The northern bunkers and towers fired thousands of rounds of ammunition into their kill zones and the Vietnamese ground attack stopped abruptly. Vietnamese dead lay scattered across the grass. Flares were sent up and anyone moving in the kill zone was killed by rifle fire.

Majewski looked out over his kill zone. Howitzer rounds had started a fire in the woods and Majewski staggered out of the bunker to get a better look at the kill zone. That was a mistake. He immediately saw movement in front of him and to his near left. A form rose from the kill zone and quickly fired. Majewski felt and heard the bullet whiz past his ear. The bullet slammed into a sandbag that supported the door to the bunker and Majewski instinctively dove for cover.

He did not see what happened to the Vietnamese that had shot at him. Someone in the next bunker fired an M-16 and the Vietnamese was shredded by the bullets.

Majewski laid sprawled on the ground on top of a low wall of sandbags. He was aware that he had been shot at but did not know how he had gotten to the ground. He recalled hearing the bullet but hadn't felt it hit anything. It had flown past his ear and not hit him at all. He was not dead. He was not wounded. He was not even frightened. He was alive and, for now, that was enough.

A soldier scrambled over the sand and helped him up.

"You all right?"

"Yeah," Majewski gasped. "What happened?"

"I don't know! You got shot at! Someone over there greased the fucker, though!"

Majewski felt weak. He held on to the soldier and the soldier helped him to the bunker. Once inside he let Majewski slide to the floor. Majewski stretched out and felt the night. It was alive and so was he. The soldier left the bunker and Majewski stretched out his arms. He was still holding his M-16. He hadn't fired it but it was still in his hand. The attack was over and Majewski had survived. That was good enough. He took off his steel pot and laid his head down on the damp sand floor. He allowed himself to remember he was going to go home.

Chapter 20

The rest of the night was filled with activity. Vietnamese artillery rounds caused considerable damage. Soldiers trapped in the collapsed bunker were freed quickly and there were no major injuries.

Shrapnel damage was extensive. Two hooches were destroyed and the infamous Bunker Nine Piss Tube received a direct hit. Shards of metal were imbedded in sandbags along the Green Line and one tower was damaged extensively enough to cause its occupants to leave it quickly before it collapsed.

Several soldiers were damaged by the concussion of the rounds. Ringing in the ears was extremely common. Blood seeping from the ears was also quite common.

One soldier in the damaged tower caught a piece of shrapnel high on his right shoulder. His flak jacket absorbed most of the impact and slowed the seering metal enough so it did not penetrate far into the shoulder. The shard lodged in the shoulderblade and singed the skin but the damage, considering what might have been, was acceptable.

Another soldier running for a bunker received a wound in his right buttocks. He laid face down in the sand screaming until he was assured that the wound would not be fatal. He then yelled, "I don't believe it! They got me in the ass!"

Majewski's bunker was away from most of the damage. The initial round had been close enough to collapse the back wall but subsequent rounds were far enough to the north to be of no consequence. It was still possible that there were Vietnamese in the kill zone but the threat seemed less important now that a great deal of damage had been done and the ground attack on the north perimeter had been repulsed.

It did not take long for Majewski to reassemble his composure. He left his bunker and walked to the bunker to his east. Soldiers had gathered and were looking past the concertina wire at the dead Vietnamese. As Majewski approached the wire the soldier who had initially helped him ran over to him.

"Are you okay?" he asked.

"Yeah," answered Majewski. "Which one of you got the dink?"

"Patterson shot him," the soldier said pointing at Patterson. "Cut him in half."

"Patterson," Majewski yelled. "Thanks."

"No sweat, 'Ski!"

"I owe you," Majewski shouted.

Patterson walked over to Majewski and extended his hand.

"I'm glad he didn't get ya," Patterson said. "I saw him just as he fired and don't even remember openin' up on him but I guess I did. He won't be fuckin' with us anymore."

"Did any of you guys get hurt?" Majewski asked.

"Miller got some sand in his eye and Dipshit cut his hand on somethin' but, outside of that, we're beaucoup fine."

"Good," said Majewski. "I'd better get back to my bunker."

"Yeah, there still might be gooks out there," Patterson said.

"Thanks again."

S. R. Larson

Majewski went back to his bunker and hoped to relax. Instead he began to tremble and his hands twitched. He became dizzy and found it difficult to breathe. The bunker seemed to be closing in on him so he scrambled out through the hole that used to be the back wall and sprawled on his stomach. He was frightened and he thought he was going to die. Lying in the sand he did not seem to be able to breathe so he lifted his head to try to get more air and saw a rat, left homeless by the collapse of the back wall, scurry past him.

"I don't believe it," Majewski gasped. "I don't fuckin' believe it!"

He pushed himself up and staggered back to the bunker. He leaned on some sandbags and tried to breathe deeply. His head was spinning and he felt weak all over but knew he would have to regain control of himself. He looked for the rat. It had disappeared. He forced himself to breathe deeply and that helped. He steadied himself and realized he was no longer holding his M-16 so he took a deep breath and went back inside the bunker. His M-16 was laying on the dirt floor. He picked it up and went back outside. He leaned against the bunker and stared at the Kill Zone. It seemed quiet but sinister and he watched it intensely until the sky began to lighten in the east.

Dawn brought new activity.

Patterson went out of the base through a gap in the wire and found the Vietnamese he had killed. Majewski watched Patterson stare at the body. Patterson reached down and picked something up. He returned through the wire and walked over to Majewski.

"Here's what he shot at you with," Patterson said as he held out a U.S. Army .45 caliber pistol. "If he'd a hit ya with this you'd be one dead son of a bitch."

Majewski took the pistol. It felt cold and slightly damp. There was a bit of rust or corrosion on the barrel but the pistol had obviously been in working order. Majewski handed it back to Patterson.

"It's yours," Majewski said. "It's all yours."

Patterson nodded. "I could never hit nothin' with a .45," he said. "You hafta be pretty close to hit someone with one of these. If your hand jerks a fraction of an inch you can miss by a lot. Just the slightest twitch'll throw off your aim."

"That must've been what happened," Majewski said. "He had me dead."

"Now he's dead," said Patterson. "and I don't even remember shootin'."

Patterson walked away with his new souvenir.

Majewski turned and looked at the bunker. There was a hole in one of the sandbags and much of the sand above the hole and spilled out and formed a small pile on the ground. Majewski stuck his finger in the hole. He felt nothing but sand. He inserted two fingers and widened the hole. More sand spilled out and something landed on his boot. He looked down and found the bullet that had been fired at him. It had flattened out considerably and was mushroom shaped.

Majewski's head would not have damaged the bullet that much. He closed his hand around the bullet and felt its sharp edges. He knew being hit in the head by such an object would have been fatal. He thought of Noland and remembered seeing his friend's head explode. His would have done the same thing. He began to sweat but would not allow himself to become dizzy again. He felt compelled to walk so he put the slug in his pocket and walked around the bunker three times. He attempted to cope.

Dawn brought the helicopter gunships. The woods was strafed and rockets were fired into suspected hiding places.

The Commanding Officer, saved from harm by a well fortified hooch, was not in a good mood. A helicopter bearing senior officers landed shortly after 0800 hours and a Medevac helicopter took out the wounded that needed more attention than the base medic was able to provide.

A Colonel walked into the CO's office and McGill was sent out to sit on the sandbags. The meeting lasted ten minutes. The Colonel left the office, climbed into the helicopter and left the base. Captain Wyandotte watched the helicopter lift off as he walked to the howitzers.

Lieutenant Melloy was standing near the artillery directing maintenance procedures. His artillerymen were good at their duties. A patrol sent out at daybreak counted nine dead Vietnamese in the north Kill Zone. None had been killed by artillery but artillery had certainly broken the ground attack. It was easy to imagine how the sound of passing artillery rounds affected the attacking Vietnamese. It had to have scared the hell out of them.

Captain Wyandotte approached Melloy and Melloy saluted.

"Lieutenant," the CO said, "I have a new target for you."

"Yes, Sir," Melloy said with a smile, "what is it."

"The village," the CO said. "Flatten it. This comes from Battalion."

"Yes, Sir," Melloy said. "I've got the coordinates right here."

"High explosive and incendiary. I don't want anything left standing."

"Yes, Sir."

"Get however many men you need to daisy chain the ammo. Blast the shit out of everything. We've got more ammo comin' this afternoon so use what you have."

Melloy followed his orders. The resulting concentrated barrage flattened the village, killed a number of villagers, destroyed every building, killed pigs and chickens and the subsequent fire ignited the buildings and everything burned.

The Vietnamese that managed to escape the initial barrage scattered into the countryside. Men, women and children ran and hid and took cover as their village was consumed by explosions and fire.

Smoke billowed high into the sky. Helicopters and a spotter plane kept their distance and the heat from the fires was so intense that many Vietnamese believed the entire world was on fire.

At the base the firing routine was conducted in due and unhurried sequence. Melloy and Wyandotte smoked cigarettes as they watched soldiers pass ammunition along the line as artillerymen loaded and fired the howitzers. Helicopters and the spotter plane reported the effects and instructions were broadcast to a radioman who, in turn, relayed information to Melloy and the CO. Dense smoke could easily be seen from the camp.

"I hope we got that old Cong," the CO said. "He pissed me off."

"We probably got everybody," Melloy said.

"Hope so. I'm tired of all this shit. They want me to send a patrol out to find that artillery piece. I don't like that idea at all."

"They couldn't've hauled it too far," Melloy said.

The CO shrugged. He knew he had to find the Vietnamese artillery.

Two squads of infantry were soon combined and sent out to find the enemy artillery. Majewski was not assigned to that patrol but was awake and restless so he walked to the remains of his bunker and watched the patrol as it crossed the Kill Zone and entered the woods near the large tree. He did not want to be with the patrol. He had sounded the warning and that was enough. He had been shot at and that was enough. He did not want the aggravation of having to deal with an infantry patrol. He wanted the enemy artillery to be found and neutralized but he did not want to do the finding or the neutralizing. Enough, after all, was enough.

The patrol entered the woods with appropriate caution. It was very easy to follow the tracks made by the artillery piece. The tracks led from the large tree about twenty meters into the woods and stopped at a pile of brush. The soldiers checked the brush for booby traps, found none and uncovered the artillery piece. It was old and Chinese. No ammunition was found. One white phosphorus grenade down the barrel and one in the breech destroyed the weapon.

The patrol did not linger. There was no point in looking for Vietnamese soldiers. It was easier to pop two smoke grenades, leave the woods and, from the safety of the base perimeter, watch helicopters strafe the trees.

On the north side of the base the dead Vietnamese were gathered and laid out on the grass. They were searched but nothing of significance was found except two good luck charms that, apparently, didn't work. The body of the soldier that had shot at Majewski lay a few feet beyond the perimeter. From the bunker Majewski could see it and curiosity eventually caused him to walk out the Main Gate so he could get a closer look.

The Vietnamese had been pulverized by Patterson's M-16. Bullets had ripped the body nearly in half and the ground around the corpse was soaked with blood. The face was contorted but the eyelids were closed and the soldier had been very young. He was one of those significant One Second People that Majewski had thought about countless times in the bunker. The soldier had appeared, fired at Majewski and died, all in a second. The Vietnamese had a fleeting chance to kill an American. He had tried and failed and the effort had cost him his life.

Time went on without the Vietnamese soldier. Had he killed Majewski time would have gone on without Majewski. Patterson had become significant in Majewski's life because he had, for a split second, done something memorable and important.

Majewski shifted his attention from the soldier at his feet to the sky above. Immediately overhead the sky was clear and blue. The sky above the village was clouded with black and gray smoke and incendiary rounds from the gunships had caused small fires in the woods beyond the Kill Zone.

He shook his head. He was tired of everything. Smoke rose, the sun shined, the air was heavy and the Vietnamese soldier was dead. Majewski was tired but alive. His world consisted of what he could see and touch.

He walked away from the dead soldier and did not intend to pause and look back but he did.

The body would be disposed of somehow and Majewski could not help but wonder what the dead man had been like. He knew soldiers were not encouraged to think of the enemy in human terms. Thinking of an enemy as subhuman or as an object or target made an enemy easier to kill. One should never think of one's enemy as having once been a child that had to take piano lessons. One should never think of one's enemy as a person with a past and a family and a life that was singular and significant. One should think of one's enemy as nothing but a target or a strategic objective. That made an enemy easy to kill.

The Vietnamese soldier lying dead had been a real threat to Majewski and a real target to Patterson. The soldier had not been a person to Majewski until he was dead. He was still not a person to Patterson as far as Majewski could know. Patterson had not considered the dead man more than an immediate target. That was fine with Majewski. Patterson probably just considered the dead man a pistol donor and that, too, was fine with Majewski.

Chapter 21

Majewski's bunker was not immediately rebuilt as the back was not strategic. He took up his position as the sun was setting. The night was clear and quiet. There was no activity in the woods that could be seen. If the Vietnamese were in the woods they were concealed and quiet. They were good at being concealed and quiet.

Sometime during the day the body of the dead Vietnamese was removed. Majewski had looked for it when he arrived at the bunker for his Green Line duty but it was no longer lying where it had fallen. The blood was still there, or at least the blood not absorbed by the ground had dried and stained the grass. In a few days the stains would be gone, too. Rain or dew or a burning of the grass would remove all traces of the death of the soldier. Somewhere in either North or South Vietnam someone would wonder what had happened to a son or a father or a brother and it was unlikely that they would ever know. The last traces of the blood would eventually disappear.

Shortly before midnight Elmore showed up at the bunker. He looked very tired.

"How's it goin', 'Ski?" Elmore asked as he rubbed his eyes.

"It's quiet," Majewski answered.

"Looks like yer bunker caught beaucoup shit last night."

"Yeah. Better it than me."

"Them wounded guys is gonna be all right." Elmore said, "an the guy what fell in the pit's gonna make it, too. They done saved his foot somehow and 'er keepin' an eye on him in case he develops some kinda 'fection. The dinks smear them bamboo stakes with shit, y'know. That way a puncture wound'll get 'fected and you'll die."

"I heard that," Majewski said. "I'm glad the kid will recover. I was right behind him when he fell."

"It's gonna take him a long fuckin' time to get better. That foot's really trashed. They done rebuilt it with pins and screws and shit like that. He's in Japan now gettin' all that done."

Majewski didn't say anything.

"The guys what got hurt last night're fine. We done got a report late this afternoon."

"I knew that artillery would bring some shit," Majewski said. "I figured they'd do more than they did, though."

"Don't count nothin' out. That gook piece's from World War Two. I'm surprised the ammo even fired."

"Long shelf life."

"Huh, well, it ain't a factor no more. The village done been wasted. They're gonna send us some pictures tomorrow of what it looks like tonight. I'm anxious to see 'em."

Majewski didn't comment.

"We still got threats out there. Ain't nothin' been settled. Keep yer eyes on them woods. I know you will but I have to say it. Things is still dang'rous."

Majewski nodded and Elmore left the bunker. If the Vietnamese were close they were quiet and Majewski began to feel anxious. He was tired and afraid he would fall asleep. There was coffee in a vacuum bottle so he poured a cup and sipped it slowly. It perked him up a bit but made him more jittery.

The edge of the Kill Zone had changed from the previous night.

Helicopters and artillery had altered the area around the big tree considerably and there were now new shadows.

Majewski took time to get used to the new terrain. He studied every shadow as each flare revealed something new and different.

The Green Line shitbirds seemed to have relaxed a bit as there were fewer flares than there had been the previous night.

Majewski drank all the coffee in the bottle and settled in for a quiet night. He thought about the Vietnamese soldier that had tried to kill him the night before and was strangely sad. He couldn't shake the image of that soldier, as a kid, taking piano lessons. Did the Vietnamese even have pianos? Majewski had no idea. He doubted there were any in the flattened village. How would you, he wondered, keep a piano from warping with all the humidity and monsoon rain?

Majewski let his mind play with such thoughts until, all of a sudden, he felt something unfamiliar. The hair on the back of his neck stood up and he was suddenly extremely alert. He looked out through the vision slot and saw nothing. He checked the landmarks he had been watching and everything seemed to be as it had appeared all night. Then he heard the woosh of a mortar round. Instinctively he dropped below the vision slot and heard and felt the round's impact.

The shell landed directly in front of his bunker about thirty meters out in the Kill Zone. Dirt and shell fragments slammed into the sandbags. Majewski swore, grabbed his rifle and scrambled out of the bunker through the gap that had been the back wall. He ran a few yard and flattened out on the sand.

The second mortar round slammed into his bunker and shredded the sandbags that had, just seconds before, protected him.

Majewski pushed himself up and staggered to his feet. He turned and ran back toward the bunker.

Sand that had been tossed into the air by the explosion fell back on him and gunfire erupted all along the perimeter.

Majewski flattened out on the sand near the destroyed bunker.

The third mortar round exploded where he had just been. It would have landed in his pocket had he still been there.

Majewski covered his head and prepared for a new shower of sand. His M-16 was lying on the ground next to him. He hadn't realized he had been holding it throughout the attack. That seemed significant to him and he mumbled "Maybe I'm finally a soldier," as he tried to push himself into the ground. Falling sand bounced off his back.

The next round hit farther away and the fifth and sixth rounds hit closer to Melloy's artillery pieces. There were no more mortar rounds after the sixth.

The perimeter was alive with M-16 fire and the sky danced with the light from flares. Majewski stood up and stared out into the Kill Zone.

"Fuck you, you fuckin' bastards!" he yelled as loudly as he could. "Fuck all of you!" He brushed the sand from his arms and realized he was not wearing his steel pot. It had stayed on the ground when he got up. He reached down, picked it up and shook out the sand. "I've had it with all you goddam' bastards!"

He slammed his steel pot to the ground. It bounced into the concertina wire.

He turned and swalked slowly toward his bunker. It had been replaced by a crater.

He walked to the next crater and realized it had replaced the space he had occupied for such a short time. He stood silently for a moment and thought about no longer existing. That could have happened. He turned and walked back to the perimeter. Sergeant Elmore had retrieved his helmet from the wire.

"You okay?" Elmore asked as he handed Majewski the steel pot.

"Yuh!"

"They done got yer bunker."

"They blew it's shit away," Majewski sighed. "if they hadn't half destroyed it last night I'd a been killed."

"How'd yeh get out?"

"Through the back before the round hit. I knew it was comin'."

Elmore shrugged.

"I ran over to where that next crater is and the round hit the bunker. Something told me to get up and run toward the perimeter so that's what I did and the shell hit where I was."

"They walk them mortars in," Elmore said. "Better to be where they were than where they're goin'."

Majewski stood silently. He seemed to Elmore to be staring out into space. Majewski's eyes were dull and he seemed unaware of anything happening around him.

"You sure you're all right?" Elmore asked.

"I used up all my luck," Majewski whispered as his eyes focused on Elmore. "I don't have any left." His voice was very weak. "It's all gone."

Elmore did not say anything. He reached out and touched Majewski's right arm. He could feel Majewski tremble.

"I think the Medic oughta look at yeh an' make sure you're all right," Elmore said. "C'mon. You're relieved. Take the rest of the night off. I'll help you back to yer hooch."

Majewski said nothing. He walked with Elmore back to his AO and laid down on his bed. He stopped trembling but felt very hollow inside. It did not take long for him to fall asleep. He slept very soundly until shortly after seven when he was awakened by McGill.

"Get up, 'Ski! CO wants to see you beaucoup ASAP."

"Shit," Majewski groaned, "what the fuck's he want?"

"Search me. He just told me to get you. Get up. He wants to see you now."

Majewski slowly rose from his bed and realized he was still fully dressed, boots and all, from the night before.

He walked with McGill to the CO's office. The CO was waiting for him.

"I hear you had a bit of excitement last night, 'Ski."

"Yes, Sir."

"Sergeant Elmore said your bunker was destroyed."

"Yes, Sir."

"Were you in it at the time?"

"No, Sir."

"Why?"

"Somethin' told me to get out."

"So you abandoned your post."

Majewski was stunned. He thought for a moment he was still asleep and dreaming but he wasn't. He managed to say "What?"

"You abandoned your post."

"What're you talkin' about, Sir?"

"You left your post."

"I knew it was goin' to get hit! I got the hell out so I wouldn't get killed."

"How did you know it was going to be hit?"

"I don't know. I just felt it."

"You had a feeling the bunker was going to get hit so you left it."

"Yes. To save my life."

The Commanding Officer was silent for a few seconds.

"I guess I can understand that," he said as he lit a cigarette and picked up a piece of paper. "Do you know when the attack occurred?"

"What do you mean?"

"Do you know the time of the attack?"

"No, Sir. I don't wear a watch."

"The official report says zero two zero two. Were you awake then?"

"Of course I was! I never sleep on guard duty. If I'd been asleep I'd be dead now!"

Captain Wyandotte looked at the piece of paper in his hand. He appeared to study it intently. Majewski was nervous and wondered what was on the paper. Perhaps it was a court martial.

"Specialist Majewski," the CO said sternly. "This came in late yesterday afternoon. You're being sent back to the States. You have about an hour to pack. The 'copter'll be here at oh eight thirty. You and a couple other shitbirds have done your time."

Majewski was stunned again.

"Excuse me, Sir, but what did you just say?"

"I said your tour's up. You're bein' sent back to the States for reassignment. Pack your shit. You're gone."

Majewski said nothing. He stood silently expecting some sort of conditions to be applied.

"Go on," the Commanding Officer said. "Get a move on."

Majewski finally seemed to realize his time was up. He came to attention, saluted and left the office. He stepped into the morning sunshine and looked to the sky. It was a brilliant blue. He inhaled as deeply as he could and felt his lungs fill with Asian air. He was going home. The day had finally arrived. He ran to his hooch, grabbed his rifle, flak jacket and the bandoliers of ammunition he kept on his footlocker and ran them back to the CO's office. He handed them to McGill. McGill smiled.

"Is all your shit here?" McGill asked.

"Yes. Check it in an' check me out."

"What about the blankets and the rest of your hooch shit?" McGill asked as he slowly copied down the serial number of Majewski's M-16 and checked it against his records.

"I'll get 'em in a few minutes," Majewski said. "Just check this shit now."

"The numbers seem to match," McGill said as he checked the rifle. "and it looks to be in pretty good shape."

"What are you? A used car salesman? Check it in!"

"Okay," McGill said, "Jeez, I'm just fuckin' with ya a bit."

"Just check it in and check me out. I've got a chopper to catch."

McGill took the flak jacket and the bandoliers. He counted the clips and wrote down all the information he needed on an Army form. Then he pushed a clipboard across the desk and said "Sign out."

Majewski signed out, shook McGill's hand and said "Thanks. We've been through a lot and it ain't been fun."

"Yeah, for sure. Now get the hell outta here."

Majewski ran to his hooch. He found his dufflebag and began tossing the contents of his footlocker into the bag. He did not have much and it did not take long for him to transfer all he had. There was room left over. He looked around and saw the fan that had belonged to Noland. He unplugged it, wrapped the cord around the base and dropped it into the bag.

He took one last look around the AO. It had been his home for ten months and he was familiar with it. He would miss and not miss it.

He sat down on the bed and felt the mattress. It was a good mattress. It had, he remembered, been Noland's. He thought of Noland again and remembered what Captain Wyandotte had said just minutes before.

"This came in late yesterday afternoon. You're being sent back to the States…"

Majewski wondered if he had remembered correctly.

"This came in late yesterday afternoon. You're being sent back to the States…"

Majewski finally realized he had nearly been killed his last night on the base. He had nearly died less than eight hours before he was scheduled to leave. The CO had known it was his last night and had said nothing. Majewski had pulled duty that nearly cost him his life. He became very angry and leaped to his feet. He ran to the hooch entrance, stuck his head out and yelled in the direction of Captain Wyandotte's office.

"You lowlife son of a bitch! I could 've got my ass blown off and it was my last night!"

The CO didn't hear him and it was unlikely anyone else did.

He returned to his AO, stripped the blanket and sheets off the bed, grabbed the empty footlocker and carried everything to the Orderly Room. He turned it all over to McGill and went back to his AO. He picked up his dufflebag, took one last look around and walked out of the hooch. He did not look back. He walked to the helicopter pad and sat down on the sand. He was going home. He scanned the sky for any sign of the helicopter that would carry him away from the Fire Base but it was not yet in sight. Two other soldiers arrived at the pad. Majewski knew them as they had arrived with him all those months before but close friendships had not developed and now they were just sharing some space and time.

The others did not conceal their joy. They were ready and happy to be going home.

Majewski was ready and happy, too, but he was a bit more reserved because he wanted to make sure the going home actually happened before he celebrated. Things could still happen.

Majewski saw the helicopter approach before the others did. He stood, shaded his eyes from the morning sun and watched a small dot on the horizon get larger and larger until it became a helicopter and touched down on the pad. Majewski let the other soldiers on first as they were eager. He hung back for a moment and looked around the camp. He noticed a work detail was filling sandbags and repairing the back wall of his old bunker. He would be gone and of no consequence but the bunker would remain and be significant.

He tossed his dufflebag into the helicopter and climbed onboard. A crewman helped him in.

"Headin' home, huh." the crewman said.

"Yep," replied Majewski.

"Hang on. We're headin' for Phu Bai."

Majewski felt the helicopter shudder and shake. It seemed as if the engine was not strong enough to pull the helicopter off the ground but it was and, in a few seconds, the helicopter lifted off.

Majewski looked out the open side as the helicopter rose. He saw his bunker and hooch and the crater where the Bunker Nine Piss Tube had been. He saw the CO's office and the mess tent and the perimeter wire.

Work crews repairing his old bunker and soldiers milling around shouted their goodbyes and waved with extended middle fingers. Someone had used his heel to scrape "KISS MY ASS" in the sand and others just waved or ignored the helicopter.

The Kill Zone looked different from the air. Majewski spotted landmarks and features and recognized the place where the soldier who shot at him had died. He saw the woods where the artillery had been hidden and fired and, as the helicopter moved beyond the Kill Zone, Majewski could see the flattened village. He knew people no longer lived there.

The woods on the village's edge had been destroyed and tall grass swayed and parted as the helicopter passed over. That dangerous tall grass. That terrifying, perilous, treacherous, menacing tall grass undulated like waves below and green tracer rounds suddenly appeared and arced harmlessly far below the helicopter.

Someone was firing at them from the tall grass.

Majewski leaned toward the open side of the helicopter and yelled into the wind "We're leaving! Shoot at the guys comin' in!"

Then he leaned back, closed his eyes and very softly said again. "Shoot at the guys coming in."

Chapter 22

Epilogue

George Bitler of Terre Haute, Indiana, went to his closet, took a shoe box from the shelf and opened it. It was empty. He checked other shoe boxes on the shelf but did not find what he was looking for. He called his wife to the bedroom and showed her the boxes on the bed.

"Have you seen my .45?" he asked.

"No. Isn't it where it's always been?"

"No. I can't find it. I wonder if the kids found it."

Four-year-old Amy was summoned and asked if she knew where the gun was. She shrugged her shoulders to show she had no idea what her mommy and daddy were talking about. She did not know what a pistol was.

Six year old Butch was called to the bedroom.

"Do you know where my pistol is?" George asked.

"No," Butch said. "I didn't know you had a pistol. That's cool."

George knew that Butch was telling the truth. Butch was allowed to leave the room.

"I can't understand what happened to it," George said.

"When did you have it last," his wife asked.

"Let's see. I guess it was during the blizzard a few days ago when we had the block party. I showed it to that guy who just got out of the VA Hospital up in Danville. You know, the guy who was tellin' about being in a rocket attack and crawlin' out the back of the bunker and a rat ran across in front of his face. You thought it was disgusting."

"Oh, ick," Dolores Bitler said, "he was a real creep. Do you think he took it?"

"I don't know. It's gone, though."

Ten days later, on the early morning of February 2, 1999, Louis Tuttle was driving his truck along a country road near Leesville, Louisiana, when he saw a car parked on the edge of the road. He slowed and noticed something strange about the car's back window. He stopped and stepped out into the damp morning air.

He looked in the car and saw a man sprawled across the front seat. There was a .45 caliber pistol lying on the floor in front of the passenger's seat and the man was dead. A bullet had been fired from very close range into the man's forehead. It had shattered the skull, exited and passed through the car's rear window.

Two notes were taped to the dashboard. One read:

020270-020299 29 years

The other read:

Once I shot a tree

S. R. Larson

434

About the Author

S.R. Larson spent the year of 1970 with the U.S. Army in Vietnam. He has worked as an artist, graphic designer, writer, editor, proofreader, and photographer in Florida, North Carolina, Illinois, and Iowa. He currently lives with his wife, Sharon, in Charleston, Illinois.

Printed in the United States
92921LV00004B/63/A